Dear Reader,

There is splendor in our swamps and mystery in our marshes. Upriver from the Gulf, at a bend in the mighty Mississippi, stands New Orleans, an American urban masterpiece. So it's no wonder that I've never wanted more than to serve Louisiana, the state I cherish. At least, I never wanted more until a psychologist named Antoinette Devereaux entered my life.

It wasn't easy for me to admit I needed her. I warned her I was a loner, but somehow, the more I warned, the more I yearned. Finally, in desperation, I showed her the things that mattered to me—bayous shrouded in moonlight, rain-drenched swamps teeming with alligators and egrets, family devoted to the most enduring of human values. And in return, Antoinette showed me love.

I can't say our coming together was easy. There was danger, and a mystery that took us to the breaking point. But we solved something even more challenging. We found a way for two very different people to come together, and now the Louisiana sun shines brighter for both of us.

Bonne chance,

Detective Sergeant Sam Long

Louisiana

MEN
MADE IN AMERICA

EMILIE RICHARDS
Bayou Midnight

Louisiana

Silhouette® Books

Published by Silhouette Books New York

America's Publisher of Contemporary Romance

SILHOUETTE BOOKS
300 East 42nd St., New York, N.Y. 10017

BAYOU MIDNIGHT

Copyright © 1987 by Emilie Richards McGee

ISBN: 0-373-45168-7

Published Silhouette Books 1987, 1993

Printed in the U.S.A.

Chapter 1

The late-afternoon sunshine oozing through the window was a punishment. Antoinette Deveraux winced and squeezed her eyelids shut, wishing for a second eyelid—like that of some lucky amphibians—to screen out every ray of light in the room. The involuntary facial contortions sent more pain radiating through her body. There was no hope for it. Her headache wasn't going away. The aspirin she had taken wasn't doing its job; three cups of coffee and the attendant caffeine hadn't made a dent in it. There was only one cure for the misery that was sucking the marrow from her bones and the breath from her body.

A cigarette.

Antoinette opened her eyes and focused them on the deceptively innocent pack lying on her desk. It was crumpled; the cellophane encasing it was tattered as if someone had nervously poked a finger beneath it and traced a circle around and around the shiny red-and-white package.

Someone had. That someone had been her. The package of cigarettes had been in and out of her desk drawer for a week. She had fondled it like a mother with her infant, toyed with it like a cat with a mouse, railed at it with the venom of a jilted lover. The only thing she hadn't done was take out one of the cigarettes, put it in her mouth and light it. And of course that was the thing she wanted most to do.

Now her hand hovered over the desk and then over the cigarettes. One finger dipped down to crackle the cellophane. Even the sound was nostalgic. How much more nostalgic would be the smell of tobacco, the inhalation of smoke, the comfort of a long-loved habit.

"That habit's killing you!"

Her hand landed back in her lap with a thud. Now she was talking to herself. It had come to that. She prided herself on her rational outlook on life; there were people all over the city who depended on her to radiate serenity and analytical good sense. And here she was, Dr. Antoinette Deveraux, talking to herself like the craziest of her clients.

Antoinette looked at her watch and then, once more, at the pack of cigarettes. She had time to succumb. She could fill her nicotine-starved body with the familiar acrid smoke and count the seconds until her headache disappeared. She would be a nice person if she did, a credit to the human community. She could consider this experiment a failure and remember it when she sometimes got impatient with people who refused to give up a habit that was damaging them.

Antoinette watched her hand take flight. It was amazing what the unconscious could do. Her hand was reaching for the pack before she had even given it permission. Obviously she had come to a crossroads. Either she was going to have to give in or give herself a dose of her own therapy. Which was it going to be?

The hand hovering over the desk punched the button on her office intercom. "Rosy?"

Antoinette waited for the reassuring sound of her secretary's voice. Rosy was an anchor. On her sloping shoulders rested the business affairs and, more often than not, the personal affairs of the five psychologists who shared the second floor of the converted Uptown mansion in the heart of New Orleans.

Rosemarie Madison was a psychologist's psychologist. She knew when to nod, when to shake her head and when to murmur, "Yes, dahlin', of course you had to." She hadn't gone through years of graduate school. She had gotten her GED after four children and two husbands, and Rosy's education in the school of hard knocks had given her a wisdom the psychologists she worked for envied.

Now Rosy's voice held the sympathy she'd been openly expressing to Antoinette all week. "Doing all right?"

Antoinette smiled, sending new shivers of pain to pierce her brain. Valiantly she ignored it. "Worst day yet," she admitted.

"Always is. My Harry always said the seventh day was the worst. Every time he quit smoking he said the same thing."

Antoinette couldn't keep from asking the obvious. "How many times did he quit?"

"Six. He never made it through the seventh day. Good thing you're stronger than Harry, may he sleep with the angels."

"Good thing," Antoinette murmured. "Listen, Rosy, I've got a five-thirty appointment. A Sam Long. If he gets here before you go, buzz me. If he's not here, just leave the front door unlocked. I'll make sure my door's open so I can hear him come in."

"It's not safe to leave that front door unlocked," Rosy scolded. "You know that. Besides, should you be alone in the building with a patient, dahlin'?"

Antoinette could almost see the worried frown that would be fighting the other lines in Rosy's weathered face. "Don't worry. He's a policeman. Detective Sergeant Sam Long."

"A cop? That's worse. A cop gone crazy is the worst kind of psycho. I'm not setting foot out of this office!"

"He's not crazy, Rosy. He's coming about a case he needs help with. Go on home."

There was silence when Rosy decided if she was going to obey her favorite boss. Then, "Okay, but you have any problems and you call my oldest boy, Deke. He just lives over on Birch Street. He could be here in seconds."

"I'll do that," Antoinette said solemnly. She flicked off the intercom and stood, moving restlessly around the room. She propped her door open with a volume of Jung's *Man and his Symbols,* and then she took care of the sunshine by pulling the heavy drapes across the large picture window that looked out on Carrollton Avenue. The window was usually a source of delight. She had fought for this particular office just so that she could enjoy the sunshine and the view of the bustling avenue, complete with old-fashioned green streetcars rolling up and down the median strip, or neutral ground as it was called in New Orleans. Today the view, the noise and the indecently bright winter sunshine only added to the pounding in her head.

Settled once more at her desk, she faced the pack of cigarettes, turning them so that they were in front of the chair at the side of her desk. She took a deep breath and then exhaled slowly, drawing another breath, only to exhale again. After the third she began.

"I don't understand the hold you have on me," she told the cigarettes. "I'm a twenty-eight-year-old psychologist who's well established in the community. I've got a good head on my shoulders and no other bad habits. You're the only thing standing between me and real maturity."

She sat quietly, staring at the pack, and then after a minute got up and moved to the chair at the side of her desk. She put her hand on the cigarettes and shut her eyes. "Well, I'm just a lowly piece of tobacco," she answered herself with a whine, "but if I had to make a guess, I'd say maybe you're just not quite ready to be perfect."

Sam Long undid the top button of his plaid shirt while he waited for someone to answer his knock. He checked his watch. He was only a few minutes late. Maybe this woman was one of those ultraprofessional types who never took anything into account except her own schedule. Maybe she'd gone home when he didn't show up at the stroke of five-thirty. He lifted his hand and impatiently knocked once more on the door with the brass sign that read Psychologist Associates.

The door leading into the downstairs hallway had been open. But there were other offices in the building, upstairs and down; there was no guarantee it had been left open for him. He tried the knob, and when it turned, he stepped into the waiting room. It was empty of people but filled with contemporary prints, thriving plants and plush upholstered furniture. The magazine rack had a larger selection than the public library; the fish swimming in a twenty-gallon tank were exotic enough to stock a South Sea lagoon. Obviously, Psychologist Associates was making money.

So where was the receptionist? Where were the patients who couldn't come during normal office hours? Where was Dr. Antoinette Deveraux?

It only took him seconds to begin to search. Sam Long was not a patient man. It was his impatience that had paid off time and time again as he combed the New Orleans streets looking for people who got their kicks putting bullets in their fellow citizens. Oh, he could wait when he had to. He could wait with every muscle of his body tensed to unleash the deadly energy that made him such a successful cop. But he never wasted time waiting for anyone less important than a murder suspect.

The reception area was flanked on either side by narrow hallways. The house had been cleverly renovated to retain the appearance of a graceful Victorian mansion on the outside and the efficiency of an office building on the inside. Sam admired the effect as he turned to the left and examined nameplates on doors.

It was only when he abandoned the hallway and crossed the waiting area again that he heard the murmur of a woman's voice. He followed it to the end of the opposite hall, pausing in front of a door that was ajar. He read the sign Dr. Deveraux as he listened to the soft, lilting voice.

"You keep bringing this back to perfection, but I have no desire in the world to be perfect. Only healthy. And if you don't stop your stranglehold on me, you'll kill me."

Sam frowned, wondering just what he'd be interrupting if he knocked. He heard the scrape of a chair and then a voice that sounded like the first voice but with a whining quality that set his teeth on edge.

"You've been using me for years to flaunt your independence in your parents' face. I won't let you give me up!

I'm the one big symbol that shows the world you're not a pretty little robot!''

The screech of wood against wood was followed by, "What do you mean you won't let me give you up! I'm a grown woman. I will not be ruled by you! Damn it! I'm going to get rid of you once and for all."

"You've been trying that for a week now," the second voice whined. "You need me. You're obsessed with me. You don't have the courage to be finished with me once and for all."

"No? Watch this. You're going out the window!"

Sam pushed the door open and stepped across the threshold. The woman with her back turned to the desk didn't even notice. She stalked across the room and furiously jerked open a set of heavy drapes. With the same angry motion she opened the window and hurled a small object to the street below. Then she stood with her hands on her hips and cheered as a truck roared by. "That'll teach you to threaten me!"

Antoinette pulled her head back in and slammed the window shut, relishing the blast of winter air. She felt all-powerful. She felt as if she could take on the world and still have energy left over.

Her triumph was temporary.

"That was quite a show. Just what did you litter the street with?"

Antoinette continued to face the window. She wiped her palms on the skirt of her raspberry-colored suit and succeeded in pulling herself back to reality. It was obviously later than she had thought. Time had a habit of getting away from her when she was in a session, especially if the session was with herself. She had no doubt whom the voice behind her belonged to. "Cigarettes," she said calmly.

"Talking cigarettes?"

"In a manner of speaking." She turned slowly and faced the blond man lounging in her doorway. "Don't policemen knock, or is that one of those things you don't have to do if you wear a badge?"

"I never knock when I think someone's about to commit a murder."

She wondered how he could deliver that ridiculous, detective-novel line with a straight face. She kept her expression blank, too. "I rarely throw people out of my window. I usually finish them off outside the office. Messy business, murder."

Sam examined the woman standing with stoic resignation in front of him. They'd met before, although at the time he'd been so involved in his job that he'd paid little attention to her. Now he wondered how he could have been so preoccupied. She was stunning, even without a smile brightening her face. Taller than average with a willowy figure, Antoinette Deveraux's greatest attraction was her coloring. The hair hanging straight and shining down to her shoulder blades was the black of many Creole beauties, but her skin was milk and roses and her eyes an incredible blue that looked like the southern Louisiana sky at midday.

There was nothing wrong with her features, either. Sam imagined an artist trying to assemble the perfection of Antoinette's face on canvas. Even Rembrandt would fail. If Sam hadn't just witnessed her bizarre temper tantrum, he still knew he would never have been able to take her seriously. She was much too beautiful. There was a place for beautiful women, but it wasn't in the middle of a police investigation. He wished he hadn't wasted his time.

"Well, aren't you going to call the men with the straitjackets?" Antoinette tilted her head to signify that Sam had her full attention. The movement was unintentional, but it always inspired confidence in her clients. When Sam didn't answer, she motioned to the chair beside her desk. Without looking to see if he would seat himself, she pulled out her desk chair and sat down.

"I won't take any more of your time."

Antoinette realized that Sam was standing exactly where she'd left him. Her lips tried to manage a tiny smile. "Sergeant Long, I'm really not crazy. I've just given up smoking, and I've had a killing headache all afternoon. I was using a perfectly reputable therapeutic technique to see if I could figure out why."

Despite himself, he was intrigued. "Did you?"

The attempt at a smile disappeared. "It was helpful. My headache felt better until I realized you'd been watching me."

"And now?"

"It's roaring like a freight train trying to get back on schedule." She put her hands to her temples in emphasis. "Please sit down."

Sam moved around the desk and sat in the proffered chair. It wasn't Antoinette's words that convinced him but the nagging realization that he couldn't tell their mutual friend Joshua Martane that he'd left without discussing his reason for coming. Joshua would accuse him of arrogance, and Joshua would probably be right.

"So," Antoinette began again, "Joshua says you're looking for a therapist to work with a little girl."

"He spoke very highly of you."

Through the pounding in her head Antoinette examined the man lounging beside her desk. Detective Sergeant Sam Long belonged on a television cop show. He was much too beautiful to be out on the streets looking for trouble. And beautiful was the correct term. Handsome was unimaginative, good-looking much too tame. He was beautiful in an entirely masculine sense, with a straight aquiline nose and perfectly drawn lips that had yet to turn up in anything resembling a smile. His hair was policeman short and sunstreaked gold, his eyes a color not quite green or brown but a compromise. The cleft in his chin was an emphatic exclamation point. He was wearing a plaid shirt and well-tailored jeans, but Antoinette imagined that in a uniform Sergeant Sam Long caused his own fair share of traffic accidents.

"We've met before," Antoinette said, remembering the day with renewed clarity.

"The day Maggie gave her statement about the kidnapping."

"Two and a half years ago." Maggie, now Maggie Martane, Joshua's wife, had been one of Antoinette's clients.

She had suffered from a hysterical amnesia that prevented her from remembering any details of her past. She had also been the victim of an attempted murder. Sam had been one of the policemen assigned to her case.

Antoinette wondered if Sam was absolutely averse to smiling, or if he would return one of hers if she gave it her full power. She decided to accept the risk and the increased pain. "Tell me," she asked, "do many of your cases end that happily?"

Sam's expression didn't change. "Rarely."

"Then it must make you glad to see Maggie and Joshua and to know that at least once in your career something turned out right."

"How many happy endings do you have in here?" Sam asked with a spare gesture that encompassed the room.

"I don't work miracles. I just see improvements."

"I'm looking for a miracle."

Antoinette nodded. "Have you decided I'm sane enough to explain your case to yet?"

A faint smile lit Sam's eyes. Antoinette was encouraged.

"What kind of therapy had you talking to a cigarette package?" he asked.

She recognized his change of subject for what it was. Sam Long didn't trust her. Antoinette guessed his trust would be difficult to win under the best of circumstances. She wasn't sure she had the energy to keep trying or even that she cared to, but she answered his question.

"Gestalt. And I wasn't talking to the cigarette package. Not exactly, anyway. I was talking to the part of me that wants to keep smoking. The package was a symbol."

"And now that you've thrown it out the window, you'll never smoke again?"

"If you weren't sitting there, I'd probably be running downstairs this very minute to scrape the tobacco off the street," Antoinette admitted.

"So it didn't work."

"Everything involving the human mind takes time. If it were that easy to quit smoking, the economy of the Carolinas would do a double back flip."

Sam let his gaze drift around the room as they talked. He'd learned to judge people by their environment. There was a lot the little office could tell him about Antoinette Deveraux. The furniture hadn't come out of the local warehouse showroom. Her desk was an antique. He wasn't an expert, but he recognized the sheen of cherry and the elegant lines of something from the nineteenth century. In the corner was a thoroughly modern sofa accented by the same rich cherry, and in front of it was an elaborate Oriental rug. She'd chosen rose and bronze and faint traces of turquoise for her color scheme. There was nothing in the room that drew attention to itself. It was a room designed to harmonize and give comfort. He wondered how many poor souls had lain on the couch and spilled their guts while she nodded and looked sympathetic.

"I quit smoking when I was twenty-four," Sam said, his gaze flicking back to Antoinette.

"And you survived?" she asked with a sigh.

"I haven't touched one in ten years."

"Did you chew gum? Suck ice? Scream at your loved ones?"

His lips turned up a little. "I just quit. No fanfare."

Antoinette's eyes narrowed fractionally. "And now you're going to tell me it didn't bother you particularly." When he neither confirmed nor denied her statement, she slumped in her chair. "Tell me about your case."

She looked so discouraged that Sam wished he could dredge up a horror story for her about his own withdrawal from nicotine. If there was one, though, it hadn't been worth remembering. He turned to the business at hand, still not sure if he wanted her to be involved.

"You've heard about the case if you read the papers. Somebody's trying to destroy Omega Oil. They've been sabotaging drilling equipment and pieces of the company fleet. And they've been setting fires."

"But that's down along the Gulf, isn't it? Why are the local police involved?"

"The Omega Oil office is here in the city." Sam could see Antoinette begin to put the information together.

"The fire down on Canal Street a couple of weeks ago," she said finally.

"That's right. It wasn't an accident. Someone set it. The top three stories of the building were destroyed."

Antoinette frowned. "Wasn't a man killed?"

"One of the vice presidents. He wasn't supposed to be there, but he'd had a fight with his wife. He'd gone in late that night to sleep in his office."

"So it's not just arson. It's murder."

Sam leaned back in his chair and nodded.

"And that's why you're here," she continued. "I remember now. You work in homicide. That's why you were on Maggie's case." She paused as Sam nodded again. "Joshua said you wanted me to work with a child."

Sam shifted in his seat. "One of the women who cleans the building brought her daughter with her the night of the fire. Laurie's seven years old. Her mom's divorced and barely makes enough to support them. She can't afford child care, so she usually takes Laurie with her when she's working. That night the cleaning staff started on the top floor, like they always do. Mrs. Fischer put Laurie on one of the couches in the president's suite, and when she came back to get her, Laurie was sound asleep."

"I don't remember reading about a little girl."

"You wouldn't have. We kept it out of the papers. Anyway, Mrs. Fischer didn't want to disturb Laurie, so she went down to the next floor and then the next, going back up to check on her every once in a while to make sure she was all right. Evidently, once Laurie goes to sleep, there's no waking her." Sam brushed a nonexistent speck of lint off his jeans, then he clenched his hand into a fist. "When the cleaning staff were down on the second floor, they heard an explosion."

Antoinette was surprised by Sam's gesture. She suspected that the clenched fist was as much emotion as he ever showed, and she was surprised that he'd allowed it to slip through his tight control. Her eye was trained to detect feelings, no matter how they were manifested, but she wondered how many other people understood that Sam Long wasn't completely emotionless about his work.

"Mrs. Fischer ran up the stairs, but by the time she got to the fifth floor, the smoke was so thick she couldn't go any farther. The firemen got there a few minutes later and found her half-dead on the steps."

"Is she all right?"

"It was touch and go, but it looks like she's going to be fine."

Antoinette wasn't sure she wanted to hear the answer to the next question. "And Laurie?"

"Laurie was found on Canal Street, sitting on the sidewalk crying her eyes out."

"Unhurt?"

"She'd inhaled some smoke, and she was hospitalized overnight, but she's fine now. She's in a foster home until her mother's released from the hospital."

"How on earth did she find her way to the street?"

"She can't remember. She remembers going to sleep on the sofa, and she remembers a policeman finding her on the sidewalk. Everything in between's a blank."

Antoinette propped her elbows on her desk and rested her head in her hands. The pounding headache had been kept at bay by sheer willpower during Sam's story, but now it was back twofold. It even hurt to think. She forced herself to speak. "It's not unusual for the mind to shut out a trauma like that. Look at what happened to Maggie."

"Joshua says one of the reasons Maggie's memory returned was because of the work you did with her."

"It would have returned anyway. I just helped her get ready for it." When Sam didn't answer, Antoinette lifted her head. He was no longer sitting in the chair beside her desk. He had moved from it, making no noise at all. She wondered if they had taught him that silent, economical use of his body at the police academy.

"Don't turn around." Sam's voice came from behind her. "Put your head back down."

Antoinette did as she was told simply because it was the easiest thing to do. She jumped at the feel of his fingers on the back of her head. She could feel him tunnel through her hair until his thumbs were pressing against the base of her skull. "What are you doing?"

"I'm taking away your headache."

"I appreciate the thought, but..."

"You have to be receptive for this to work." Sam stroked his thumbs up and down the taut skin of her neck and scalp. Finally, he settled on two spots, letting his fingers rest on the top of her head. Then he began to squeeze until his thumbs were digging into the sensitive flesh and his fingers were holding her head captive. "Shut your eyes and concentrate on breathing slowly in and out."

"That's my line," she murmured, her eyelids fluttering shut even as she said the words. She began to pay attention to the rhythm of her own breath, deepening it and drawing it out. In a matter of seconds all she could feel was the touch of Sam's hands and a burgeoning sense of peace.

"The headache's not from lack of nicotine. You're as tense as a guilty man on the witness stand."

"That tension's the only thing that keeps me from falling into a million pieces. You have no idea how much I want a cigarette."

Sam tried to remember wanting anything that badly. Standing with his hands buried in Antoinette's hair and her subtly exotic perfume tantalizing his senses, the only thing he could remember ever wanting with that kind of energy was a woman.

"You smell like a New Orleans spring."

Antoinette was surprised by the personal observation. She was also surprised that she was sitting in her office with a stranger massaging her headache away. But the surprise in no way detracted from the fact that whatever Sam Long was doing was working.

"There are actually people in the world who don't know what sweet olive is," she murmured.

"And you pity them."

"I'm a dyed-in-the-wool New Orleanian."

Sam drew a deep breath and confirmed his impressions of her. "You buy your perfume in the French Quarter, your

antiques on Magazine Street, your groceries at Langen
stein's and your clothes over in the Riverbend.''

''Guilty as charged.'' Antoinette began to rotate her head
in rhythm to the pulsing of Sam's fingers. She found her
self hoping that he'd never stop.

''You were born in the Garden District, went to school a
either Sacred Heart or McGehee's. You went away to col
lege for one year and came home to make your debut dur
ing carnival season, when you were the queen of one of the
old-line krewes. You haven't lived out of town since.''

''You forgot to mention the year I took the grand tour
and visited French relatives outside Paris,'' Antoinette said
with a laugh. ''Are you always so good at ferreting out the
facts?''

''Always.''

''Then have you also figured out that I graduated from
Tulane with honors, established my practice without the
help of my wealthy parents, made a name for myself in the
community by the sweat of my perfectly formed brow and
learned enough about people to make me a damned good
psychologist?''

Sam's thumbs missed a beat. ''No.''

''Then you have something to learn about getting information,'' she said sweetly. ''How could you have wallowed
in your prejudices and missed the obvious?''

Sam let his fingers slide the length of her hair. It was fine
and soft, as shiny as polished jet. But it was the spirit of the
woman beneath it that intrigued him more. As soon as he
withdrew his hands, he missed touching her.

Antoinette moved her head from side to side. Her headache was gone.

She waited for it to return, but even when Sam was once
again sitting beside her desk, the headache was still a thing
of the past. Antoinette opened her eyes and smiled at him.
''Don't tell me that was part of your training?''

''I'm supposed to take care of anything that gets in the
way of getting my job done.''

''Where did you learn to do that?''

''From a Cajun *traiteur*. A folk healer.''

Her smile widened. "Joshua said you were a man of many talents. He was right. Thank you."

She *was* too beautiful, but Sam realized that time was running out. His choices were limited. Antoinette Deveraux would have to do, even if he still had reservations about her.

He nodded for his own benefit. The decision had been made. "We need somebody to work with Laurie. Specifically, we need a woman, and one who's been trained in hypnosis. The police psychologist thinks that we might be able to get some information from her that her conscious mind is blocking."

"What kind of information?"

"Laurie didn't get down to the sidewalk by herself. It's obvious that somebody helped her. We want to find out who."

Antoinette stretched, amazed at the well-being that filled her body. "Why is that so important?"

Sam leaned forward, and Antoinette stopped stretching to meet his eyes.

"It's important," he said, "because the person who helped her may very well have been the person who set fire to the building."

Chapter 2

"What makes you think so?" Antoinette completed her stretch and then sat forward on her seat. She might have reservations about Sam Long; she might have doubts that they could ever work together with the ease and confidence necessary for a professional relationship, but whatever her doubts, she was intrigued with the case he was presenting.

"As far as we can tell, there was no one else in the building that night, certainly no one who's come forward to assist in the investigation. But the arsonist was there. The fire was set after the cleaning staff left the top floors."

"You think he was trying to avoid harming anyone?"

"That's our guess. He'd done his homework, although not thoroughly enough."

"A sloppy, well-intentioned arsonist with a grudge against Omega Oil." Antoinette tapped her finger against her lower lip, a gesture that didn't take the place of a cigarette but helped a little. "Do you think he just happened to run across the little girl?"

"I think the explosion woke her up and she started to scream. The fire started on the top floor but in the opposite wing. Our man was heading for the exit on Laurie's side of the building and heard her. He found her and carried her to safety. Then he disappeared.''

''A sloppy, well-intentioned arsonist with a soft spot for children.'' Antoinette tried to imagine the scene as Sam had presented it. ''And Laurie doesn't remember anything that would support your hypothesis?''

''If she does, she's not telling anybody.''

''Why don't you want one of your own psychologists working with her? I know your staff. They're good, competent people.''

''They're men. Laurie's been raised without a father.'' Sam paused, and his face took on a grim set. ''Actually, Laurie was beaten by her father when she was a preschooler. That's why her mother got a divorce. Laurie's scared to death of men. Our psychologist thinks that, if she's hypnotized, she might be able to remember something that would help, but he says that Laurie will never trust him enough to let him put her in a trance.''

''Why didn't your psychologist find someone suitable? Why are *you* here?'' Antoinette leaned back in a casual posture that belied the importance of her question.

''Because I don't want somebody working with her of whom I don't approve.''

Antoinette took in the even grimmer expression on Sam's face. She felt the second stirring of interest in him. The first had come when his fingers had taken away the pain in her head. Now she was curious about the tough, bitter cop who had a vulnerable spot for one little girl. ''You're really involved with her, aren't you?''

''I don't want to see her hurt. I don't like the idea of hypnosis in the first place. I don't think the information that we'll get will be that helpful, and I don't think the possible aftereffects are worth taking a chance on.''

''What aftereffects?''

Sam stood and walked to the window. ''If she's forgotten the whole thing and suddenly she remembers it, it'll be like reliving the whole damned trauma. I don't want her going through hell again. Not even for the sake of the investigation.''

"Then why did you come?" Antoinette stood and joined him at the window. She leaned against it with her back touching the panes of glass and her arms crossed.

"I was overruled."

And he didn't like it. Not one little bit. Antoinette guessed that Sam was seldom given an order, and when he was, it took all his willpower to comply.

"Let me tell you what I think is happening here," she said, observing the muscle jumping in his jaw. It was the only thing that disturbed the male perfection of his profile. "I think you're very angry that your opinion wasn't accepted. To gain some time, you got permission to find the 'right' therapist to hypnotize Laurie. Only you're so averse to the idea that every person you interview is going to fall short."

"Should I lie down on the sofa over there while you continue, Doctor?"

"If you'd be more comfortable," Antoinette answered calmly. "You've already decided against me, or if you haven't, you will when you leave this room. I'll be too young, or too flighty, or too pretty, or not pretty enough."

"Too pretty," Sam affirmed.

"Thank you," she said without missing a beat. "You'll find fault with the next two or three people you interview, and in the end you'll go back to your superior and tell him that there's no one in the city qualified to work with Laurie. And you'll do all of that without realizing you've done it, or if you do realize it, you'll push the realization to the back of your mind and ignore it."

"Do I pay you now, or will you send me a bill for your services?"

"It's too bad, too," she said, ignoring his sarcasm again, "because in the case you've described, hypnosis might be helpful. And it certainly won't harm the little girl. Not if it's done with sensitivity and concern for her well-being."

"If hypnosis is such a miracle, why didn't you hypnotize Maggie?"

Antoinette defended herself without a trace of irritation. "Maggie's memories were beginning to surface even before

I started working with her. Hypnosis is really just a process whereby we help people achieve a state of receptivity to suggestion. In Maggie's case, it wasn't necessary to put her in a trance to suggest she'd begin to remember events at the rate with which she could cope with them. She already was.''

"In other words, you didn't want her traumatized by remembering before she was ready."

"Under hypnosis I might have been able to get Maggie's whole story and, as it turned out, that might have been good for the police. But at that time I believed there was no hurry and that we should let it unfold naturally. In the case you're describing, there is a reason."

"So you made a mistake."

"No. I made a judgment I'd make again under the same circumstances. And may I remind you that Maggie did remember everything when she needed to, and she coped just fine."

Sam turned his back to the window and copied Antoinette's posture. "How would you help Laurie cope?"

She smiled. "I thought you'd never ask."

"I'm asking."

"First of all, we're not sure Laurie will allow herself to be hypnotized. But let's say she does. Once she's in a hypnotic state, I'd probably suggest to her that she's watching the entire event on a television screen. Then I'd ask her to describe what she saw, what was said. Afterward I'd suggest to her that when she wakes up, she'll only remember the parts of the session that made her feel good. And I'd tell her that as she feels better about remembering, she will recall bits and pieces of what happened until the whole event is clear."

Sam's response was a snort. "And you think that would work?"

"It would work."

"Because some book tells you so?"

Antoinette didn't let the flash of anger she felt show. "I know it would work, Sergeant Long, because I understand the human mind. I realize that the general public associates the practice of hypnosis with a nightclub act where a man in a long black cape insists some poor fool squawk like a chicken, but I've seen its benefits in therapy. I use hypnosis whenever it's called for, and I use it well.''

''Have you ever used it with children?''

''Occasionally.''

''Have you ever used it to get at buried memories?''

''Yes, although I won't pretend that's what my practice routinely consists of. Hypnotherapy's just one of the techniques I use.'' She took a deep breath. ''And just so you and I understand each other, let me tell you this. I appreciate your concern for Laurie, but I don't appreciate your attitude toward me. I won't even pretend to guess if it's women or just psychologists that you dislike, but if you communicate any of those feelings to Laurie, I couldn't possibly work with her.''

Sam turned so that he was facing Antoinette. She turned, too. They were only a scant foot apart. ''Do you always say exactly what you think?''

''I find it saves time.''

''Then I'll do the same. I'm not happy about this. I'd have preferred a gray-haired matron with a lap wide enough for a seven-year-old to sit on and a little more sense of her own fallibility. But you'll do, Dr. Deveraux.''

She drew in a breath of pure outrage, and then she caught the sparkle in his eyes. The sparkle surprised her so much that she expelled the breath and gave him a brilliant smile. ''I like you, too, Sergeant Long.''

''Sam.''

''Antoinette.''

''You'll take the case?''

Antoinette nodded. ''Yes.''

''Good.'' Sam checked his watch. ''I've kept you long enough. I'm sure you have better places to be.''

She wished it were true. She suspected that this conversation with Sam was going to be by far the most interesting part of her evening. Now that they had called a truce, she had to admit that Sam Long and the case he'd described were the most interesting things that had come her way in a long time. "Actually," she said, "I'm just going home and pretend I really don't want to smoke anymore."

"Go for a good run if it gets too bad."

"If I ran a block, I'd drop dead. That's one of the reasons I quit smoking." Antoinette followed Sam to the door.

"You must have been good and hooked."

"Two packs a day. I started when I was sixteen."

He paused at the threshold. In spite of himself. "That doesn't fit with Sacred Heart and carnival debuts."

"Precisely why I did it."

It made a peculiar kind of sense. He mulled it over as he changed the subject back to his reason for coming. "I'll call you about setting up an appointment with Laurie."

"I'll want to meet her and get to know her a little before we try the hypnosis. Does she like her foster home?"

"She misses her mother, but she's happy enough where she is."

"Then why don't I meet her there the first time."

"Fine. I'll call you tomorrow to schedule an appointment."

Antoinette reached out and touched Sam's arm. "Thank you for helping me with the headache. Will you teach me that someday?"

Sam could feel each separate finger on his skin. He could have guessed that touching people was easy for Antoinette Deveraux. He wondered if she understood the full effect that such a gesture had on a man. He wondered if she understood the full effect that *she* had on a man. He gave a perfunctory nod, surprised at the strength of his own reaction. Then he turned and disappeared down the hallway.

Antoinette watched him go. Idly she wondered if Sam Long had any idea the effect his strong, silent routine had on a woman.

Driving through New Orleans rush-hour traffic was a job best done with a cup of coffee and chicory on the dashboard, jazz on the radio and a cigarette perched between index and middle fingers. Antoinette sat at a stoplight on

Carrollton Avenue the next morning, fulfilling the first two but not the third prerequisite for a tolerable trip.

Her headache was back, although it no longer threatened to turn her brain into dog food. She had awakened that morning from the first real night's sleep she'd had since giving up smoking, and she was beginning to believe that she was going to survive her withdrawal symptoms. She still wanted a cigarette worse than she wanted food or a roof over her head, but she no longer wanted one so badly that she'd lie, cheat or steal for it. She was definitely improving.

After crossing the neutral ground and dodging streetcars going in both directions, she parked in front of her office and let herself in with her key, leaving the door unlocked for those who would follow. From the foyer she noticed that it was strangely silent upstairs. Although two of the psychologists Antoinette shared the building with worked evenings or weekends, the others were as compulsive as she was about arriving early to start the day. And Rosy was always there before nine with the coffeepot steaming and the typewriter clattering.

The suite of offices was unlocked, but the waiting room was empty. No Rosy, no associates. Antoinette shrugged and headed for her office. She was pushing her door open when she heard the sound. It was an ill-disguised cough, and it was coming from behind the door. Before she had time to realize she should be frightened, a voice boomed out "Surprise!" and a chorus of voices shouted a repeat.

Antoinette stepped inside to an office transformed from Freudian chic to childlike splendor. "It's not my birthday," she said, examining the purple balloons and the purple, green and gold streamers that had obviously been left over from someone's Mardi Gras celebration. Then she grinned at Rosy and three of her associates who had lined up in front of her. "But if you don't care, I don't care."

"We know, dahlin'. But it's been a whole week now since you smoked a cigarette. That's even better than a birthday!"

Antoinette gave Rosy a hug, then hugged each of her cohorts in turn. John Simmons was an elderly man who specialized in working with families. He was everybody's father figure. Daffy Brookes was a flamboyant redhead who looked like a young Shirley MacLaine and dressed entirely as she pleased, with no regard for style or public opinion. Daffy was a Gestalt psychologist whose passion was psychodrama and dream interpretation, and she was Antoinette's closest friend. The third psychologist present, Jeremy Miller, worked exclusively with children referred through the school system. He had a quiet strength and a gentle sense of humor. He was exactly the kind of man Antoinette knew she should fall in love with and never seemed to be able to.

Daffy was regarding her friend with interest. "So you went and kicked the habit."

"That's a bit optimistic. But I did kick it for a week."

"You're never going to smoke again," Rosy prophesied, settling her arm around Antoinette's waist. "And to celebrate, I baked an apple strudel."

"If I quit smoking, will you bake me a strudel?" John stepped over to Antoinette's desk to begin slicing the flaky pastry.

"You don't smoke."

"I'd start and stop again for one of these."

"I'll pour the coffee." Daffy swept over to stand beside John, her long skirt rustling as she went. Today Daffy was imitating an eighteenth-century Russian peasant.

"This is trading one form of oral gratification for another," Antoinette warned as Rosy broke away to get her a piece of strudel. "If I start eating as often as I smoked, we'll have to widen the doorways to get me into the office."

"You couldn't get fat," Daffy scolded. "You're too tall. It's little people like me who get dumpy after a dose of calories."

"Both you girls need more meat on your bones." Rosy nodded for John to cut seconds. "More of you to love."

"Is that how it works?" Antoinette chewed slowly; the strudel was much too wonderful to hurry, and despite Rosy's urging, she was not going to have a second slice.

"All these years I've been trying to stay slim so some man would be smitten, and the problem was that there wasn't enough of me to love." Daffy, who had a string of men in her life long enough to wrap around the globe, passed the last cup of coffee to Rosy. "Give me the biggest piece, John."

"If there was more of you to love," Jeremy predicted, "no man in New Orleans would be safe."

Daffy gave Jeremy her most alluring smile. "Is that a challenge or a warning?"

"An announcement. I wanted that piece of strudel myself."

Antoinette watched the affectionate byplay among her friends. The first year of her practice had been conducted in a modern building with her own completely private office. Most of her earnings had gone to pay her rent. She hadn't been able to afford secretarial help, and the isolation had almost driven her to seek a job with one of the social-service organizations in the city.

John Simmons, a mentor from her graduate school days, had lost the lease on his office about the same time Antoinette was contemplating dropping hers. Over drinks one night they began to explore the possibilities of sharing a space somewhere. Daffy had learned of their plan and asked to join them. Daffy had mentioned it to Jeremy, and Jeremy had told another psychologist who was looking for an office he could use in the evenings and on weekends.

The five had searched and found the converted house on Carrollton, and although there were occasional disputes, they had managed to work out a comfortable, friendly arrangement. If there were times when one of the associates resented another's methods or successes, there were more times when they were grateful for advice or even for a trusted place to refer a client they weren't getting through to themselves.

"Has it been bad?" Jeremy asked Antoinette.

"Awful," she said cheerfully. "Last night I seriously considered lighting a fire in my fireplace just to inhale the smoke."

"Isn't the fireplace in your house blocked off?" Daffy asked.

"That's what stopped me. But just barely."

"Take deep breaths," John counseled. "Smoking's just a socially appropriate method of getting more oxygen."

"Did you try talking to the cigarettes like I suggested?" Daffy asked, starting on her second slice of the pastry.

Antoinette remembered the session that Sam had witnessed. "I'll get you for that," she warned.

"If all else fails, come into my office and I'll let you work through your problems with my dollhouse," Jeremy offered. Jeremy had an assortment of toys that he used to reach the children he worked with. It wasn't unusual to see him down on the floor building elaborate cities with blocks as he listened to a little boy or girl talk about what was bothering him or her.

"My mother warned me about playing house with good-looking men," Antoinette teased.

"May I help you?"

Antoinette turned to see who Rosy was addressing. Sam stood in the doorway, dressed in brown slacks and a tweed sports coat. "Sam. Come in."

Antoinette waited until Sam had joined her before she introduced him to her colleagues. "I'm going to be working on one of Sergeant Long's cases for a little while," she explained.

"I don't want to interrupt," Sam told her. "I just wanted to find out if you had time after school hours today to meet with Laurie."

"My whole afternoon is free. Wednesdays are my day to catch up on dictation."

Rosy rolled her eyes. "Thursdays are my worst days! Dr. D oughta write encyclopedias." She began a story about the typing Antoinette made her do that demanded everyone's attention except Sam's and Antoinette's.

Sam had watched the lively camaraderie in the tiny office full of people long enough to be surprised by it. He'd expected serious, quiet professionals going about their business with chronic nods and narrowed eyes. Then he thought about Joshua Martane, who was a psychologist, too, and wondered where he'd picked up his own stereotypes. He also wondered just what there was about Antoinette Dever-aux—besides physical beauty—that had made him take the extra time to see her in person rather than calling and leaving a message with her secretary.

He'd wanted to see her, even though he'd known that he'd be seeing her soon anyway. He'd wanted to start his day with another conversation, another chance to size her up and, yes, damn it, another chance to just enjoy her. He was only human, a fact that he and most other cops had to remind themselves of from time to time. He was not immune to women, especially when they were raven haired, five foot eight and movie-star beautiful.

"Would you like some coffee or apple strudel?" Antoinette found herself hoping Sam would accept her offer. She was in no hurry to see him leave.

"I can't stay."

She wondered at her own disappointment. "Then where shall I meet you this afternoon?"

Sam forced his attention to the business at hand. "Why don't I pick you up here about three? That'll save you from trying to find the house on your own. It's not a great neighborhood."

Antoinette started to refuse, but the thought of being alone with Sam for the minutes it would take to get to where Laurie was staying was enticing. "Fine. I'll be downstairs so you won't have to park."

Sam nodded. In a moment he was gone.

Daffy left the group around Rosy, wandering over to Antoinette's side. "Married, divorced or eternally single?" she asked, watching Antoinette, whose eyes were still trained on the doorway with a faraway stare.

"I don't know."

"Then I'd guess the latter. The man thinks he's too smart to let himself get caught."

"What else did you see?" Antoinette focused her gaze on her friend.

"Possibilities." Daffy reached behind her for another piece of strudel and held it out to Antoinette. "Here. You're going to need the fortification."

* * *

Sitting next to Sam in his car later that afternoon, Antoinette decided Daffy was probably right. She'd had no trouble resisting men in her twenty-eight years, except once. That man and that marriage had taught her all she wanted to know about the perfidies of the male sex. But there was something about Sam Long that made her forget all her lessons. He was going to be a difficult man to ignore.

"Where are we headed?" Antoinette asked as he turned his car off Carrollton and onto Orleans Avenue.

"Not too far. But if you're not familiar with Mid-City, you can get lost."

"I live about half a mile in that direction," Antoinette said, pointing to the right.

"So does Laurie."

"It was my neighborhood you were insulting."

"I had you pegged for a condo over on St. Charles."

"Nope. A plain little white frame number with a screened-in front porch and absolutely nothing to recommend it except a fenced-in yard for my dog and a clear shot at the Endymion parade. If I'm ever out of work, I can rent out my bathroom by the minute on the Saturday before Mardi Gras and make a fortune."

"Why?"

"Why what?" Antoinette turned a little so she could see Sam's face.

"Why here? You can afford better."

"Because the neighborhood is full of real people."

"Do you study them?"

Antoinette turned back to stare out the windshield. "People fascinate me, but I don't put them under a microscope, if that's what you mean. I like people and I respect them—people with problems included."

Sam just continued to drive.

"Why are you trying so hard to put me in a category?" Antoinette asked finally.

Sam had been asking himself the same question. He was surprised to hear Antoinette verbalize his thoughts. "I haven't figured it out yet myself. Maybe I don't like unknowns. That's part of my training."

"When you're dealing with people, you can never know everything," she pointed out.

Sam pulled his car into a space in front of an old two-story house with a balcony that tilted at a sad angle from the second floor. "You can never know everything, but you can know enough to make fairly accurate predictions. That's what police work is all about."

"Psychology, too. But it's a professional hazard to carry it into your personal life."

Sam got out and came around to open Antoinette's door, but she was already standing on the sidewalk when he got there. "Let's go meet Laurie."

"Sam."

He stopped and turned to face her. "Yeah?"

"It would be easier for both of us if you'd just forget what you think you know about me and give me the benefit of the doubt until I do something to prove I'm guilty."

"Guilty of what?"

"Of being a beautiful, spoiled rich girl."

"You're definitely guilty of the first," he said. Before he knew what he was doing, he reached out to touch a long lock of black hair that lay over her shoulder. He withdrew his hand when he realized what the simple movement was doing to his insides. "And I have been guilty of reverse snobbery."

She was glad he could see it and was surprised that he could admit it. She smiled her answer.

"Now let's go meet Laurie," he said again. In a moment Antoinette was following him up the steps and onto the porch.

"She's shy, even with women." Sam raised his hand to knock. The door opened, and two small bodies hurtled out, followed by a dog who was not as purebred but just as large as a Great Dane.

"Laurie?" Antoinette asked, one eyebrow raised.

Sam shook his head. "The foster parents here have six kids of their own and three other foster kids besides Laurie. They collect children like some people collect stamps." He stepped aside as another child followed the first two.

Before Antoinette could tell their ages, or even their sex, the children had disappeared down the street.

"Mrs. Patterson?" Sam shouted through the door that was still ajar.

"Come on in."

Antoinette stepped inside the door that Sam held open for her. Then she followed him through the house and into the kitchen.

"I thought it was probably you." Mrs. Patterson, a plump, frowsy woman with her hands deep in bread dough, looked up to give them both a big smile. "You'll have to excuse me, but if I stop kneading this bread, it won't be any good."

"No problem. This is Dr. Deveraux. Dr. Deveraux, Mrs. Patterson."

"Glad to meet you." Mrs. Patterson kneaded rhythmically as she talked. "Laurie's upstairs with her nose in a book. I've never seen a child read as much as that one does."

"How has her adjustment been?" Antoinette asked.

"She's real quiet, hardly says a word unless you ask her something directly. But she never gives us any trouble. If you ask me, the ones who never give you any trouble are the ones who're *in* trouble. Give me a kid who acts out anytime."

Antoinette nodded. "How many kids have come through here? Obviously you've learned a lot."

"We've had fifty-four kids, some for a day or two, some stayed until they graduated from high school. Six of them became ours for life." Mrs. Patterson pushed and pulled, pushed and pulled.

"I'd say they were lucky kids," Sam told her.

"Oh, we're the lucky ones. Had a few come through who caused no end of trouble, but most of them have been fine little people. I miss them something terrible when they go."

Antoinette nodded. The Mrs. Pattersons of the world never ceased to amaze her. Their kind of unqualified love was the glue that held society together. "When is Laurie scheduled to go back to her mother?" she asked.

"Next week, if everything goes well. She'll be glad, too. She and her mother have been alone so long she's not used to the noise and the push and shove around here. But I think it's good for her."

"It is," Sam affirmed. "I want Dr. Deveraux to meet her. Would it be all right if I went upstairs and brought her down?"

"Sure thing."

"Sam—" Antoinette stopped him with a hand on his arm. "If Laurie's afraid of men, is it a good idea for you to be the one to get her?"

Mrs. Patterson's belly laugh filled the kitchen. "Laurie may be afraid of men," she told Antoinette, "but there's one man in the world she's not afraid of and that's Sergeant Long. She's almost as crazy about him as he is about her."

"Is that so?" Antoinette said, her hand still on Sam's arm.

"I'll tell you what I think," Mrs. Patterson continued. "I think Sergeant Long has done more to help that child than years of therapy would ever have done. She needed a man she could believe in, and she found one."

Antoinette met Sam's gaze. He definitely looked uncomfortable. "I think Laurie chose wisely," she said softly. She squeezed his arm and then dropped her hand. "I'll look forward to meeting her."

Chapter 3

Laurie was coming today.

Antoinette stood in the doorway of her office and tried to picture the comfortable room as seen through the eyes of a scared little girl. Laurie would be scared. Of that there was no doubt. Two days before, at Mrs. Patterson's house, she had hardly spoken a word to Antoinette. She had blinked her huge brown eyes and twisted the ponytail that had been lovingly brushed into one long golden curl. She had nodded solemnly and bitten her lower lip. She had only smiled once . . . at Sam.

Sam would be coming, too. Detective Sergeant Sam Long, the stereotypical cop with the one-word answers and the cynicism that dripped out of every pore. But Antoinette knew now, without a doubt, that he was very different from the image he tried so hard to project. The real Sam Long was a man with magic fingers that could take away pain, and the compassion to care about a frightened little girl. From the beginning Antoinette had sensed a vulnerability in him that he struggled to hide. Now, after seeing him with Laurie, she knew she had imagined nothing.

The hypnosis session wasn't going to be simple. Hypnotizing children never was. Hypnotizing children with a suspicious adult hovering in the background was the worst possible scenario, but Antoinette knew that it was the scenario she would be dealing with. Sam was allowing her a chance with Laurie, but he wasn't enthusiastic. He was fiercely protective of the little girl. She knew nothing of his history, but if he wasn't a father already, he should be.

Idly Antoinette walked to her desk and began to rearrange items on it for something to do while she waited. Mentally she prepared herself for what was to come. She had few doubts about the ease with which Laurie would go into a trance. Antoinette had visited Mrs. Fischer, Laurie's mother, in the hospital to obtain a history. According to Mrs. Fischer, Laurie was an intelligent child who already, at age seven, could lose herself in a book and while away an entire afternoon. She had an active imagination and, considering what traumas she had been through in her short life, was well adjusted. All those factors were promising.

The social history had been enlightening, both to help Antoinette understand the child and to help her understand Sam's protectiveness. Laurie had been badly beaten by her father more than once. Mr. Fischer was the son of a wealthy family in a small Mississippi town, and when Mrs. Fischer had divorced him and reported him to the authorities, no one but Mrs. Fischer's own immediate family had supported her story. In fear for Laurie's life, Mrs. Fischer had fled the town, bringing Laurie to New Orleans where Mrs. Fischer had eked out an existence by cleaning office buildings. Even her family didn't know where she was, and she lived in terror that she would be found and Laurie taken from her by her former husband or his parents.

The story was a sad one. Because of her experience Laurie disliked and distrusted men, although play therapy at the local mental health center had helped her learn to tolerate them. Then Sam Long had come along, and the little girl, traumatized by the fire and her exile to a foster home, had broken her own rules and chosen him as a person she could trust. According to both Mrs. Patterson and Mrs. Fischer,

Laurie couldn't have made a better choice. Sam had spent hours with the little girl, drawing her out of her shell, reassuring her, listening to her concerns.

Antoinette suspected that Sam was even more involved with the child than he'd admitted. As he'd driven Antoinette back to pick up her car after meeting Laurie, she had asked if he had any plans to help the family after Mrs. Fischer was released from the hospital. His reply had been noncommittal, but Antoinette was sure that something was in the works. If Sam had anything to say about it, Laurie was not going to spend any more nights sleeping on office building couches, and Mrs. Fischer wasn't going to spend her life on her hands and knees scrubbing floors.

It was amazing, really, that such a sensitive man could hide under Sam's tough, arrogant veneer. Antoinette recognized veneers better than most people. Not only was she trained to see beyond them but also she had developed the skill from her personal experience. She had been married to a man with one, although his had been the sensitive-on-the-outside, thoroughly-corrupt-on-the-inside variety. There was no question that she found Sam's combination more appealing.

Actually, there was no question that Sam Long appealed to her, period. And that feeling was new and definitely scary. Since her divorce she'd been careful not to let herself in for another self-destructive relationship; there had been no more Ross Dunlaps in her life after their marriage had ended. In exchange for that security, however, she had chosen to have no one in her life at all.

Antoinette knew enough about her own responses to recognize the unusual nature and depth of her interest in Sam. She also knew enough about her own needs to recognize the foolishness of her attraction. Sam Long would not be able to offer her the kind of sharing, the kind of intensity, that she wanted in a relationship. He was a far cry from her ex-husband, but in the last analysis he and Ross had one thing in common: something else would always take precedence over their personal lives. If she allowed herself to pursue this attraction to Sam, she would be repeating history.

By the time Sam's knock sounded on her office door, Antoinette had put away all thoughts of him as anything other than a policeman who needed her help. When she answered the door, it was Laurie on whom she focused her attention.

"Hello, Laurie." Antoinette smiled at the little girl dressed in a navy blue jumper and a polka-dot blouse. Laurie's answer was an expression of sheer terror. Antoinette straightened a little and met Sam's eyes. "Sergeant Long," she said with a nod. "Come in and let's get comfortable."

"She didn't want to come," Sam said with no preface.

"I'm sure she didn't." Antoinette focused her attention on Laurie again. "It's scary doing new things, isn't it? But you're seven now, and you understand that even though grown-ups can make you do things you don't like, you still have lots of control."

"I don't want you to hypnotize me."

Antoinette's heart went out to the little girl whose chin was wobbling as she fought to hold back her tears.

"I can't do anything without your permission, Laurie. Come inside, and we'll talk about it."

Laurie turned her tear-filled brown eyes to Sam. "Are you going to stay?"

"Sure."

"You won't let her hypnotize me if I don't want her to, will you?"

"No."

Laurie crossed the threshold with tiny steps. Once inside she stopped, checking each detail of the room before she went any farther. As Antoinette watched, Laurie seemed to visibly relax. She gave a little sigh and then took a few more steps.

"What did you think you were going to find, Laurie?" Antoinette asked softly.

The child lifted her shoulders in a weary shrug. "I thought it'd be dark in here, like it was on TV."

"I like the sunshine. There's nothing I ever do that can't be done in the sunshine." Antoinette walked to the sofa and sat down, patting the space beside her. "Can you tell me more about what you saw on TV?"

"I don't want to."

"Okay."

Antoinette motioned for Sam to sit in the chair beside her. Laurie continued to stand in the middle of the floor as Sam sat down.

"It was just a dumb cartoon."

Antoinette nodded. "A cartoon you didn't like." Laurie walked to the desk and picked up a rosy-hued conch shell that Antoinette used as a paperweight. "Sometimes when I watch cartoons," Antoinette observed, "I get scared."

"Not me." Laurie set the shell down. "Maybe once."

Antoinette made an educated guess. "A cartoon about being hypnotized?"

"Gargamel made Papa Smurf do things he didn't want to do."

"Gargamel sounds like a bad man."

"He's always trying to get the Smurfs."

"Does he ever get them?"

Laurie shook her head.

"Not even when he hypnotized Papa Smurf?"

Laurie shook her head again. "Where's your necklace?"

Antoinette understood immediately. "I don't have one."

"Gargamel did. How can you hypnotize people without swinging a magic necklace in front of them?"

"I don't use magic. I talk to people, and they relax and start to feel good. Most of the time they shut their eyes, but they don't even have to do that. They hear every word I say, and unless they don't want to, they remember everything that happens."

"Papa Smurf didn't remember."

"But you will, if you want to."

Laurie just stared at her.

"There's nothing inside you to be frightened of, Laurie. But sometimes we don't want to remember something because we just don't like the way it makes us feel. It's the same if you're hypnotized. If you don't want to remember when you're not hypnotized anymore, you don't."

"Have you ever been hypnotized?" Laurie came to stand in front of Antoinette.

"Hundreds of times. I hypnotize myself, and I've been hypnotized by other people, too."

"Why?"

"Sometimes just to help me relax, sometimes to help me remember things. I even hypnotized myself to help me quit smoking." She wrinkled her nose at the little girl in a conspiratorial grimace. "It didn't help much."

Laurie giggled in spite of herself.

Antoinette stretched her arm along the back of the sofa. "Would you like me to tell you about the time I found a missing diamond ring while I was hypnotized?"

Laurie's eyes brightened, and she nodded. She couldn't resist the thought of a mystery. As if she realized that the story would be more fun to listen to if she were comfortable, she sat on the sofa, too, perching on the edge at the opposite end from Antoinette.

Antoinette pretended to ignore the small victory. "Right before she died, my grandmother gave me a beautiful diamond ring that had been in my family for almost a hundred years. I was so happy to have it that I wore it everywhere. It was too big for me, and I kept thinking I ought to go to the jeweler and get the ring made smaller or buy a guard for it, but I kept putting it off. One day I was at work, sitting on this sofa, and I looked down at my hands. The ring was gone."

"Did you cry?" Laurie asked with interest.

"I did."

"I cry sometimes," Laurie admitted.

"We all do. After I cried, I realized I was going to have to try and figure out where I might have lost it. But I was so upset, I couldn't remember a thing."

"What did you do?"

"I went home and searched my house and my car, but the ring wasn't anywhere to be found. So I decided to hypnotize myself and see if I could remember when I last saw the ring and everything that happened afterward."

"Did it work?" Laurie's imagination had been captured, and her rigid defenses were softening.

"It did. I remembered having the ring on that very morning. I remembered seeing it while I was washing my hands after breakfast. So I went back to that moment and replayed everything I'd done before going to work. I remembered locking my house, getting into my car and driving to work. I remembered stopping by the side of the road to buy some vegetables from a man who parks his truck off Orleans Avenue. I remembered reaching for a head of lettuce and then drawing my hand back quickly because a fly landed on it. Then I remembered picking up the lettuce, transferring it to the other hand and paying the man." She paused. "At that point I woke myself up, went into the kitchen and checked the lettuce. Right in the middle of the head was my ring."

Sam gave a long whistle. "There are insurance companies who could use your talents."

"You didn't do anything bad," Laurie observed.

Antoinette followed the little girl's train of thought. "No. Hypnosis is good. I couldn't make myself do anything bad if I tried, and I couldn't make you do anything bad if I wanted to."

"And if you hypnotize me, I'll wake up like you did?"

"You won't even be asleep. Not really. If you were asleep, you wouldn't be able to do what I ask you to do. You'll just be very relaxed and comfortable. You'll be very, very safe. Sergeant Long will be right here." Antoinette played her trump. "You know he won't let anything happen to you."

"Do you want her to hypnotize me?" Laurie asked Sam.

Antoinette waited. Sam's answer would make all the difference.

"You'd be doing me a favor if you let Dr. Deveraux hypnotize you," Sam said after a hesitation. "I really need your help."

Antoinette wondered if he had any idea how perfect his answer was. Enlisting Laurie's cooperation was the key to success.

"It would be a little like trying to find the ring," Laurie said thoughtfully.

"Yes, it would be," Antoinette agreed.

Laurie sat back against the sofa cushions and squeezed her eyes shut. "Go ahead and do it."

Antoinette caught Sam's eye and smiled. Despite the encouragement he'd offered Laurie, he still looked concerned about what was to take place. His hand was gripping the arm of his chair, and she covered it with her own for a moment. Then she stood. "Sergeant Long, I'm going to need your seat. Why don't you trade with me."

She waited until Sam was settled on the sofa before she pulled the chair in front of Laurie, whose eyes were open wide again. "Do you swim, Laurie?" she asked as she seated herself.

"My girlfriend's apartment has a pool. Her mom's taught me a little."

"Do you float?"

"I can float real good," she said proudly.

"And you like it?"

"It's fun."

"What we're going to do might feel like floating to you. When you float in the pool, does someone stay near to help you?"

"Becky's mom."

"I'm going to be here to help you, so you can feel perfectly comfortable if you start to float. You can just let go and enjoy it. You're going to like the way you feel."

"What if I don't?"

"If you don't like it, then you won't float."

"Really?"

"Really."

"You're not like Gargamel."

"Not at all," Antoinette assured her.

"Okay."

"Lie back against the sofa now and close your eyes," Antoinette instructed. "I'm going to tell you a story. It's a special story about a cottage deep in an enchanted forest.

The story is special because if you listen hard enough and believe what you hear, then you can really go there.''

Sam listened to Antoinette tell the story to Laurie. As he watched, the little girl seemed more and more relaxed until finally her face lost most of its rigidity. She was such a beautiful child. He rarely worked with children; there were few opportunities in his life to be with children at all. He hadn't realized how easy it was to become attached to one. Adults were a different story; they made their own decisions. But a child was so helpless.

Right now Laurie was especially helpless. There she was, sitting on the sofa, putting her trust in a woman she didn't know. He'd asked Laurie to cooperate, but there was a feeling deep inside him that he'd made the wrong decision. He'd made the only decision a cop could make, but he wasn't sure it was the best thing for the child sitting next to him. Now he could only sit quietly and watch Antoinette take her deeper and deeper into a trance.

Antoinette seemed to know what she was doing. She looked perfectly calm and professional. No, that wasn't quite true. She'd always be just a shade too beautiful to look completely professional. Today she was dressed in a suit—as she had been the other times he'd seen her—but it was a brilliant royal blue, and the blouse she wore with it was the brightest of whites with a high lace collar that caressed her throat. Her hair was pulled back in a simple knot at the nape of her neck, and his fingers itched to pull it loose and watch it settle like black satin over her shoulders.

Antoinette had been on his mind entirely too often. It was almost as if she had used one of her trances on him. He never daydreamed, he never lost his concentration, and yet recently he'd found himself thinking of her when his mind needed to be somewhere else. He'd never been able to understand cops who let their personal lives interfere with their jobs. He'd had a partner once who was going through a divorce, and the damned fool had almost gotten them both killed taking unnecessary chances during a high-speed automobile chase. All because he was angry at his wife.

And now here Sam was letting a woman interfere with his job, too. He struggled to pull himself back to the business at hand. He was here to find out what Laurie knew. He wasn't here to indulge in his attraction to the woman hypnotizing her; he wasn't here to let his own sentimentality interfere with his job. He was just here to listen. Period.

"We've drunk the water from the mystical spring and we've explored the enchanted forest. Now we've taken the path to lead us to that very special cottage where everything I tell you will happen just as I say it will." Antoinette's voice grew even quieter, almost droning the final words. "We don't want to wait any longer to go there. As we come up over the hill, we see the cottage. Its door is wide open, and we hurry inside. We are finally there, at that special enchanted place in the enchanted forest, and now everything I say and everything I describe will happen just as soon as I have said it. As long as we stay here, even my words will seem enchanted."

Sam turned his attention to Laurie. She looked perfectly relaxed. Her eyelids had fluttered at the beginning of the trance induction, but now they were perfectly still. She looked comfortable and not at all unhappy. As he watched, Antoinette instructed Laurie to let her right hand float above her head. The hand rose as if it were weightless, hovering over her blond curls until Antoinette instructed her to let it drift back into her lap.

"Laurie," Antoinette continued, "after your long walk through the enchanted forest, you are feeling very tired. You want to rest and you see a sofa in the living room that looks very comfortable. It looks so comfortable that you know it's where you want to sit and rest. You walk over to it and sit down. The sofa is very soft, it feels like you're sitting on a wonderful cloud. You feel very good sitting on it, so good that you know nothing can hurt you as long as you continue sitting there. As you sit, you notice a television set across from you. It's a magic television set. All you have to do is tell it to turn on and it will."

As Sam watched, Laurie smiled a little. He knew she loved watching TV. In fact, she had told him once that the thing she liked best about living at the Patterson's house was the large color console in their living room. Obviously the image was one she would relate to with enthusiasm.

"Now, when I tell you to turn on the set, you will. There is only one station that this television can get. And on this station is the story of a little girl, seven years old, whose name is also Laurie Fischer. You will be able to watch everything she does and tell me about it. You might even feel sad or happy for her, like you would for anyone on a television show. But you will not feel scared because the things that happen are happening to the other Laurie Fischer, the one on television. If you understand what I'm saying, will you please say yes?"

"Yes."

Antoinette nodded as if Laurie could see her, although the little girl's eyes were still closed.

"All right, Laurie. Turn on the television set. The first picture you are going to see is Laurie Fischer getting ready for bed last night. She is at the Patterson's house. Will you tell us what she is doing?"

"She is getting her pajamas on. They aren't hers, they're Ginger's, but Ginger doesn't like them, so she gave them to Laurie. Ginger always wears Jonas's T-shirt to bed. Laurie likes the pajamas. Ginger tells her she looks pretty and says she'll brush Laurie's hair. Laurie lets her. Then she has to go to the bathroom and brush her teeth, except there are already people waiting to get into the bathroom, so she has to wait."

"Can you tell us how she feels when she has to wait like that?" Antoinette asked after Laurie had been quiet for a few seconds.

"She's sleepy. She doesn't want to stand in the hall, but she has to, so she does."

"After she brushes her teeth, what does she do?" Antoinette asked.

"She goes to bed and starts to cry." Laurie's voice was matter-of-fact. "Mrs. Patterson comes in to tuck her in and strokes her hair and tells her that her mother will be coming to get her one day very soon. Then, when Mrs. Patterson goes away, Ginger crawls into bed with Laurie and hugs her. Laurie feels better and goes to sleep.''

''That's very good. You did a good job of telling us what you saw. Now we're going to start watching a new show.'' Antoinette took a deep breath. She realized she was feeling anxious about the next part of the session. She had faith in her own abilities; she believed that what she was doing was not going to hurt her little patient, but there was always that twinge of doubt that something could go wrong. Rationally she knew that Laurie was deeply in the trance and quite able to divorce her own feelings from what she saw on the television screen. Emotionally she wondered if she was taking even the smallest of risks by continuing. She caught Sam's eyes, and for a moment his doubts were her own.

Her experience and training won. She focused her gaze on Laurie once more. ''The new show is about Laurie Fischer, too. You are still sitting on the couch and feeling very comfortable. You are looking forward to the next show because it's about Laurie being rescued from a fire and you know it will be exciting. The best part is that you know Laurie is going to be all right, so you don't have to be frightened for her. When you turn on the set, you will see Laurie and her mother. Laurie's mother is putting her to sleep on the couch where Laurie's mother works. Turn on the set now, and tell us what you see.''

Laurie's voice was as even and natural as if she were truly describing a show she was watching. ''Laurie's mom tells her to lie down on the couch while she cleans another office. Laurie likes the couch—it's big and soft. She can hear her mother singing as she goes down the hall. Laurie doesn't want to go to sleep, but she does.'' Laurie stopped.

Antoinette sensed Sam's movement, although she didn't take her eyes off Laurie. She knew this was the moment he'd been waiting for, and she guessed that he was listening intently.

After a long silence Antoinette prompted the little girl. ''Tell us about when Laurie wakes up.''

Laurie sniffed. ''The air is all smoky. Laurie can't see.'' She sniffed again. ''She's very scared. She starts to cry.''

One sparkling teardrop trailed down Laurie's cheek. "She shouts for her mommy, but her mommy doesn't answer."

"This is a sad show," Antoinette sympathized during Laurie's silence. "Can you tell us what else happens?"

"She starts to cough. It's hard to breathe. She's choking. She sits up, but she can't see anything. The smoke makes her cry, and she starts to scream." Another tear ran down Laurie's face, followed by another. In a second she was overcome by her own tears, sobbing as if her heart was broken.

Antoinette was so intent on watching Laurie that she didn't even realize that Sam was standing until she felt his hand on her shoulder.

"Bring her out of it right now," he commanded in a whisper.

Antoinette shook her head. "It's all right, Sam," she reassured him quietly. "She needs to feel the sadness, even indirectly."

"Bring her out of it!"

Antoinette covered his hand with her own in reassurance. "Trust me," she said softly. "Just trust me, please. We're very close."

"I don't want her hurt!"

Antoinette could feel his fingers dig into her shoulder. She continued to cover his hand with her own, as much to stop him from moving toward Laurie as to continue to reassure him.

"What is happening to Laurie now?" she asked the little girl.

"She sits up," Laurie said in a tone still choked with tears. "And then she stands. She tries to find the door, but she runs into somebody. He puts his arms around her and lifts her up and carries her like a little baby." Laurie sniffed, but by now her tears were beginning to dry up.

"Laurie, I want you to stop the picture. This is a magic television set, and it lets you stop anytime you want, just as it lets you start again when you're ready. You are looking at the man who is holding Laurie. Can you tell us what he looks like?"

Laurie frowned. "He's big. Bigger than Laurie." She stopped.

"Good. Can you tell us anything else?"

"It's dark and smoky. Laurie can't see anything."

Antoinette pushed down her disappointment. "Okay. Now the television picture is moving again. What happens next?"

"Laurie is still crying and coughing, but the man doesn't stop. He just keeps carrying her. The hall is smoky, too. She can't breathe. The man opens a door, and then they're going down. Everything is black."

Antoinette realized Laurie must have fainted at that point. "Tell us about the next thing Laurie sees."

"She's outside now, on the sidewalk. She opens her eyes, and a man is bending over her. He starts to go away."

"Good. The television picture has stopped again. Can you tell us what the man looks like?"

"He has black hair."

"Long hair or short?"

"Short."

"A big nose?"

"No."

"A beard or a mustache?"

"No."

"Any moles or scars you can see?"

"No."

Antoinette felt a pang of frustration, but she kept it out of her voice. "Anything else about his face that's interesting or scary?"

"No."

"What is he wearing?"

"A dirty shirt and jeans."

Antoinette waited, but no more description was forthcoming. She didn't doubt that Laurie had noticed more, but she knew that a seven-year-old's power to describe what she'd seen was limited. There would be no vivid, incriminating descriptions of beaklike noses or beady eyes.

"Bring her out of it now. This is futile," Sam told Antoinette.

Antoinette ignored him. "Laurie, I've asked you to tell us how the man looks. Can you tell us if he says anything?"

Sam squeezed Antoinette's shoulder in protest.

"Yes," Laurie answered.

"Please tell us what he says."

"I can't. The picture's not moving."

Antoinette nodded at the literal response and ignored the pain in her shoulder. "The picture is moving again. The man is talking to Laurie. You can hear what he says now. Please tell us his words."

"Sa me fait de la pain. C'est ein affaire a pus finir."

Antoinette blinked in surprise. The French words had been said with a remarkable accent. "Does Laurie speak French?" she asked the little girl.

"No."

"Does Laurie understand what those words mean?"

"No."

Antoinette turned to look at Sam. His face was contorted into a frown, but he had stopped squeezing her shoulder.

"Does the man say anything else to Laurie?" she asked, turning back to the child.

"No. He goes away. Laurie cries and then a policeman finds her."

Antoinette focused her attention on Laurie's face. "And now Laurie is safe."

"Yes."

"She is sad and still scared, but she is glad that the man carried her out of the building."

"Yes."

"And now the television show has ended. It has been a sad show, but like many sad shows, it has ended happily. Laurie has been saved."

As Sam watched, Antoinette continued, beginning to bring Laurie out of the trance. She told her that, when she came out of the forest, she would no longer remember any parts of the television program except the parts she wanted to remember. She told her that, as the days went by, parts of the program would come back to her, but they would not frighten her, until one day she remembered everything. Then slowly and carefully Antoinette took Laurie back through the forest, suggesting finally that, when the little girl opened her eyes, she would feel very good and have lots of energy.

"Now you're back. You can open your eyes."

Laurie did as she was told, looking around as if she were in a strange place.

"How do you feel, Laurie?" Antoinette asked.

"Did you do it?"

"Sure did," Antoinette said with a smile. "Tell me what you remember."

"I was in a forest and then in a cottage. There was a TV set, and I watched it for a while. Then I came back here."

"Very good."

"That's not hypnotized," Laurie said with a frown. "That was just my imagination."

"It's all part of the same thing," Antoinette assured her. "Do you remember what you watched on TV?"

Laurie puckered her face in a frown. "Some of it," she said cryptically.

"Do you remember more about the fire than you did before we went into the forest?"

"I think so." Laurie changed the subject. "I feel good."

"I'm glad. I knew you would."

"I cried."

"Crying is just fine." Antoinette took a tissue off the table beside the sofa and handed it to her.

Laurie blew her nose.

Antoinette rose. "Would you like to go into the waiting room and wait? You can feed the fish if you tell Rosy I said it was all right."

Sam stood, too, and together they watched as the little girl, fish food in hand, scampered out of the room.

"She really is all right," Sam said, betraying his own skepticism.

"When I was bringing her out of the trance, I made sure she'd feel good."

Sam was silent for a moment. "I owe you an apology."

"Yes." Antoinette faced him.

"I shouldn't have interfered."

She cocked her head to examine him. "I'll bet that was one of the most unprofessional things you've ever done."

He narrowed his eyes a little, but he nodded. "I didn't want her upset just so we could find out that the man who might or might not be the arsonist had black hair."

"There's never any guarantee that the information a child can give will help."

"It helped."

Antoinette knew Sam was referring to the French phrase that Laurie had remembered. "How helpful was what he said to her?"

"Do you speak the language?"

"Despite the grand tour, I couldn't make heads or tails of what she said."

"That's because it was Cajun French," Sam explained. "Laurie's accent was remarkably authentic. *Sa me fait de la pain* means 'I'm sorry.' *C'est ein affaire a pus finir* roughly means 'It's a thing that has no end.' Chances are our black-haired arsonist lives or had lived down in southern Louisiana in Cajun country. It's not the best lead in the world, but it's a lead. And at this point, we'll take anything we can get.'

Chapter 4

"You're staying late again? That's the third time this week. One of these days you'll try to walk out that door and your foot'll be rooted to the floor."

Antoinette listened patiently to the intercom as Rosy extolled the virtues of rest and relaxation. She knew Rosy was right. She had been staying late too often. But she'd found that working decreased her need for a cigarette. She'd never been the type for active hobbies. Those things she did to relax she'd inevitably done with a cigarette in her hand. Now she found it difficult to read or watch television without one.

And tonight she needed a cigarette worse than she had for days. The session with Laurie had gone well, but it had left her with pent-up energy. Her nerves seemed to be dancing a jig right under the surface of her skin. At home she was sure she would succumb to the lure of a tobacco tranquilizer. Here she could bury herself in dictation and paperwork.

Antoinette realized that the intercom was silent. "Rosy, I know you're right, but believe me, staying is better than going home and smoking."

"Well, at least get some dinner and then come back."

"I'll order a po'boy."

Rosy's sigh was audible through the intercom's static. "I'll order it for you. Shrimp or oyster?"

"Shrimp. Just tell them to bring it to my office. Dr. Hollins is going to be here seeing clients tonight, so the door'll be unlocked."

"I'll order milk to go with it."

"Milk? With a po'boy?"

"Somebody's gotta take care of you." The intercom clicked off.

Antoinette smiled at the small gesture of defiance. She stretched, pushing her chair away from her desk as she did. She really didn't want to stay tonight. If there were someone at home to distract her, going home would be a pleasure. She allowed herself a moment of fantasy. What would it be like to know that when she walked through her doorway, someone other than Tootsie, her English sheepdog, would be there to greet her? What would it be like to lose herself and the tensions of the day in the arms of a lover?

She was obviously in need of a cigarette. This was the second time that day her thoughts had drifted in this direction. It had to be stress.

The intercom buzzed, and she leaned over to answer it.

"I'm going now, dahlin'. I ordered your sandwich and I told them to take it right to your office." Rosy's voice dripped disapproval. "They said they know which one is yours. You're keeping them in business these days."

Antoinette murmured her thanks and cut Rosy off before she could say another word. She reached for the top file on the pile she had made on her desk. Shutting everything else out of her mind, she began to make notes.

Half an hour later a knock sounded on her door. "Come in," she called without looking up. "How much do I owe you?"

"It's on me."

She recognized the voice before she lifted her eyes. Sam was standing in the doorway, a white paper bag balanced on the palm of his hand. And there he was, she realized with sudden insight, the source of the crazy fantasy she had indulged in earlier. She was surprised she had deluded herself into believing that her wistful longing was due to nicotine withdrawal. Obviously that longing had been spurred by the intimacy of the hypnosis session with Laurie. And all that energy she'd been trying to suppress? It didn't take a psychologist to understand exactly what part of her body was generating it.

"Moonlighting as a delivery boy?" she asked lightly, standing to greet him.

"Reassure me. Tell me this is for lunch tomorrow, not dinner tonight."

"I'm a very poor liar."

"You can't stay beautiful on a diet of po'boys." His eyes swept her body with the practiced thoroughness of a cop analyzing a suspect.

The words and the visual caress, as calculating as it had been, sent ripples of heat through her body. Enlightenment number two followed the sensation. It had been much too long since she'd had a man in her bed.

She strove to be casual. "I grew up in a home where seafood po'boys were considered food for the plebeian masses. I had my first one in high school—on the sly—and I haven't stopped since." Antoinette walked around her desk and held out her hand for the bag. "You must have paid off the delivery man. What do I owe you?"

"Dinner." Sam held the bag just out of reach.

"I guess it's big enough for two."

Sam shook his head. "This goes in the refrigerator. Let me take you out." Before she could decline, he continued. "My thank-you for your patience today."

"Patience with Laurie? Or patience with you?"

"Both."

"How'd you know I'd still be at the office?"

"I had a talk with your secretary right before she left." One corner of his mouth turned up. "She coached me on the best way of getting you out of here."

"Which was?"

"Coming over instead of discussing it on the phone. If all else failed, I was to callously withhold your po'boy until hunger lowered your resistance."

She focused on the thought of hunger and resistance for a moment, thinking of her recent enlightenment. It was funny what meaning could be present in words with absolutely no intention on the speaker's part. She shrugged off her thoughts with difficulty. "We need to put Rosy in one of these offices and give her a few clients to keep her happy."

"Come with me."

"I haven't eaten out since I stopped smoking. I might go into a convulsion if I don't light up after the meal."

"The company'll be too interesting."

She suspected he was right, and she couldn't find the words to disagree. "Even I get tired of sandwiches for dinner. But nowhere fancy, please. I'm not dressed for it."

"There's no place in this town you couldn't go. Especially..." He reached across the space separating them and touched her hair.

"Especially what?" Antoinette asked, meeting his eyes.

"Especially if you take your hair down first."

So it wasn't to be a business dinner, or even just a simple thank-you. The admiration in Sam's eyes was too frank, too completely unveiled for her to pretend that the evening wasn't a preliminary to something. Antoinette wondered if Sam himself knew exactly where the evening was supposed to lead.

As he watched, she lifted her hands and began to slowly pull out the pins holding her hair in a knot at the nape of her neck. Her hair had been confined all day, and she always enjoyed the resulting sense of freedom when it was loose once again. But as the first strands were set free, she caught the flicker in Sam's green-brown eyes. For a moment she pictured a nineteenth-century wife taking her hair down for her husband to admire at bedtime. A century later the act had some of the same sexual overtones. She almost stopped. Instead, she forced herself to continue, setting the record straight as her hair tumbled to her shoulders. "I need to know if you're married."

"I'm surprised you haven't asked Joshua."

"I hadn't realized I needed to."

"No, I'm not."

She combed her fingers through her hair, and she realized her hands weren't quite steady. "What else would Joshua have told me?"

"There's nothing much to tell."

"Will you tell me that 'nothing much' over dinner?"

"If you'd like." He stepped forward and brushed a strand of hair over her ear. "For the record, I did ask Joshua about you."

"Mutual friends can really save time, can't they?"

Sam recited the facts with just a hint of interest in his voice. "You were divorced at twenty-two, never remarried, almost but not quite had an affair with Joshua. He says you've been so busy learning to be the best psychologist in the city you've neglected your personal life."

"Spoken like a man with a beloved wife and a beautiful daughter." She realized she wasn't breathing normally, and to compensate she took a deep breath when Sam removed his hand. "Ever since Joshua married Maggie and had Bridget, he's been matchmaking."

"If that's what he's doing, it's an irony. I did everything I possibly could to keep him from falling in love with Maggie."

"Have they forgiven you?"

"Apparently. I'm Bridget's godfather."

"A real honor."

"I thought so."

Antoinette forced herself to break eye contact. She turned and went to her desk, gathered her files to put them in a desk drawer and locked it. "I'll be right back." She went into the adjoining bathroom to brush her hair, emerging a minute later with her poise in place. "Okay, I'm ready. We can drop the po'boy in the refrigerator on the way out."

Tonight Sam was not driving the four-door white sedan that was obviously an unmarked police car. He ushered her into a late-model Toyota and found a radio station playing blues before he pulled out into Carrollton traffic. "Do you have someplace special you'd like to go?"

"You can't miss in this city."

They settled on a quiet little restaurant in the Riverbend section of the city. It was a converted bargeboard house, a short walk from the Mississippi, and they were given one of two tables on the tiny glassed-in porch looking out over a side street of sedate boutiques and crape myrtles. They surprised each other by ordering the same redfish topped with crabmeat, and preferred the same wine.

"Who'd have believed our tastes were so similar?" Antoinette asked, holding up her glass for a toast.

"To thank-yous," Sam said, tapping his glass against hers. "And to information that might help catch a murderer."

"If you investigate every black-haired man in Louisiana who speaks Cajun French, it'll take the entire New Orleans police force the rest of their lives."

"If Laurie begins to remember the facts, do you think she'd be reliable if it came to an identification?"

Antoinette frowned, trying to imagine the little girl picking someone out of a lineup. "I couldn't say. It was dark and smoky inside, then she fainted. When she woke up on the sidewalk, she only had a few seconds to see the man's face. Who knows how bright the light was there? On the other hand, the man had just saved her life, and when someone's undergone a trauma, information sometimes imprints itself so clearly on the unconscious that he or she never forgets it."

"If she did identify the man, it wouldn't be admissible in court. Not from a seven-year-old who's been hypnotized to remember details. But if Laurie did point out the man in a lineup, we could dig for evidence."

"It seems like such a long shot."

"We're not without suspects."

Antoinette settled back in her chair. "You enjoy this, don't you? It's like putting together a giant jigsaw puzzle. This piece fits, then this piece. Eventually you have the whole picture."

"I like solving crimes. I don't like the fact that they were committed in the first place. The last thing I think when I walk into a room and see a dead body is how glad I am to have a new case to play with."

Antoinette wasn't hurt. Sam's words had been matter-of-fact, almost as if he was convincing himself. "And sometimes you feel guilty because you like what you do."

One corner of his mouth lifted in a half smile. "How much fun is it analyzing everything you hear for the hidden message?"

"It has the same attraction as solving crimes, I guess. I don't like the fact that my clients are suffering, but I do like trying to figure out what's causing their problems. And I really like helping them resolve their difficulties if I can."

"How many men does that ability scare off?"

"Just the ones who threaten easily."

"Did your ex-husband threaten easily?"

Antoinette was surprised at the personal nature of the question and even more surprised that she didn't mind answering it. "When I was married, my analytical ability was so limited as to be nonexistent."

"You were very young."

"I was very naive. I married a man who wanted me as part of his collection of assets."

Sam could understand a man wanting her for any reason. She looked particularly lovely sitting across from him, the fading light of day and the solitary candle on their table illuminating the ivory-rose of her complexion and the satin blackness of her hair. He'd been battling himself since the session with Laurie that afternoon. A phone call would have sufficed as a thank-you. For that matter, the generous check from the NOPD would have sufficed. There was no reason to be here except that he hadn't been able to convince himself to stay away.

"You were twenty-two when you figured that out?" he asked, turning his thoughts from his own puzzling action.

Antoinette gave a wry smile. "I suspected something wasn't right from the beginning, but I ignored it. I married at twenty and went into therapy at twenty-one. At twenty-two I realized my only problem was immaturity and Ross Dunlap himself. I divorced him immediately."

"Ross Dunlap?" Sam's eyebrows lifted in surprise.

Antoinette had known the name would be familiar to Sam. It would be familiar to anyone in Louisiana who'd ever read a newspaper. "I was Ross's New Orleans connection to old money and social status. Quite a coup for a man on his way to the governor's mansion."

Sam remembered the Dunlap case only too well. The man had been the worst kind of high-powered con, insinuating himself into people's lives, fleecing them and moving on until he'd built a power base on broken dreams and blackmail. It sickened him to think of Antoinette caught up on the Dunlap train to hell. "Did you get out before the house of cards tumbled down around him?"

Antoinette heard the concern in Sam's voice and was gratified by it. "Years before, although Ross was probably involved in shady dealings when we were married. I never saw enough of him to know what he was into. I've wondered since if the money I took as a divorce settlement was embezzled from some poor sucker who'd trusted him as much as I had."

Sam's face was grim. "I worked on that case. Undercover. It was my first step up from driving a patrol car."

"I'm glad you got him."

"Bitter?"

"Sure," Antoinette admitted. She was silent while their waiter arranged their salads in front of them, and then she continued. "But it's more than personal satisfaction that Ross got what was coming to him. The penal system in this state isn't terrific, but I'm hoping he'll get some help while he's doing his time. Ross is a sick man."

"Sick? He's not sick. He's a slime ball, plain and simple."

"Nothing's ever that simple."

"Nothing's ever much more complicated. There are good, honest people, and there are the other kind. Your ex-husband fit solidly in the last category."

Antoinette took her first bite of salad and shut her eyes in sheer appreciation. "Do you know how long it's been since I had a vegetable? I'm glad you rescued me tonight."

Since she didn't seem upset by what he'd said, Sam pushed her a little harder. "Do you actually believe that Ross Dunlap is going to change into an honest man after a little heart-to-heart talk with a prison psychologist?"

"I believe he can. That's not to say that he will. If I didn't believe people could change, I'd be in a different field."

"Would you take him back?"

Antoinette swallowed her salad and washed it down with the last of her wine, holding out her glass to Sam for a refill. "Ross Dunlap could turn into God incarnate and I wouldn't take him back. I'm not that forgiving."

The answer gave Sam a peculiar sense of relief, which he promptly ignored. "Then your interest in seeing him change is purely professional."

"Purely human. I don't like to see anyone suffer." She smiled a little. "Not even a slime ball like Ross."

"What makes you think he suffers because of what he is?"

"He's driven by needs he doesn't understand. He was an unloved little boy who learned to manipulate the world to get back some of his self-esteem. It's really a classic story."

Sam waved away the rest of her explanation. "Do you really believe that people commit crimes just because of the way they're raised?"

"It's not that simple, but if I had to distill my thoughts on the matter, I'd say basically yes. The way they were raised along with their biological potential."

"I'm eating dinner with a bleeding-heart liberal."

"And I'm eating dinner with an opinionated reactionary cop who's still the best company I've had in a long time." Antoinette reached across the table and touched Sam's hand. "Why do you think people are bad?"

"Not because they've been neglected or thwarted or bottle-fed or sent to the wrong schools."

"Then why?"

Sam looked down at their hands, joined in a casual gesture by the woman who touched so easily. "Because they decide to be."

"You think it's a conscious decision? Something they just decide out of nowhere?"

"I know it is."

"Then you must think psychology is so much mumbo jumbo. You've simplified the world so that it's just God and the devil all over again. People openly choose which one they're going to follow and that's it. No more decisions." Antoinette pulled her hand from Sam's as the waiter cleaned off their salad plates and served the redfish.

Sam smiled with an easy grin that surprised Antoinette. She realized it was the first full smile she'd seen from him, and it was a knockout. She felt its warmth bloom inside her, and she was glad she was no longer touching him because she was sure he'd have felt her reaction.

"There's a place for psychology," he said, "but not to make people feel sorry for criminals. Someone who does the things I see every day doesn't deserve pity or understanding. I don't care what their motives are. I just care about seeing justice done."

Antoinette changed the subject, realizing that both of them had given their final speech in defense of their positions. "Can you talk about the Omega Oil case? You mentioned you have suspects."

Sam gave a short, humorless laugh. "If all our suspects stood shoulder to shoulder along the Mississippi riverbank, they'd stretch up to Minneapolis and back down to the Gulf."

"Why are so many people under suspicion? Why does everyone hate Omega Oil?"

"Pick a reason. It's not a well-run company. There's been mismanagement for years generating harsh feelings among competitors and employees alike. The drop in oil prices hit Omega harder than other better companies who ran a tighter ship. Omega had to lay off almost twice as many employees as some of the bigger companies, to the point that they now have only skeleton crews working, and they're working those people to death."

"Sounds bad."

"Then last year during Hurricane Eileen they lost a handful of men on one of the oil rigs."

"I remember that," Antoinette mused. "But I'd forgotten that was Omega Oil."

"The families and friends of those men haven't forgotten. One of my cousins works on an Omega rig, so I know. There're bad feelings toward Omega down in the bayous where those men came from. They should have been evacuated, and nobody blames anybody except Omega's board for the fact that they weren't."

"It sounds like most of Louisiana had a grudge to settle."

"That's just one level of bad feeling," Sam continued. "About three months ago Omega began trying to clean up its act. There was a major reshuffling of positions in management here in the city. The whole executive branch of the company now has a gripe about the way they've been treated."

"I don't envy you your job," Antoinette said with a shake of her head. "Even if you did find the man who carried Laurie out of the building and even if he really was the man who set the fire, there's no guarantee he's working alone or for himself. He could just be some flunky who's been hired by somebody else."

"No, but if he is the man who set the fire, then he's the man who killed the executive who died in it. And that's my particular piece of the puzzle to solve." Sam's words were punctuated by a buzzing under the light blue sports coat he wore. Antoinette recognized the sound of a beeper. "Excuse me," he said, standing. "I'll be back in a minute."

The waiter came and cleared away their plates. He was just in the process of pouring coffee when Sam came back to the table. Without ceremony he waved the man away. "Antoinette, I've got an emergency. Can you get a cab back to your car?"

She nodded before she realized he was shaking his head at his own words. "No, look, why don't you come with me? You should find this interesting."

"I won't be in the way?"

"No. But I've got to go right now." He pulled out his wallet and dropped several bills on the table. "Come on."

They were in his Toyota and speeding toward the Central Business District before Antoinette could ask another question. "Can you tell me where we're going?"

"Heard of a place called Tadlows?"

Antoinette had been there several times with friends. It was a bar where business people on their way home from work and employees from City Hospital often stopped off for a drink. It was respectable and usually crowded, not the sort of place for a brawl.

At her nod Sam went on. "The message was from a friend of mine, Skeeter Harwood. He and Joshua were at Tadlows having a drink tonight after Joshua got off his shift at the hospital. A customer started some trouble, and the bartender asked him to leave. The guy pulled a gun and threatened the bartender and everyone else in the room. They all got out safely, but the guy's still there behind a locked door, threatening to shoot anyone who comes in after him and daring them to try in the same breath."

Violence wasn't unknown in New Orleans, but Antoinette shuddered to think that Joshua had been involved. "Anybody who'd lock himself in a room and practically dare the cops to come after him is a sick man. He sounds suicidal."

Sam's laugh was derisive. "Do you feel sorry for him? God, woman, don't you realize that it's nothing more than luck that kept him from killing a roomful of people? If Joshua hadn't been there to talk him into letting them all go, we'd be heading for the morgue right now."

"He's a sick man. That doesn't condone what he did, Sam, it's just a statement of fact."

"Would he have to kill a friend for you to stop sympathizing?"

The only sound in the car was the soft purr of the engine as they sped toward their destination. Finally Sam spoke again. "I'm sorry. I don't know what got into me."

Antoinette could have told him what had gotten into him. A very human emotion called anger provoked by a picture of two friends suffering at the whims of a crazy man. "It's all right," she said gently. "I understand."

Sam could feel her words—soft as they were—in every part of his body. She did understand, possibly better than he did, and she didn't hold it against him. She was the most accepting individual he'd ever known and the easiest to be around. Since he wasn't looking for either acceptance or that kind of companionship, his answer was a curt nod.

Antoinette watched Sam as he expertly guided his car through the heavy New Orleans traffic. His face was still set in grim lines. She wondered how in control of his own impulses he was at that moment. She wondered if he was carrying a gun concealed under the deceptively innocent sports coat. She wondered how often he'd been called on to use one and how often in a situation where his own emotions were involved.

"Why did Skeeter call you? I'm sure the place is swarming with policemen by now."

"He knows I'm working on the Omega case."

Intrigued, Antoinette sat forward a little. "What does this have to do with Omega?"

"Before the guy started waving a gun, he was rambling on and on about what Omega had done to him. Skeeter and Joshua were sitting close enough to hear it all. Seems he was fired about three months ago after twenty years with the company. He was within a year of being eligible for a generous pension. Skeeter thinks the guy was waiting for some of the Omega executives to stroll into Tadlows so he could blast them."

"Do you think he might be connected to the fire?"

"I think it's a possibility. I also think it's a possibility that he had absolutely nothing to do with it at all."

"Has Joshua been able to talk to him since he locked himself in?"

"Joshua and the police have been talking to him through the door."

"Good."

"A lot of good it will do."

"It sounds to me like the choices are limited," Antoinette pointed out.

Sam's answer was apparent in the whiteness of his knuckles gripping the steering wheel. The rest of the ride was silent, culminating in Sam's thoroughly illegal parking at a taxi stand down the street from the bar.

There was a crowd around Tadlows, although the immediate area in front had been cordoned off and was populated entirely by uniformed police officers and one man in a suit, Joshua Martane. Sam grabbed Antoinette's hand and pulled her to stand at the edge of the crowd next to an exotic-looking man with a dark tan and a neatly trimmed mustache.

"What's happening?" Sam asked with no preliminaries.

"Nothing since I called you." The man swept his black eyes over Antoinette and gave a stunning grin. "Not here, anyway."

"You must be Skeeter," Antoinette said, smiling back at him. "I'm Antoinette Deveraux. I think I met you the day Maggie gave her statement to the police."

"I haven't forgotten."

Antoinette remembered a much different man, one with hair to his shoulders, a gold hoop in one earlobe, a flamboyant handlebar mustache. This man had the same snapping eyes and easy grin, but he was much more civilized, although he would never fade into a crowd.

"Skeeter, stay with Antoinette. I'm going up front."

"You invited me to come with you, and that's what I'm going to do," she said confidently. "I'll stay out of the way, but Joshua might need my help."

Sam didn't have time to argue. If the situation proved to be dangerous, he'd insist. And she wouldn't dare disobey.

At the front of the crowd, they were stopped by two police officers who apologized as soon as they realized Sam's identity. Joshua was standing close to the door, apparently talking to the man inside.

"Is he getting anywhere?" Sam asked, inclining his head toward Joshua.

Before the police officer could answer, Joshua turned and saw them standing there. He said a few words to the man inside and then strode toward them.

Joshua was a large man, larger by several inches than Sam. He looked more like a prizefighter than a minister turned psychologist. He had none of Sam's Apollonian good looks but much of his magnetism for women. He nodded to Antoinette before he directed his attention to Sam.

"He refuses to budge. He's threatening to kill anyone who comes in after him."

"Nice guy."

"He's not responding to me at all. I've put in a call for one of the female psychiatrists who practices at City. He might respond better to a woman. He lost his wife a year ago."

"When does she get here?"

Joshua shrugged. "She wasn't on call, so she's not carrying a beeper. Who knows?"

"I'll talk to him myself," Sam said.

"Let me do it." Antoinette waited for both men to face her. She only had to wait a split second. Sam's expression was a study in seething anger. "Sam, you're a man and you're angry at this guy. It shows in every word you say. Let me talk to him. I know the history, I have the training. Let me give it a try."

"Don't interfere, Antoinette." Sam's voice was ice-cold.

Joshua was frowning at them both. "I don't know what's going on here," he said, "but Antoinette's right about one thing. You do sound too angry to deal with this guy appropriately. You'll provoke him into doing something he really doesn't want to do. And besides, you're not a woman. I still think a woman might get through to him."

"I won't have Antoinette risking her life on your say-so."

"The risk is minimal at worst. Frankly, I think the only person he's in danger of killing is himself," Joshua said wearily. "And if Antoinette can prevent that from happening, then we have to give her a chance."

"It's all right, Sam," Antoinette said, reaching for his hand and squeezing it. "I'll be careful. I know what to do."

Sam felt the softness of her hand over his. She was reaching out to him again in that casual, reassuring way she had. He knew he had to let her go, but he knew one thing more. The next time they touched, it wouldn't be at her initiation, and it wouldn't be casual.

And when they were done, they would both be in need of reassurance.

Chapter 5

"Has he told you his name?" Antoinette asked Joshua. "Howard Fauvier."

"Has he said anything about a family we might be able to get in touch with?"

"Like I said, his wife died last year. They didn't have any children."

"Anything else?"

"Nothing except the business with Omega. I assume Sam told you about that." At Antoinette's nod Joshua stepped beside her to escort her to the door. In an instant Sam was between them.

"My job, Josh." He took Antoinette's arm firmly and walked with her, shielding her body with his own as they got closer to the door. Joshua watched them from behind the cordon.

Antoinette wasn't frightened, but she did like the feeling of Sam beside her. She suspected, in fact, that she might like it entirely too much. At the door Sam waved the other police officers back and positioned himself so that he would be between Antoinette and any possible gunfire.

"Mr. Fauvier?" Antoinette waited for an answer and then tried again. "Mr. Fauvier, my name is Antoinette Deveraux, and I'm a friend of the man who's been talking to you. I'd like to talk to you myself."

The snarl from behind the door sounded only half human. Antoinette would have given anything to see the man's face at that moment for a better reading of his mental state.

"I thought you might like to talk about why you're angry," she continued calmly. "Sometimes talking can help."

Antoinette felt a hand on her arm. She turned to face Sam. "You have two minutes," he mouthed. She frowned and shook her head, turning back to continue her one-sided conversation. Sam moved closer, fitting his body against hers in a pose that was instinctively protective. She felt the warmth and strength of it, and she forgave him for trying to rush her.

"I don't believe you want anyone to get hurt," Antoinette said to the closed door. "I think you want to make a point. The problem is that if you don't talk to me, no one will ever understand what you're trying to say by doing this."

"Go away!"

Antoinette knew the words, hostile as they were, were encouraging. "I understand you lost your wife and your job in the past year," she continued. "That's very hard to live with."

Her words were met by silence.

"You must miss your wife very much. How long were you married?"

There was a muffled sound, almost like a sob.

"I've never lost anyone I was that close to," she continued, her heart going out to the man. "I'd be kidding if I told you I know just how you feel, but I think I know a little of what you're going through."

Sam's hand tightened on her arm, as if he couldn't bear to hear her express her sympathies so genuinely.

"Go away! Leave me alone!"

Without thinking, Antoinette tried to step closer to the door, as if by doing so she could give comfort, but Sam pulled her back. "Mr. Fauvier," she said, trying to shake off Sam's hand, "I know you loved your wife. When she died, you must have been devastated. Then Omega fired you after you'd given them all those years of your life. You're entitled to be upset and discouraged."

The voice that answered was thick with tears. "I have nothing left. Nothing!"

Antoinette wondered if she would ever be hardened to the sound of human misery. What had begun purely as an attempt to get the man to give up his gun was now an emotional drama. Her intuition told her that Mr. Fauvier, like many people who are swept along on the tide of emotion, wanted someone to lead him away from the path of self-destruction. She searched for a way to do just that.

She tried to put her feelings into her voice. "Let me tell you what I think. I think you're a man who's never hurt anyone. All of a sudden, life takes a big swat at you, and then, before you've gotten back on your feet, it takes another one. That's enough to make anybody feel angry."

"I'm not angry," he said in a voice that was strangely like a plea. "I'm a killer. Didn't they tell you that before they let you come near me?"

"No. No one here believes you're a killer. I believe you were a loving husband and a good employee. I think you're fighting fate in the only way you know how, but I'm here to tell you there are better ways."

"There's nothing left for me," Mr. Fauvier said in a broken voice.

"Do you remember how you felt before all this happened to you?" she asked. "Can you remember what it was like to feel at peace with yourself, to feel good about waking up in the mornings?" Out of the corner of her eye, Antoinette saw the cynical set of Sam's mouth. She knew he thought she was wasting their time on pie-in-the-sky philosophy.

"I remember."

"If you get help, you'll feel that way again," she promised. "I've seen it happen more times than I can count. With help you can start over. Your life will be different, but you can be the man you used to be."

"I don't know what's wrong with me. Something's wrong with me, and I don't know what it is."

"Mr. Fauvier," she said in her most soothing voice, "I don't know you at all, but just from talking to you this little bit, I can tell that you can be helped. Every one of us has to keep fighting when life gets us down. It doesn't take courage to take out a gun and kill yourself or someone else. But it does take great courage to admit you need help."

She continued in the same vein, reassuring him about his basic worth and promising him that, if he let them help him, he could begin to feel better. Sam's hand no longer punished her arm, although he didn't remove it. He continued to stand beside her, his body fitting even closer against hers, and she felt its reassurance all through her. Endless minutes passed as she played the desperate game of cat and mouse with the man who was only a heartbeat away from ending his life.

Finally there was a ragged sob from behind the door and a voiced fear. "If I come out now, the police will shoot me."

"No. No one wants to shoot you," she reassured him. "A friend of mine is standing right here with me. He's a policeman, and when you're ready, he'll tell you what to do to stay safe. I'll stay right here to make sure no one hurts you."

"The world would be better off without me."

"I believe the world would have lost someone very special."

There was another long silence. Antoinette leaned forward a little and held her breath. Beside her, Sam tapped his foot impatiently.

"I need help," Mr. Fauvier said finally.

She relaxed a little. "I promise you'll get the help you need," she told him.

"I want to come out."

"I know you do. Are you ready to talk to Sergeant Long about the best way to do that?"

"Will you be there when I come out?"

"Right here."

Sam stepped in front of the door, still shielding Antoinette with his body as he did. "We'll make this simple," he said, his voice devoid of emotion. "You put your gun on the floor and then unlock the door. Crack it a little and then slide the gun out onto the stoop with your foot. I'll come in to get you with my hands empty. That way neither of us can get hurt."

There was another long silence. Finally they heard the sound of a lock turning. The door opened a little, and a moment later a small handgun, pushed by the toe of a scuffed Loafer, appeared on the floor in front of Sam's feet.

Antoinette let out the breath she had been holding as spontaneous applause sounded from the crowd behind them.

"I'm coming in now," Sam told him. "Just put your hands on top of your head so I'll be sure everything's okay. We'll have this over within a few seconds." He pushed the door open.

Antoinette waited, but there was no sound from inside. Finally she stepped into the doorway, just in time to see Sam putting handcuffs on a small older man with a receding hairline.

"Is that necessary?" she asked Sam softly.

"Absolutely."

"You'll get the help you need," she told Mr. Fauvier, eyeing the handcuffs distastefully. "You did exactly the right thing."

Mr. Fauvier sniffed, turning his face into the sleeve of his shirt to wipe his eyes.

"Sam, he needs to be in a hospital. Can't we bypass the police station?"

Sam shook his head. "You should know better than that."

Antoinette knew he was right. There was a procedure for dealing with cases like this. As other police officers began to straggle into the bar, she rested her hand on Mr. Fauvier's shoulder, surprising him with her touch. His head snapped up at the same moment that Sam narrowed his eyes at her gesture. "You're going to make it," she told the man in handcuffs. "It's not going to be easy, but you're going to make it. This is a beginning for you."

He turned his head away, and Antoinette could see tears rolling down his cheeks. She removed her hand. "I'll come see you when they get you settled," she promised him.

"Come on," Sam said, his hand on Mr. Fauvier's arm. "I'm going to read you your rights and take you down to the station."

Antoinette watched them go. It was only when the Tadlows patrons began to swarm back into the bar that she went to find Joshua and Skeeter to say goodbye.

"Hey, Toots!" Antoinette ignored the fact that her suit was going to be quickly covered with dog hair. There were those who said that sheepdogs who were groomed regularly didn't shed. She agreed and lived her life accordingly, brushing her clothes every morning as payment for the small fantasy.

Now she knelt and braced herself for Tootsie's on-slaught.

"Did you miss me? Did Carly take you for a walk?" She suffered the dog's wet caresses, remaining on the floor until Tootsie regained her canine poise. Then she stood and checked the kitchen to be sure that the teenager who lived next door had been in to feed Tootsie and give her a late-afternoon walk as promised.

Later, settled on the sofa in a long, plum chenille robe with Tootsie's head on her lap, Antoinette shut her eyes and commanded her body to relax. It had been a long day, the kind of day best ended with a cigarette and a loving back rub. It was just over a week since she'd had the former and too many weeks since she'd had the latter. Years would be more like it.

She was feeling sorry for herself. She could write a scientific paper on nicotine withdrawal and its correlation to self-pity, all based on the experience of one subject. Herself.

She opened her eyes and regarded her faithful pet. "Tootsie, we need someone else to share our lives with. This you-and-me-against-the-world stuff isn't working."

Tootsie's ears perked up and then flopped close to her head again.

"Does that mean yes or no?" When no answer was forthcoming, Antoinette shut her eyes again. She rarely carried her work home with her. One of the things she had learned to do in the first year of her practice was to say goodbye to her caseload when she walked out of her office and hello when she walked back in. She did not shoulder burdens she couldn't handle; she did not take responsibility that belonged solely to the people she was trying to help. Tonight, however, she could not get Howard Fauvier off her mind.

She was still sitting exactly the same way a half hour later when her doorbell rang.

"Answer the door, Toots."

Tootsie wagged the stump of her tail but did not move any other part of her furry body.

"Some watchdog you are." Antoinette pushed Tootsie's head off her lap and went to the door herself. Pulling her robe tighter and retying the knot in its sash, she peered through the window. Sam Long stood on the front porch, surrounded by her potted jungle of tropical plants. He was still wearing the blue sports coat, but the shirt beneath was unbuttoned several new inches, and his hair was ruffled by the chilly March wind. If she could have put all her longings into one image, they would have looked surprisingly like the man in front of her. Antoinette unlocked the door and beckoned him inside.

He didn't smile. "Were you asleep?"

"I don't think I'm going to be able to sleep for hours."

"I know what you mean."

"Is Mr. Fauvier in jail?"

"Until tomorrow. They'll decide what to do with him then."

Antoinette turned. She knew that Sam was following her by the sound of his footsteps. In the living room she faced him. "Can I get you something? Coffee? A drink?"

"I'll take a beer if you've got one."

She returned from the kitchen with a glass and a Dixie longneck to find Sam pinned to the couch by Tootsie's rag mop body.

"If you let her, she'll smother you."

His mouth curled up in a half smile. Until tonight he had never seen a woman who could still be called beautiful wearing a fuzzy robe and no makeup. He realized that pretending he'd come to thank Antoinette again was really just that—pretending. He might convince her, but he knew better himself. He'd come because he hadn't wanted the evening to end on such a bitter note. He'd come because he wanted more of her than the scene at Tadlows had allowed him to have.

He reached for the beer and caught her hand instead. "Sit with me."

Antoinette felt the touch of his fingers in parts of her body far from his reach. She was exhausted, lonely, sad. She wanted to give something of herself to someone whole and strong. She realized just how vulnerable she was to the man in front of her. "I'm not sure that's a good idea," she said honestly.

He didn't question her. He just pulled her toward him. "I'm not sure it's a good idea, either," he admitted.

Tootsie seemed to understand that her presence on the sofa was no longer desirable. She jumped to the floor and meandered toward the kitchen. With such an obvious cue Antoinette knew she could do no less than submit to Sam's invitation. She set the beer and glass on the coffee table and allowed him to pull her down beside him. When his arm came around her, she rested her head on his shoulder. She could feel his fingers brush lightly across the top of her head.

She had been aware of Sam Long the man right from the beginning. She had related almost exclusively to Sam Long the policeman, but under all their interactions had been the twanging string of sexual attraction. She had pretended that it was just comfort or sincerity that made her want to touch him so often, but there was no pretending now. It had been the kind of day that needed to be ended with comfort, with sincere sharing. Now, mystifyingly, she found herself inclined to want neither. She wanted the feel of Sam's arms around her and the taste of his mouth on hers. She wanted a wildness that would blot out all thoughts of anything except him and the world they could make together.

"I must be losing my mind." She pulled away, just as he was turning her head to his.

"I know the feeling."

"I don't know you."

"I thought we were about to take care of that."

"See? I didn't even know you had a sense of humor." She tucked her knees under her and moved so that her head rested on the inside of his arm.

Sam curved his arm behind her head and began to stroke her hair once more. "Did you know I've wanted to kiss you since the day I found you talking to a pack of cigarettes?"

She'd had no doubt the attraction she felt was mutual, but it was nice to have it confirmed so openly. "I'm glad." She tried to lighten the tone of their exchange. "Crazy ladies turn you on?"

"Only if they have black hair and blue eyes." His hand touched her cheek. "And skin soft enough to get lost in."

She turned her face into the palm of his hand, appreciating the feel of its callused hardness. "It's been a long time since anybody kissed me."

"Why?"

"Because I haven't wanted anybody to."

"And now?"

"Now I do, only I don't know the man at all. He's a cop. He acts like a cop, talks like a cop, thinks like a cop. Underneath all that's a man I get little glimpses of now and then. He loves kids, hates to see anybody hurt, believes in justice to the point he'll put his life on the line for it. Other than those few things, I don't know him." She shifted so that her eyes met his. "I want to know him."

"You need all that information before a kiss?" Sam let his hand travel to her back. He pulled her closer.

"I think," she said softly, "that with this man a kiss would only be the beginning."

"Shall we see how accurate your prediction is?" His other arm closed around her until her mouth was only inches from his. He watched her close her eyes and he felt her relax against him. It was only when he felt the willingness in her whole body that his lips met hers.

It took him one full second to realize how he'd been deluding himself. He'd wanted to kiss her, to hold her, as much to convince himself that she was like any other woman as for the pure pleasure of it. But she wasn't like any other woman. No one else had made him question the decisions of a lifetime. No one else had eased past his defenses as if he hadn't spent a lifetime fortifying them.

Antoinette sighed and let the last remnants of tension drain from her body. She was right where she was supposed to be. She was too good a psychologist to believe that everything in life had to be understood completely. She had a feeling she would never understand this attraction to Sam. She didn't care.

When he deepened the kiss, she was grateful. There was no need for hesitancy, no place for doubt. She shifted her legs to bring herself closer, balancing with her hands on his shoulders. He settled her across his lap, never taking his lips from hers. His hands tangled in her hair, his thumbs caressed her face. She heard a low moan and knew it was her own. She felt the caress of his tongue against her lips and opened her mouth willingly.

Sam let the black silk of her hair slide through his fingers. There was nothing of her that wasn't an explosion to his senses. Her hair, her mouth, her skin. He didn't trust the feelings she engendered. He could make love to a woman and still keep most of himself inviolate. With Antoinette, he couldn't even risk a kiss without feeling as if the most elemental parts of him were exposed. And worse, he couldn't stop himself from wanting more.

Antoinette was the first to break away. She pulled back with regret, reclining in his arms to search his face. One hand lifted to caress his cheek, then smoothed over his chin, resting for a moment in the deep cleft. She drew her fingers up to his mouth and traced the curve of his lips before she spoke.

"That felt like a beginning."

"Do you analyze everything?" Sam parted his lips to pull one of her fingers into his mouth, nipping it lightly.

"Do you ignore everything?" She leaned forward, brushing kisses as weightless as butterflies across his forehead.

"Was I ignoring you?" He turned her so that she was more solidly against him. He could feel the softness of her breasts through the chenille robe, and his body responded in such a way as to make the question foolish.

"Your beer is getting warm." Antoinette tried to pull away, but Sam anchored her against his chest.

"If you leave now, the beginning will be an ending."

"I'm going just far enough to keep us from doing anything stupid and staying just close enough to keep you from forgetting what we've already done." This time when she pulled away, he let her go. She settled on the sofa beside him, leaning over to pour the beer and hand it to him before she made herself completely comfortable.

"So what now?" Sam asked, toasting her with the glass before his first swallow.

What now? Her head was spinning, and her body felt like every ounce of will had drained out of it. She had been in enough trances to recognize the feeling. She was completely relaxed but, oh, so suggestible. And under all that giddiness was an awareness of the man beside her that was so strong she could almost believe they were one being.

"Tell me about you," she said after a long pause.

"How much do you have to know to be sure what's happening is really all right?"

"I'll just know."

He fingered a dark lock of her hair, bringing the ends of it to his cheek in an unconscious caress. "I'm from here,

Irish Channel born and raised. Joshua, Skeeter and I grew up together. I was what they call uncontrollable. My father spent all his time in bars. My mother spent all the hours she wasn't working to feed us on her knees in church. I spent my time on the streets getting into trouble.''

Antoinette put her hand on his shoulder and moved a little closer.

"Eventually Joshua started playing basketball on a Garden District church team. I wanted none of that, and I started hanging out with some characters who made Joshua and Skeeter look like saints. My father sobered up long enough to realize what was happening, and my mother convinced him to send me down to the swamps to stay with her brother, Claude.''

"And you went?''

"Sober, my father was a man to contend with.'' He smiled a little. "I went. I stayed for two years. They were the best two years of my life.'' He fell silent, finishing the contents of his glass but not his story.

"Will you tell me about those years?'' Antoinette touched his cheek.

Sam realized that he'd never tried to explain that time in his life to anyone before. He'd chosen to keep the memories inside, untainted by casual conversation. There'd never been anyone who would understand the emotional investment that he had in them. Not until now. Realizing that Antoinette would understand made him even more cautious.

"There's not a lot to tell,'' he said finally. "That whole side of my family is Cajun. They've always lived along the bayous and in the swamps. Centuries ago they came to this part of the world with the first wave of Acadian exiles and vowed never to let anyone or anything push them from their home again. My mother was cut off from her family when she left to marry my father. Seventeen years later, when she had to write and ask for their help, they relented and agreed to take me in. They'd have taken her back, too, but she was too proud to ask. My father borrowed a car and drove me down to Bayou Midnight to live with my uncle. My mother stayed behind.''

''Did she ever reconcile with them?''

''No. She died while I was there. I came back to New Orleans for her funeral and decided to stay. By then I had a different view of life.'' He paused, deciding to condense the next sixteen years of his life into one sentence. ''I worked, went to school part-time and finally joined the force. That's where I've been ever since.''

Antoinette looked at the fabric of his story, rent with holes though it was, and was grateful that he had shared even that much. ''Will you tell me the rest of it someday?''

''Why?''

A lifetime of distrust seethed under his question. Antoinette shook her head. ''We're so different. This is really crazy, isn't it?''

Sam pushed her away, standing to wander the room. Both of them knew exactly why he was putting distance between them.

''Put this place in a lineup and I could make a positive identification,'' he said with a quick gesture that encompassed the room. ''This belongs to Antoinette Deveraux.''

Since she had worked long and hard to be sure it reflected who she was, Antoinette wasn't hurt by his words. ''What do you see in it, Sam?''

He narrowed his eyes, shooting her an irritated glance. ''You want to treat this like a giant inkblot test?''

''That's how your comment sounded to me.'' She stood, too. ''I'd like to hear what you think you know about me. I've told you what I know about you.''

''What you *think* you know.''

''My mistake.''

He turned away, examining the room. ''There's nothing in here that's not genuine. That landscape,'' he said, pointing to a delicate watercolor, ''is an original. That vase,'' he said, lowering his finger, ''came off a potter's wheel, not an assembly line. You have to understand everything you live with. It has to speak to you in some way. It has to be real.

"You chose pieces of furniture as the mood struck you, mixing antiques and contemporary, woods and upholstery, with no regard for propriety. The antiques show your background, the contemporary your attempt to break away."

He went on before she could congratulate him on his astuteness. "You use cool, feminine colors, but the warmth is always there in the accents. You don't let it overwhelm you, but no one could miss it, either. You surround yourself with plants to make the room live, and as if that's not enough, you keep a dog who likes to touch as much as you do."

Her laugh tinkled across the room, and he turned to face her. "You rarely entertain."

"How did you know that?"

"One couch, one armchair, only two chairs at your dining room table. No bar, no wineglasses turned upside down on the buffet. No space that would flow well for a party."

"And what does that say?"

"That you can't devote the kind of attention you like to give people if there's a crowd. You're happier with small groups, happiest with one other person."

"Remarkably accurate."

"You scare people with your honesty, scare them with your need to really know them."

"Are we talking about me now, or you?" Antoinette walked across the room to stand in front of him.

Sam lifted his hands to her shoulders. She had her head cocked in her own unique way so that he knew she was listening on all levels to what he said. Irrationally it irritated him. He didn't want the kind of intimacy she was capable of.

"I'm not scared of you, Antoinette. I just don't want what you're offering."

Her eyes widened, and he heard her draw in a breath. "I didn't realize I was offering anything," she said softly.

"Let me tell you about the place I live," he said, squeezing her shoulders in emphasis. "It's the same house I lived in when I was a boy, only it's mine now, not some slum landlord's. It's a big old house chopped into three apartments. I live in the smallest one. I change the light bulbs when I have to. Other than that, I haven't changed anything since the day I moved in. It says nothing about me."

"And is that the way you want to live the rest of your life?"

"I have no plans to change anything, ever."

"Tell me why you're here, then."

He was there because he hadn't been able to stay away. It had been a mistake not to try harder. His voice was harsh. "I find you more attractive than any woman I've met in a long time. We're adults. Do I have to spell it out?"

"It shouldn't be too hard. It's only a three-letter word. S-e-x." She waited for his answer.

"I'm not ashamed I want you." He moved toward her, holding her still.

"No? Then why the warning?"

"I don't want an entanglement. I want you in my bed, and when we're ready to move on, I want us to part friends."

"And if you're ready to move on and I'm not?"

His face was only an inch from hers. She had not closed her eyes; her gaze was steady and clear. "Don't let that happen," he answered. "For either of our sakes."

Her hands crept around his neck as much to hold him off as to bind him to her. "Sam," she whispered, "look at me. I haven't slept with a man since I slammed the door in Ross Dunlap's face. Do you think I could give myself to you after what you've just told me? One thing I'm not is a masochist."

Her refusal was predictable. The vulnerability in her voice and the news that she had been chaste for six years was not. If anything, it increased his certainty that he'd been right to be so blunt. "There must be plenty of men out there willing to make the kind of commitment I can't, just to make love to you. What have you been waiting for?" he asked, blunter still.

A cop with eyes the colors of a winter-burned meadow? A man who protected and challenged with the same ease? An enigma in plain clothes who needed exactly what she had to give? "A man I could love," she said with a catch in her voice. "Nothing more complicated than that."

"Then be glad we talked."

She pulled his mouth to hers in answer, giving herself up to the last kiss they would share. If he was not to give them a chance, then she would be sure he remembered what he had lost.

Her mouth moved against his with a hunger to know all its secrets. There was nothing to hold back because there was no place left for them to go. She was surprised by the mixture of sadness and sheer sensual pleasure she felt. Standing with her body pressed against his, she knew, for the first time, exactly how they fit together. There were no adjustments to make, no compromises to reach.

His lips parted, and he plundered the moist recesses of her mouth, hauling her against him until she could feel the strength of his arousal. She could feel her breasts swell and her nipples peak at the intimate contact. Deep inside she could feel the rush of heat that signaled the building of her body's ultimate response.

Antoinette dug her fingers into Sam's hair, trying to find a way to bring him closer. She began to pray the kiss that was to be a goodbye would never end.

It was Sam who pushed her away, Sam who stepped back and shook off the slender arms around his neck. It was Sam, breathing hard, who found his way to the front door and closed it without a sound.

It was Antoinette who stood and watched him go, wishing that life would learn to be kind.

Chapter 6

The soft knit shirt was the same vivid green as the sunlit fields of the Emerald Isle. Antoinette pulled it over her head and nodded with approval at her image in the full-length mirror in her bedroom. Her pleated skirt was the same color as her shirt, and the effect was exactly right for this Saturday before St. Patrick's Day. Just to be sure everyone got the point, she pulled her brush through her hair and tied it back from her forehead with a ribbon of the same green.

It was only when she tried unsuccessfully for the third time to fasten tiny emeralds in her earlobes that she realized she was nervous. She wasn't trembling; it was just that her fingers refused to coordinate. Each one was working independently of the others.

It had been two weeks since she had seen Sam Long, two weeks of alternating periods of acceptance and sadness. He had not called; she had not asked about him when she happened to run into Joshua. Then two days ago Joshua had stopped her in the hall while she was visiting Mr. Fauvier, who had been admitted by court order to the City Hospital Psychiatric Unit. Joshua and Maggie were having a party before the annual Irish Channel St. Patrick's Day parade. They wanted her to come.

Antoinette had accepted without considering the potential consequences of her decision. It was only when Joshua had gone and she was already committed that she realized Sam would probably be at the party, too. By then it was too late to manufacture an excuse. Or perhaps it was just that her pride wouldn't let her. After all, she and Sam hadn't done any more than exchange a few kisses. There was no reason to let that stop her from accepting an invitation for what promised to be a fun afternoon.

Now she stopped for a moment, forcing herself to relax completely. This time when she tried to insert the earrings, they went in easily. She wasn't about to let Sam Long shake her self-control.

The drive to Joshua and Maggie's gave Antoinette time to rehearse what she would say to Sam if he was there. She would ask him about Laurie, whom she hadn't seen since the hypnosis session, and she would ask him about the Omega Oil case. She would be friendly, but not too friendly, warm, but not warm enough to make him think she wanted to give their relationship another try. Except for a mutual friendship with the Martanes, she and Sam didn't travel in the same circles. But New Orleans was a small enough city that she was bound to run into him someday. She might as well get that first meeting over with when she could prepare for it.

The streets of the Irish Channel were already crowded with cars. Antoinette found a parking spot several blocks past Joshua's house. As she walked back, she admired the tidy houses decorated with green streamers and balloons, along with the natural decorations of lavender wisteria and scarlet azaleas.

The Channel was one of the first sections of New Orleans to define and describe itself as a neighborhood, although there were those who argued that the neighborhood was more a state of mind than a section bounded by particular streets. The houses had been built for working men during the nineteenth century, many of whom were Irish

immigrants. Today they belonged to working men and
women of every nationality and color. Like almost any urban neighborhood, some streets were lined with houses on
the verge of collapse, and others sported houses that anyone would be proud to own. There was an eclectic mix of
architectural styles, but most of the houses had one thing in
common. They were strong, solid examples of construction
built to last, and even years of neglect had not diminished
their essential character.

The Martane's house was located on a street on its way
back up. There was hardly a house for blocks on either side
that had not at least received a new coat of paint. More
common was partial or total renovation. Antoinette stood
in front of the iron-rail fence that enclosed Maggie and
Joshua's yard and admired the changes they had made. The
house was large, large enough to have been broken up into
apartments before Maggie hired an architect to have it re-
stored. Now it was a one-family dwelling again, a graceful,
two-story blend of porches, balconies, wrought iron and
New Orleans charm. Brightly colored annuals and azaleas
set off the soft gray paint and rose-colored trim.

"Antoinette!" Maggie stepped onto the porch, Bridget
perched comfortably on one hip.

"I was just admiring what you've done to this place."
Antoinette opened the gate and walked up the brick sidewalk.

"Has it been that long since you've been here?" Maggie
leaned over and brushed a kiss across Antoinette's cheek.
Bridget's blue eyes widened, and she grabbed a fistful of
Antoinette's hair before her mother could straighten. Maggie calmly extracted each strand. "No, Bridget. It's to look
at, not touch."

"Come here, Bridget, and I'll let you play with it all you
want," Antoinette promised. Without a moment of hesitation, Bridget extended her arms, and Antoinette settled her
against her own hip. "She looks like you," Antoinette told
Maggie. "Every time I see her, she looks more and more like
you." Both Martane females had the same chin-length
brown curls, the same huge blue eyes and the same heart-

shaped faces. Today they were even dressed alike in kelly green dresses with large round buttons pinned on the bodices proclaiming Kiss Me, I'm Irish.

"If she looks like me, that's a compliment," Maggie said with a grin. "She's obviously the most gorgeous child ever to set foot on this planet."

"Agreed," Antoinette said solemnly.

"Get down," Bridget announced, pointing to the porch floor. "Get down, now."

Antoinette stooped and set the little girl on the porch, watching her toddle into the house. "She's so big already. They grow so fast."

"I'm with her every day, and the changes still happen too fast," Maggie said as Antoinette stood. "I'm glad I run the hospital day-care center, or I'd be one of those women who just has to have a new baby every two years like clockwork."

"And you're immune now?"

"Actually, I'm pregnant now," Maggie admitted. "But I don't plan any more than one or two—" she hesitated "—or, at the most, three kids."

Antoinette laughed and hugged her in congratulations, and then the two women, arms around each other's waists, strolled into the house.

Inside, the living and dining rooms were full of people Antoinette knew by sight from the work she had done with patients at City Hospital. A quick census assured her that Sam Long was not one of them. Skeeter was there, however, tending bar, and Maggie guided Antoinette toward him, making sure that Antoinette's request for Irish coffee was given top priority.

Antoinette leaned against the counter and watched Skeeter combine a generous shot of Irish whiskey, strong black coffee and thick sweetened cream. He was wearing a white shirt printed with shamrocks and long strands of green beads. On top of his thick black hair was a green felt derby.

"Shall I tell you again how expertly you handled the situation at Tadlows?" Skeeter asked, handing her the brimming mug. "Someone who should know says you saved the guy's life."

"Joshua's always been one of my biggest fans." Antoinette licked the cream off the top of the drink and decided it was her favorite part.

"I heard it from Sam."

Antoinette looked up and saw the frank assessment in Skeeter's eyes. She examined her mug once again. "Obviously you're one of the select few Sam talks to."

"That's right."

"And obviously I'm not."

"No, you're one of those select few he talks about."

The cream was gone. Antoinette took a big sip of the whiskey-laden coffee and felt its warmth spread through her whole body. Or was it Skeeter's words that had affected her that way? "And what does Sam say when he talks about me?" she asked finally.

"How well do you know Sam?"

"How well does anyone?" she countered.

"I've known him since we were children. He doesn't have to spell things out for me to understand what he's saying."

Antoinette set her mug on the counter and met Skeeter's eyes. "What do you understand?"

"That you've got a hell of a time ahead of you and so does he."

"We have nothing ahead of us. Sam's made that quite clear."

"I believe Joshua once made that same thing quite clear to Maggie." Skeeter pulled a long strand of green pearls from around his neck and leaned on the counter to drop them over Antoinette's head. Then he kissed her cheek. "Best of luck, babe."

She wanted to ask him what he meant, but before she could, he was serving drinks to other partygoers. A recording of Irish harp and penny whistle accented the conversations buzzing through the downstairs, and Antoinette drifted from group to group, introducing herself to people she didn't know and greeting those she did. It was a friendly crowd, growing friendlier still with the consumption of alcohol in the combined traditions of Ireland and New Orleans. Joshua came over for a hug and smiled with pride when she congratulated him on the impending addition to his family.

It was only when she had tired of adult conversation and the nostalgic smell of cigarette smoke that Antoinette decided to investigate the backyard, where she knew Bridget and some of the other children invited to the party were playing. The day was sunny and clear, cool enough to enjoy, warm enough to hint at subtropical temperatures still to come.

The promise of fresh air and a quiet place to think about what Skeeter had said drew her through the kitchen and out onto the back porch, where she could see the tiny plot of grass that had been turned into a child's fantasy world.

She had been prepared for jungle gyms and huge sandboxes. She hadn't been prepared for the sight of Sam pushing Bridget and another little girl on a redwood swing set. She wondered if he had come out here to avoid seeing her, then she wondered just when she had gotten so paranoid.

As she tried to decide whether or not to go back inside—her eyes helplessly riveted on the lean, muscular man clad in a green knit shirt and jeans—she realized it was too late.

"I could use some help," Sam said casually, his gaze grabbing and holding hers across the feet that separated them.

"You look like you're doing all right."

"I'd be doing better if you were here pushing, too."

She neither shrugged nor smiled. She put one foot in front of the other as casually as she could and walked across the yard to stand beside him. He moved slightly, giving her clear access to the little girl who was swinging with Bridget.

"That's Martha," he said. "She wants to go up to the sky."

Obligingly, Antoinette began to push, smiling despite herself at the gurgling laughter of the little girl whose two short black braids flopped back and forth in rhythm to the accelerating speed of the swing.

"How have you been?"

Antoinette pondered Sam's question. She had no intention of telling him the whole truth. He didn't need to know that she'd been strangely unhappy since the evening they'd shared. He didn't need to know that she'd begun to get in touch with just how lonely her life was. There were some things best left unsaid.

She settled for part of the truth. "I'd say I've been busy. I've been filling in for emergencies while a colleague vacations. Unfortunately, there've been a lot of emergencies."

Sam watched the steady ebb and flow of Martha's swing and the graceful hands of the woman pushing her. He wondered if there was anything that Antoinette didn't do with quiet self-assurance. He wondered how those long-fingered hands would feel moving slowly down his body. The last thought was an unpleasant surprise, and he searched for a topic that would rid him of his yearnings.

"I understand you've been visiting Howard Fauvier."

"I have. He needs support."

"How's he doing?"

Antoinette turned a little to view Sam's expression. She had expected to see cynicism; instead, she saw curiosity. She also saw the way the sunlight turned his hair a mellow gold and warmed the honeyed tan of his skin. She focused on Martha's back again.

"Actually, Joshua'd be able to give you more information than I would. He's working with Howard. I'm just visiting him as a friend."

"Howard? Friend?"

"He's certainly in need of one."

"Why you?"

She didn't think she could ever explain it to Sam's satisfaction, but she tried. "Something happens when you save a life. I don't think Howard would have killed himself even if I hadn't come along, but as it turns out, I was instrumental in getting him out of that room. That created a bond between us. I know who he is and what he did, but I care about him anyway. That's powerful medicine. It won't change him, but it might help him be more receptive to things that can."

"No wonder you're busy. You take the problems of the world on your shoulders."

"No, I don't. I just reach out where and when I can. I get as much as I give. When the balance changes, I'll change my way of doing things." Antoinette realized she had increased the pace of her pushes until Martha was soaring so high her braids sailed out from the side of her head like wings. She stepped back to let the little girl come down to earth again.

Sam thought about her words. Antoinette's commitment to others amazed him. She would be the same way in a relationship, giving all she had and fooling herself into believing that she was getting as much as she gave. Ross Dunlap must have been the ultimate fool as well as the ultimate con man to shake her loyalty so disastrously that she would leave him.

Antoinette waited for Sam to disparage what she'd said. When he didn't, she began the conversation she had rehearsed in her head. When she had her answers, she would go back in the house and join the rest of the party again. The worst would be over. "How is Laurie doing now that her mom is out of the hospital?"

"Much better. Did you know they're both living with the Pattersons?"

"No, I didn't."

"Mr. and Mrs. Patterson wouldn't let them go back to the apartment where they'd lived before the fire. Mrs. Fischer still needs a lot of rest, and Mrs. Patterson convinced her that she'd be insulted if they didn't come to her house where she could fix their meals and do their laundry."

"Will she be going back to work soon?" Antoinette began to push Martha again.

"She and Laurie'll be going back to Mississippi as soon as she's well enough. She's planning to go to school there and get a degree."

Antoinette was thrilled to hear such good news. "How did that happen?"

"Someone from her hometown was here on a convention, saw an article in the paper about the fire and recognized her name. Her parents and her in-laws came up last weekend to see her and Laurie. Laurie's father is out of the picture now. His parents finally realized that he had problems and sent him to a treatment center out of state. They've been searching for Laurie and her mom ever since. Mrs. Fischer says they're very supportive and they want her to go back home and get a fresh start.''

Antoinette realized she'd sighed. She loved happy endings, and she saw them too rarely. ''I'm so glad it's worked out for them. They both deserved a better life.''

''And four grandparents in a little Mississippi town are getting their granddaughter back.''

''Listen to you. You like happy endings, too.'' Antoinette turned, momentarily forgetting the tension between them, and shot Sam a big smile.

Sam could feel the impact like a cannonball in the gut. If he'd managed to convince himself in the intervening weeks that his attraction to Antoinette had just been a passing fancy, that one smile destroyed his conviction. ''What made you think I didn't?''

Her smile faltered and died. She wasn't about to get into a discussion that could turn personal. ''Can you talk about the Omega Oil case or is it top secret?''

Silently he congratulated her on such a neat change of subject. She was right—neither of them should be digging beneath the surface. ''Unfortunately, there's nothing to tell. We could still fill the Superdome with our suspects.''

''What about Howard Fauvier?''

''Angry is not the same as guilty. We're still looking into the possibility he had something to do with the fire, but personally I don't think it's likely.''

''Has Laurie's description been helpful?''

''No. I'm not sure it ever will be.''

''I wanna get down!'' Antoinette turned her attention back to the little girl in the swing in front of her.

''Hold on, Martha.'' Antoinette grabbed the slender chains and pulled the swing to a stop. She unhooked the safety bar, and the little girl slid to the ground. From the corner of her eye, she could see that Bridget was also getting down. Both little girls ran to the porch and disappeared inside.

"I imagine we'll be heading for the parade soon." Antoinette checked her watch. "It left Felicity Street at two. I think I'll go inside and see what the plans are."

"Antoinette."

She was halfway across the yard before Sam's call stopped her. She turned, glad that so many feet separated them.

Her name had come out of his mouth with absolutely no permission from his brain. Why had he called her? He had what he'd claimed he wanted. She was friendly but distant. There had been no touching, no particular warmth except for that one smile. There was no danger of a relationship between them anymore. She understood exactly how little he had to give a woman, and she wasn't interested. He wondered what he was going to say next.

"Will you walk to the parade with me?"

Antoinette noted the surprise in Sam's eyes at his own question. It was nothing compared to the surprise she felt. "What's happening here?" she asked him after a long hesitation.

"Damned if I know."

"Sam, you made it clear you didn't want me."

"That's not what I remember. I wanted you."

"You know what I mean."

"I'd like to be friends."

"That would be something new."

He smiled at her stubbornness. He hadn't suspected it existed. "Would it help if I told you I've regretted what happened?"

"Which part did you regret?"

What part? He regretted he hadn't kept his mouth shut. He regretted he hadn't let their passion build until it culminated the way they had both yearned for it to. He regretted not knowing what her body felt like under his, what it felt like to be rid of this desire for her.

"Never mind." Impatiently Antoinette tossed her hair over her shoulder, but she couldn't keep her lips from turning up. Sam was a master at hiding his feelings, but he couldn't hide the way his eyes were devouring her body. She knew what he was thinking. "I guess I can hazard a short walk with you." She was up the stairs and in the house before he could think of a response. He stared at the door for long moments before he followed her inside.

As it turned out, the walk to the parade was a study in innocence. Joshua refused to let Maggie leave until the last possible second so that she wouldn't have to stand longer than necessary. Sam volunteered to take Bridget so that she wouldn't miss a moment of the preparade chaos, and then he handed her to Antoinette because he was carrying a ladder with a specially built seat on top.

"I don't see anyone else carrying a ladder," Antoinette remarked after they had covered three blocks. Bridget was heavy enough; she imagined Sam was regretting his offer.

"Then Bridget'll have the best seat on the route."

"And the brightest." The ladder was painted in Day-Glo stripes of purple, green and gold. The seat was padded with plush shag carpeting of a different gold so that the effect was shattering to the eye.

"Are you criticizing my ladder?"

"*Your* ladder?" Antoinette eyed Sam, who looked as if he were carrying a toothpick. He wasn't even sweating.

"I made it for her at Mardi Gras. Then I had to paint it to convince her to get on it."

"Mine," Bridget said helpfully, pointing to the ladder.

Antoinette digested the new piece of information. Obviously Sam's love was next to impossible to win, but once it was won, it was boundless. She remembered him admitting that he had disliked and distrusted Maggie at first. Clearer still was a picture of Sam at the party, before they left, ushering Maggie to a chair and standing guard over her so that she wouldn't jump up to play the perfect hostess. His expression had been tender, and it had given Antoinette a strange jolt to see it aimed at another woman, even one as happily married as Maggie Martane.

"You love all of them, don't you? Joshua, Maggie, Bridget."

Sam's answer was a grunt.

She wondered how many other people he'd loved in his lifetime. She wondered why she wanted to be included on the list.

Three blocks later they stopped on Magazine and Washington, and Sam unfolded the ladder. The Irish Channel St. Patrick's Day parade was a tradition in a city where there was never a reason not to parade. No holiday, no matter how solemn, passed without floats, bands and handfuls of doubloons and beads thrown into the streets. The St. Patrick's parade added the unique touch of bestowing cabbages and other assorted vegetables on the expectant crowds. And following the floats and the clowns were the marching clubs, seemingly endless lines of men dressed in formal attire who exchanged a paper carnation or string of long beads for a kiss.

"Have you ever been to this parade?" Sam asked Antoinette after the ladder was secured and Bridget was clapping her hands from her seat on top.

"I used to come all the time when I was a kid. I grew up right down the street."

"I had you pegged for the Garden District."

"You were right. My parents still live in the house I grew up in." Antoinette watched as a group of Shriners' clowns moved a bright green sound truck into the street in front of them. The off-key tinkle of "Danny Boy" filled the air. One of the clowns jumped off the running board of the truck and began to make a balloon sculpture for Bridget. He left as suddenly as he'd arrived, giving the little girl a pink balloon poodle before he disappeared into the crowd on the other side of the street to honor another child.

Vendors passed, selling green felt derbies and plastic leprechauns. Family groups perched on the curb, eating peanuts and drinking soft drinks and beer. The streets were lined in anticipation of the parade, but there weren't the hordes of people that a Mardi Gras parade would have produced. The atmosphere was relaxed and friendly. This parade, like other parades throughout the year, was a party New Orleans gave itself.

Police officers assigned to control the crowds wandered over to talk to Sam. Antoinette watched the mixture of affection and deference with which he was greeted. She was introduced as Sam's friend, but she saw the assessing looks that came her way. She wondered if she was passing the test.

Little by little guests from the Martane's party came to stand around them. Just as the Jerusalem Temple clown cars began to buzz the street in front of them, signaling the beginning of the parade, Joshua and Maggie arrived to take over the ladder. Sam stepped down, pulling Antoinette to stand next to him. His arm slipped around her waist, and his hand rested on her hip. The only person in the crowd who didn't seem perfectly clear about their relationship was her.

The next half hour was a free-for-all of people scurrying for beads, bronze and green doubloons, plastic cups with Irish slogans and lethal vegetables that seemed to come flying through the air from nowhere.

"What's our count?" Sam asked Antoinette, peering into the plastic bag that Maggie had given them.

"Two cabbages, six potatoes, three carrots and too many Brussels sprouts to number."

"Watch out!"

Antoinette ducked with a reflex that had been honed by twenty-eight years of New Orleans parades. She felt something whiz past her head, ruffling her hair.

"Got it. Make that three cabbages."

"All we need is corned beef and we've got dinner."

Antoinette felt Sam's fingers dig into her shoulder as he leaped for some other piece of Irish booty. The float passing them was partly populated by a group of the New Orleans Saints, the city's own football team, and the crowd was going wild.

"This was thrown to you." Sam held up a green silk garter trimmed in dime-store lace. "You should wear it."

Antoinette lifted her eyes to his and saw the challenge there. She realized he didn't know her well enough to understand just what a challenge did to that tiny part of her that was never going to grow up. "I've got my hands full," she said, drawing out the words. "Why don't you put it on for me?"

Nothing moved except his eyes. They neither narrowed nor widened; they only seemed to heat until they were the leaping gold of an autumn bonfire. "My pleasure," he said. The sound came from low in his throat, and Antoinette willed her heart to beat as he stooped in front of her.

She was aware of the continuous passing parade, but time seemed to stop as Sam coaxed her to lift her foot and removed one of her low-heeled sandals. He ran his fingers along her instep and up to her ankle before he began to smooth the garter over her stockinged toes. He worked slowly, inching the silky fabric over her foot and ankle, up the calf of her leg, over her knee, to finally rest above the hem of her skirt. His hands slid down the way they had come, making a torturous, unhurried exit. Then he slipped her shoe back on her foot and fastened the tiny silver buckle. When he finally stood, Antoinette could think of nothing to say.

"I thought it was over, but it's just begun," Sam said, taking care of the silence between them.

Antoinette knew he wasn't talking about the parade.

The streets of the Garden District were quiet and serene. The shamrock and leprechaun charm of the Irish Channel was absent, although only a mythical line separated the two neighborhoods. The Garden District streets were lined with homes that often qualified as mansions, and yards that only a professional gardener touched. The Garden District had not been built for working men. It had been built before the Civil War for the American entrepreneurs of New Orleans who had not been accepted by the Creole aristocrats already in residence in the French Quarter. These "Americans" had surrounded themselves with stately gardens instead of enclosed courtyards, and they had created their own aristocracy.

The block-long gardens had given way to more houses through the years, and today it was common to find families with old Creole names living in them. Still, the Garden

District kept its unique flavor of old money and older charm. As Sam and Antoinette walked along one of the quiet side streets, the differences in their backgrounds were perfectly obvious.

"Bow your head. We're about to step on hallowed ground." Antoinette rested her head against Sam's shoulder as they walked, arms around each other's waist, along the sidewalk.

"Your house?"

"The one with the widow's walk." She pointed in front of them. "That was my favorite part of the house, only I was never allowed to go up there. My mother didn't think it was safe or respectable. She insisted that the neighbors would think we were spying on them."

Sam examined the huge mansion with stained-glass windows and Victorian furbelows and tried to picture the child Antoinette playing there. The house lent itself to visions of children hopscotching on its wide curving porch or peering over the railings of the widow's walk, but something about the way it was maintained canceled the vision. The whole picture was too immaculate, too perfect. The pristine white paint looked as if it were touched up twice a day; the yard looked as if no leaf had ever dared to fall on its landscaped perfection. Sam wondered if her childhood had been equally stultifying.

"Were you an only child?" he asked, testing his theory.

"I have a sister two years younger than me."

"Still in New Orleans?"

"No. Mignon left home when she was seventeen and never came back. I hear from her about twice a year, always from someplace new. She's happy, I think."

He wanted to know more, but a movement on the front porch of the house caught his eye. "Your mother?" he asked softly.

"We've been caught. Do you mind?" Antoinette lifted her arm to wave at the woman waiting for them with her hands on her hips. She moved away from Sam and took his hand. "We won't go inside. Just let me introduce you, and we can be on our way."

Sam let her pull him up the brick walkway bordered by perfectly spaced clumps of purple alyssum. The woman on the porch had yet to smile, and he got an image of what Antoinette would look like in twenty years if she ever soured on life and learned to expect more than she could possibly get.

"Hello, Mother. This is my friend Sam Long. Sam, my mother, Martha Deveraux."

Mrs. Deveraux looked as if she was considering whether or not to offer her hand, but she finally extended it for a brief, limp handshake. "Hello, Mr. Long."

"Sam and I were touring the neighborhood. We've been over at the St. Patrick's parade."

"You always did love that parade."

Sam registered the disapproval in the words that could have been warm and conspiratorial.

"I always did. How have you been, Mother?"

"Well. Your father and I just got back from a trip to Bermuda."

"Did you enjoy it?"

Mrs. Deveraux lifted her shoulders a weary inch. She and Antoinette continued their polite, stilted exchange, although Sam noticed that Antoinette was the only one asking questions.

It wasn't until they had said their goodbyes and were back in the Irish Channel that he felt Antoinette's body soften against his. He felt as if he'd been given a long, intense lecture on her childhood, complete with slide show and Dolby sound. "How did you survive?" he asked finally.

Antoinette understood exactly what he meant. She had asked herself the same question often enough. "I did exactly what was expected of me. I incurred my parents' wrath as little as possible and waited for the first chance to get out of the house. Ross was that chance, and, of course, I leaped right out of the frying pan and into the fire. After that it took a while to put my life in perspective, but when I did, I knew I wanted to spend the rest of my life helping other people do the same."

Sam had guided her down a street paralleling the Martane's, and now he stopped, pointing at the house in front of them. It was in sad need of paint, but it stood proudly, waiting for someone to care about it. In style, it was much like Maggie and Joshua's house. In spirit, it was a million miles away.

"I get a three-week vacation this summer. I'm going to spend most of it painting this monstrosity."

Antoinette tried to imagine Sam growing up in the dilapidated old house. "It needs love as much as paint," she said finally. "It needs commitment."

"I don't have either to spare."

She faced him, no measurable space between them. Her hand lifted to touch his cheek, smoothing a path along the line of his jaw. His eyes were green now, as green as the crepe-paper streamers on the house next to his. "I don't think you know yourself very well," she said, standing on tiptoe to brush her lips against his.

His arms came around her waist, and he stopped her from retreating. "I know what I want and what I don't," he said, his mouth against her ear. "I just don't know if I can have one without the other."

"Then you'll have to choose. And you'll have to learn to live with your choice."

"Or you'll have to choose and learn to do the same," he answered just before his lips found hers for a kiss that taught them both that choices were never easy to make.

Chapter 7

Dr. Daphne Brookes, better known as Daffy to her friends, stood on her head in the corner of the darkened office, her scarlet-tipped toes pointed toward the ceiling. Antoinette stood in the doorway, right side up, and waited patiently as her friend attempted to increase blood flow to her brain.

"Hard day?" Antoinette asked when Daffy was sitting cross-legged on the floor in a position that made Antoinette's joints creak in protest. Daffy did yoga when she was under stress. Judging from the level of activity at that moment, Antoinette knew the day must have been a monster.

"Extremely hard. The worst. Unsurvivable."

"Break a fingernail?"

Daffy's grin was like sunshine in the midst of gloom. "Think you know me, huh?"

"As well as anyone ever will. What happened?" Antoinette took a seat on the Japanese futon catercorner to Daffy's contorted body.

"My car died. Died, as in no resurrection possible. They're hauling it to the junkyard for me, and it's so far gone I have to pay them to do it. They don't even want the parts!"

Antoinette tried to look properly saddened. The car in question was a 1960 Volkswagen Beetle, although there was little left of it that was still circa 1960. Everything had been replaced at one time or another, even the sporty little sunroof, which Daffy had reupholstered in chartreuse Naugahyde. "Have you thought about a replacement?"

"Shame on you." Daffy shook back her unruly mop of red curls. She had confided to Antoinette recently that she was letting her hair grow so that when she stood on her head, she'd have more padding. Antoinette hadn't questioned her logic.

"Well, when you're done grieving, I'll be glad to lend you my car so you can buy a new one."

"It'll be years before I recover."

"I know the feeling."

Daffy shifted slightly so that she was facing her friend. Daffy had no qualms about following her impulses and living out her fantasies, but she was also one of the most perceptive therapists Antoinette had ever known. As a friend, those qualities were just as evident. "What is it you're recovering from?" Daffy asked now. "Does the sinfully handsome police sergeant have anything to do with those circles under your eyes?"

Since she and Daffy never played games, Antoinette nodded. "He does. I haven't seen him for two weeks, and today, out of nowhere, he called and invited me to take a little girl to the park with him tomorrow. I can't figure out what our relationship is or isn't. I could adjust if I knew, but as it is, I feel off balance."

"Then he's just what you needed."

Antoinette tilted her head to regard her friend, who was now arched like a bow with only her palms and the soles of her feet touching the bare wood floor. "What's that supposed to mean?"

"I mean you need someone or something to shake you up," Daffy said, gasping. "I've been hoping it would happen before you turned thirty. The thirties are too good to waste being careful and doing what you think you're supposed to."

Antoinette ignored the fact that Daffy was only twenty-eight, too. "I don't do things I don't want to."

"And you don't do things you *do* want to." Daffy collapsed on the floor, rolling onto her stomach. "Walk on my back, will you?"

"I'm not a chiropractor."

"Just put your feet on each side of my spine and walk. Dare to be different."

Antoinette made a noise between a sigh and a grumble. She took off her shoes and straddled her friend. "I'm going to break something. Don't you sue me!"

"I'm waiting."

Antoinette put one foot on Daffy's back and tried adding her weight little by little. Daffy's response was a pleased moan. Shaking her head, Antoinette added her other foot, distributing her weight evenly. She began to inch along. "What do you mean I don't do things I want to?" Since Daffy's back was in perfect proportion to her five-foot-two body, the walk was over before it had begun. Antoinette stepped down, turned around and walked back the way she'd come. Then she resumed her seat.

"Thanks." Daffy sat up and began to rotate her head. "You're a beautiful woman with a woman's normal drives, but you keep every man who comes near you at arm's length. You're too busy, or too considerate, or too blind to what a man wants."

"You're saying I don't sleep around and I'm really dying to?"

"I'm saying something always stops you from taking a lover. And I think it's because you're still not over the fact that you made one real doozy of a mistake."

Antoinette didn't like having her fears so easily dismissed. "I couldn't survive another man like my ex-husband."

Daffy heard the hurt in Antoinette's voice, but she went on anyway. "You've grown into a new person, but you don't trust yourself yet. You still think you could be fooled again."

"Sam's not trying to fool me. He's honest about what he wants. Me. On my back."

"Are you waiting for marriage?"

Antoinette shook her head. "I guess I'm waiting for a signed statement that says I won't get hurt again."

"Fat chance."

"I know."

"What's the worst thing that could happen?"

"I could go to bed with Sam, and after a night or two together he could decide he didn't want me anymore."

"And you'd feel hurt and angry. Then, after a while, you'd see that you really weren't any worse off than you'd been before Sam and that at least you'd reached for something wonderful."

"Well, here's something even worse." Antoinette leaned forward. "What if it weren't just a matter of one or two nights? What if we developed a real relationship, I fell totally in love with him and then he left me?"

"Are you the kind of woman who lets herself fall in love if there's no hope it'll be reciprocated?"

"I don't think I'd do that. Even with Ross I thought he loved me when I married him."

"Then is Sam the kind of man who'd drop a woman he'd made an emotional commitment to? Does he fall in and out of love as often as he washes his shirts?" Daffy stopped revolving her head and met her friend's gaze.

Antoinette might not understand everything about Sam, but she had seen enough evidence of his commitment to those he cared about to know the answer to Daffy's question. "No, he doesn't. I think once Sam loves, he's loyal to death."

"There's your answer. The very worst couldn't happen. The risk is small. You have to decide if it's worth taking."

"Why does everything always sound so simple coming out of your mouth?" Antoinette stood and stretched. After watching Daffy's yoga exercises, her own body felt tight and unfit.

"Generally, I find if something's not simple, it's because people are making it difficult on purpose."

"You think I should have an affair with Sam?"

"I think you should reach for what you want."

"Why does that put butterflies in my stomach?"

Daffy stood and gave her friend a quick hug. "Because you haven't had much practice."

"That's definitely true where men are concerned."

"So now you want to hear the good news?"

Antoinette smiled wryly and nodded her head.

"Even at your advanced age, you're not too old to learn."

Antoinette watched Sam demonstrate the intricacies of scooping minnows from the water with a small net. Laurie stood beside him, her brow wrinkled in concentration. "What do I do if I get one?" she asked doubtfully.

"You put it in this jar. Then, before we go, we'll put them back in the water."

"Do they bite?"

"Not unless you're good to eat."

Laurie giggled and took the net. In a moment she was absorbed in the pleasure of outsmarting minnows. Sam came to sit on the blanket beside Antoinette, his back against a huge live oak tree draped with lacy Spanish moss.

"You realize this could take all day," he said lazily.

"All day for her to catch a minnow?"

Sam made himself more comfortable and his expression was smug. "We can't leave until she does. If we do, she'll feel like she's failed."

"And in the meantime you get to be lazy."

"I planned it this way."

"I got one! Come see, Sam! I got one!"

Sam groaned and got to his feet again while Antoinette laughed. Shooting her a grin, he walked to the shore to peer over the little girl's shoulder into the net. "That's a minnow, all right."

"Get me the jar, quick."

Sam held out the gallon jar filled with water, and Laurie deftly plopped the tiny silver fish into it. "He's a beauty," he complimented her.

"It's a girl fish."

"How do you know?"

"She looks like a girl. I'm gonna see if I can catch a boy next."

"Good thinking." Sam set the jar in the shade where Laurie would have easy access to it and joined Antoinette once more.

"This could be a very short picnic," Antoinette observed, closing her eyes and letting the warmth of the April sun work its magic.

"Well, it's a big park. If she catches all the minnows in sight, we can take her over to the merry-go-round or rent a paddleboat."

"I'm going to catch a whole family! A mother, a father, kids. Everything!" Laurie called from the bank of the little lagoon. "Then I can tell my grandmas."

"You're going to miss her when she goes, aren't you?" Antoinette reached over and rested her hand on top of Sam's. Today was a farewell celebration for Laurie. Tomorrow she and her mother were going back to the town where she'd been born.

Sam turned his hand palm up and wove his fingers through Antoinette's, magnifying the intimacy of her impulsive gesture. His thumb caressed the sensitive skin on the inside of her wrist, and he could feel the resulting increase in her pulse rate. "I'll miss Laurie, but I'm happy she's going. Life'll be easier for them from now on."

Antoinette pulled her hand from Sam's and reached for the battered old picnic basket that Mrs. Patterson had insisted on filling with her homemade bread and other assorted goodies, including dozens of spicy boiled shrimp. She still wasn't sure where the day was supposed to go. As she'd told Daffy, the off-again, on-again quality of their relationship had knocked her off balance. Every time Sam touched her, she wondered just exactly where it would lead. Every time she touched him, she wondered just exactly what she was trying to do.

Antoinette set the shrimp between them and began to remove shells as she changed the subject of the conversation.

"Last time I saw you, you still weren't close to solving the Omega Oil case. Has anything broken on that yet?"

There was no reproach in her words, but Sam heard only the beginning of the sentence. *Last time I saw you.* He had waited two weeks before giving in to the urge to contact her again, but not a day had gone by without thoughts of Antoinette. Not that all his thoughts had been good ones. Along with the vision of her body pressed against his came the vision of chains. She was a woman who wanted more than a casual affair, a woman who deserved more. If she gave herself, it wouldn't be easily, and it wouldn't be temporarily. He was a man satisfied with his life. He was a loner, and being alone suited him. So why had he called her? Why couldn't he let go?

"Sam?" Antoinette held a shrimp between her thumb and forefinger, tantalizingly close to his lips. "Are you hungry?"

Sam opened his mouth, and Antoinette dangled the shrimp over it, dipping down to run it along his bottom lip. He tasted cayenne and allspice, the rich tang of shellfish and desire. His fingers closed around her wrist, capturing it to hold it in place as he took the shrimp between his teeth. When he'd finished it, he savored the flavor of her fingers.

Antoinette closed her eyes at the unexpected pleasure of his lips gently sucking her fingertips. Sam watched the long sweep of eyelashes against her cheek, heard the involuntary sigh. Antoinette was a woman who enjoyed being touched as much as she enjoyed touching. And yet she was a woman who had denied herself more than the most casual affection. He wondered why a woman who obviously took such delight in human contact had denied herself the ultimate human contact for so many years.

Sam released her hand, and Antoinette pulled her fingers from his lips to reach for another shrimp. She was trembling; she realized that her needs and her vulnerability to the man beside her were going to make it impossible to say no to him again. She had passed the crossroads, and she hadn't taken the safest path. The wise decision would have been to tell Sam she wouldn't see him anymore when he'd called. That decision hadn't even occurred to her.

"I could starve on one shrimp."

"Better start peeling, then." Antoinette sat forward and began to strip the shell off another shrimp for herself. She let her hair fall across her shoulder to hide her face and, she hoped, her thoughts. As a psychologist she knew what happened to people who let their feelings build until they erupted with volcanic force. For all her training, for all her experience, she was no different. Her feelings for Sam were reaching volcanic proportions.

Sam sat forward, too, and picked up a shrimp. "You asked about the Omega Oil case."

Antoinette tried to sound casual. "I was curious. If you can't talk about it, that's okay."

"I wish I had something to talk about."

"It's still up in the air?"

"The team working on it is evenly divided. One of the prevailing theories is that someone in management's got an ax to grind, the other is that the arsonist's a relative of one of the men killed during the hurricane last year. There's evidence that either one of those theories could be correct and evidence that points away from them."

"Which one do you subscribe to?"

"Neither. I'm working on it without a theory."

"Has anyone tried to develop a psychological profile of the man responsible?"

"There's not even positive evidence only one person is responsible."

"Do you think one man set the fire?" Antoinette felt Sam touch her shoulder. His hand lifted the heavy mass of black hair and pushed it behind her ear.

"Probably."

"How about a psychological profile of him?"

"There's too little to go on, and our staff is too small."

"I could do it for you." Since she was no longer hidden from Sam's view anyway, Antoinette twisted so that she was facing him. "Gratis."

"Why?"

"Because I'm interested in the whole case. The man who rescued Laurie isn't your ordinary psychopath. If he's really the one who set the fire, then he's quite a complex individual. I already have some ideas about him. It won't be a truly professional profile, more a series of hunches and impressions. But it might help."

Sam examined the woman leaning toward him. Today she was dressed in designer jeans and a turquoise sweater that molded the slender curves of her body to perfection. The dappled sunlight emphasized the luminescence of her skin and the jet black of her hair. He remembered the day he'd come to her office to ask her to work with Laurie. He'd thought she was too beautiful to be truly professional. She was no less beautiful now, but today he knew better than to let that prejudice him.

He nodded. "I'd be glad to have your help." I'd be glad to have you, he added silently, and then wondered why that thought had come so easily when the reality was much more complicated.

"Now I just need an uncle." Laurie came back to the blanket and deposited the gallon jar filled with minnows at the edge. "There were lots of aunts but no uncles."

"How about a shrimp instead?" Antoinette peeled one and held it out to the little girl.

"Minnows don't eat shrimp."

"Young ladies do, don't they?" Antoinette patted the place beside her. Laurie dropped to the blanket and wiggled her way between them. She ate the shrimp Antoinette had peeled for her, peeling another for herself when it was finished.

"Will you come see me in Mississippi?" Laurie asked, her face lifted to Sam's.

"Sure."

Laurie turned to Antoinette. "You can come, too."

"Thank you."

"I like you. You're the one who made me remember the fire."

Antoinette looked at Sam, who was frowning at Laurie's innocent comment. "So you remember it now," Antoinette said with studied nonchalance. ''Does it seem scary to you?''

''No. I don't remember much of it, just lots of smoke and crying. Stuff like that. And I remember the man who carried me out.''

''He helped you.''

''He was a good man,'' Laurie agreed. She turned to Sam, her eyes wide and trusting. ''When you find him, will you tell him I'm glad he found me?''

Antoinette watched Sam's face. Not a muscle twitched. ''Sure will,'' he promised the little girl. ''Just as soon as we find him.''

''Good.'' Laurie popped another shrimp into her mouth.

''Finish up and we'll take you for a ride on the paddleboats.'' Sam rummaged through the picnic basket, searching for napkins, and Antoinette shut her eyes and listened as he made sure Laurie got enough to eat. Sam Long, the man who said he wanted no ties and no changes, would make a wonderful father if he ever changed his mind. She wondered if, in his quest for absolute independence, he realized how many people he already loved.

''You look sad.'' Antoinette stood in front of Sam on the porch of her house. The picnic had been a success with Laurie chattering freely to both of them. A full family of minnows had been returned to their watery home, an hour in a paddleboat had taught them more about City Park than they'd ever wanted to know and three of the old-fashioned horses on the carousel had been graced with their presence until Antoinette finally had pleaded motion sickness.

Laurie had clung to Sam at the end, aware that it would be a long time before she saw him again. He had kissed her on the forehead and promised he'd write. Then he'd sent her into the house and into the waiting arms of her mother and Mrs. Patterson. He'd had nothing to say on the short trip to Antoinette's house.

The sun had gone down, and the sky was a collage of rose and apricot. The cool air was fragrant with sweet olive, and as they'd walked up the sidewalk, a mourning dove with a long string in her beak had flown across their path to add to a nest in a nearby hedge. Antoinette had experienced it all, as if every one of her senses was heightened to these ordinary events of a New Orleans spring. It was her twenty-eighth April, and she knew that it was the first that had affected her this way.

Now she moved closer to Sam and reached out to touch his hair. It slid through her fingers, each separate strand a tactile pleasure. "Laurie's a lovely little girl," she said softly. "I know you'll miss her."

"I can think of a great comfort." Sam's hands settled at her waist, neither drawing her closer nor pushing away. Both of them knew he was waiting for Antoinette to make the next move.

"I don't want you to leave."

"I'm in no hurry to go."

Antoinette stepped closer, her fingers weaving among the golden tendrils until his face was only inches from hers. His expression was a mixture of caution and desire. There had been no promises made, no answers to the questions whirling through her head. For the first time in her life, she wondered if promises and answers were irrelevant. "Would you like to come inside? I think I have something we can fix for supper."

"I'd like that."

She continued to hesitate, sighing finally as she breached the distance between them by lifting on tiptoe to find his mouth with hers.

It was all the response he needed. His hands left her waist to slide into the pockets at the back of her jeans and fit her body against his. His mouth slanted over hers in a kiss that demanded everything she could give him. Antoinette clasped her arms around his neck and gave herself up to the peace of a decision made.

Sam could feel the exact moment when she relaxed completely, letting the kiss take them both somewhere they had never been together. Her lips parted willingly, and their tongues met in a mutual caress. He could feel his body tighten with desire; he could feel liquid fire pouring through his veins at her uninhibited response. He hadn't known what it was like to go from wanting a woman to needing one, all in the space of a heartbeat. With his last ounce of self-control, he found her waist again and set her away from him.

Antoinette's eyes were half-shut, and her face was still turned up to his. She wondered how she had lived for twenty-eight years without the wonder of the feelings that had suffused her body. She wondered why Sam had so abruptly ended them.

"Let's go inside." Sam released her and stepped back to put more distance between them.

Antoinette heard the caution in his voice. Fear flickered through her, and it became an antidote for the remnants of passion. She had been told often enough that she was a lovely woman. She had seen the approval in men's eyes and heard it in their voices. And always, as she did now, she had wondered if all that was desirable about her was the empty shell of her beauty. Was the gift of herself, her heart, her soul, so worthless that when she gave it, it meant nothing?

She turned to find her key and unlocked the door. Fear continued to play its skillful, diabolical game with her confidence.

"Antoinette, if you'd like me to leave, I will."

She could hear her own vulnerability in her answer. "Do what you want, Sam."

He followed her inside, watching as she bent to greet Tootsie. The big dog was going crazy with joy, and some emotion he refused to name shot through Sam at the sight of Antoinette dropping to her knees to hug the wriggling bundle of fur. He'd had more women in his thirty-four years than he could remember names. Not one of them would have been seen on the floor hugging a dog. Not one of them would have cared about a man intent on killing himself or about a little girl's fears or about one of his cases. Not one of them had ever kissed him with the same intensity, the same total giving of herself.

He wanted to run.

Antoinette stood and brushed dog hair off her jeans, laughing as she apologized. "I'm sorry she's so awful, but she's a sociable dog and she's been cooped up all day. I should have brought her with me to the park, but she's so exuberant I thought she might scare Laurie. Mrs. Patterson told me Laurie's afraid of their dog."

"When did you talk to Mrs. Patterson?"

"Last night."

"You called her about the dog?"

"Well, actually, she called me. She's got a new foster child who's giving her problems, and she wanted my advice."

"Does anyone pay you for what you do? Do you always give your services for free?"

"NOPD paid me. Remember?" Antoinette started toward the kitchen. She sensed something in Sam's voice that she didn't understand. It seemed to be a close relative to disapproval.

"Where are you going?"

She turned in the kitchen doorway, leaning there for support. "To find us something to eat."

Sam counted all the sources of the anger welling up inside him. He was angry at Antoinette for being the person she was, angry at himself for wanting her even though he knew just how dangerous it would be to have her, angry at a world where people who could never be good for each other still fell in love. "Don't make anything for me."

Antoinette heard the anger. "What have I done?" When he didn't answer, she moved to stand in front of him, her body a careful distance from his. "Sam, talk to me."

The shake of his head was barely perceptible. "We've already said it all. And what good did it do? We're standing in the same place, wanting each other, and neither one of us has changed."

She thought she understood, and her face lit up in a smile of pure relief. "Not true. Did you think I was teasing you? Promising something I had no intention of delivering?" She laughed a deep, throaty laugh that went straight through him. "Is that why you pushed me away?" To test her theory she moved closer, circling his waist with her arms. "I wouldn't do that, Sam."

Nor would she give herself with no thought of tomorrow. He knew her well enough to understand that. "I haven't changed," he warned, even as he pulled her closer. "I'm not looking for a relationship."

"I know. Shall we just take this one step at a time?"

He understood—even if she didn't—that one step at a time meant you had to be heading somewhere. The only place they were headed for was trouble. He had the absurd desire to protect her from her decision, and at the same time he wanted to guide her into the bedroom and spend the night getting her out of his system.

"So what's the next step?" he asked, one hand threading through the glossy hair cloaking her shoulders.

"Kiss me, and this time don't push me away."

His hands met under her chin, tilting her head so that her mouth was in line with his. He hesitated for a second, then brushed her lips lightly.

She leaned forward, capturing the next kiss and drawing it out until neither of them could continue. She felt his hand move down her spine, his fingers tracing the pliant ridge until they settled momentarily at her waist before lifting her sweater to begin the journey back up.

He stopped at the clasp of her bra, unsnapping it with a deftness that spoke of practice. His fingers fanned out to caress the sides of her breasts as his mouth worked a skillful magic on hers. Antoinette felt heat streak through her body, beginning at the very core of her and spreading out until it reached her fingertips. She knew she was trembling.

Sam opened his eyes to meet her gaze. Her summer-sky eyes were wide and vulnerable. He'd seen that look once today on the face of a little girl who thought the sun rose and set on him. He did not want to see it in the woman he was sure to hurt.

She smelled of spring, had the look of an innocent child and felt like the most desirable woman he'd ever known. Even the briefest kiss, the briefest caress, sent desire raging out of control.

The wariness had never left his face, but Antoinette saw it intensify, felt his hands drift back to her waist. She hoped she was wrong, and she waited for magic. When it wasn't forthcoming, her body tightened with tension. Her words were traced with bitterness. "If ambivalence had a name, it would be Sam Long." Antoinette forced herself to step back away from him. "Look, don't feel obligated to make love to me. I've never thrown myself at a man before. I guess I don't have the technique down yet."

"Don't kid yourself. I want you."

"Yes, I could see that," she said, tainting her words with sarcasm. "Look, I've misinterpreted what's been happening here. I'm sorry, but I think we'll both be better off if you leave now."

Her voice was calm, but her eyes glistened both with anger and unshed tears. Sam wanted to make her understand. "Just tell me one thing," he said. "How would you feel in an hour or two when I got out of your bed to go home? You're not that kind of woman."

"I expected that you'd stay the night."

"I sleep alone."

"I see."

"Do you?"

"Yes, you're telling me I'm not even worth a one-night stand. That's all the humbling any woman would ever need." She lifted her chin and willed the tears just below the surface to dry up. "And now I remember clearly why I sleep alone, too."

"There are plenty of men out there who can give you what you want."

"It's a pity, isn't it, that I never seem to want them." She crossed her arms in front of her to ward off the sympathy she thought she saw in his eyes. "Thank you for the picnic. But don't call me anymore, Sam. I've already had one man in my life who didn't need what I was offering. God knows, I don't want another one."

It was over, ending just the way he had known it should. But if that was true, why did he feel as if a terrible mistake had just been made? He reached out to comfort her, to convince her she was not at fault in any way, but she moved out of the range of his touch. She stood stiffly, her chin still lifted defiantly, and met his gaze without flinching. He turned, almost tripping over Tootsie, who had stretched out behind him in anticipation of more attention.

At the door he paused, his hand on the doorknob. But there was nothing left to say. He stepped across the threshold and into the soft, scented darkness. Antoinette watched him go and cursed herself for being a fool.

Chapter 8

Antoinette forced herself to respond to the fervent affection of the dog at her feet. She thought again, as she had often lately, that she should find another home for Tootsie, one where the dog's new owner wouldn't leave her alone all day and most of the evening, too. Tootsie needed more than just an infrequent pat on the head. The dog needed love and attention.

"Don't we all," she said out loud, kicking off her shoes and stripping off the jacket of her blue suit. She snapped on the kitchen light and rummaged through the refrigerator, settling on a carton of yogurt. She stood at the sink eating it, too tired and too dispirited to bother setting the table.

The week had drained her vitality—taken what little had been left of it after the scene with Sam. She couldn't shake the feeling that she was on some supreme being's hit list. Not only had she made a fool of herself over a man again, but in the same week she had also been forced to hospitalize one of her favorite clients and watch two others lose significant ground in their fight against depression. Setbacks were to be expected. If she weren't depressed herself, she might have been able to cope with them better.

Lethargically she flipped on the VCR to catch a taped rendition of the evening news, which she never got home in time to see anymore. Her mood quickly went from bad to worse as she watched nations war, people starve and politicians mouth platitudes. She made herself finish watching the show, certain that something that had happened somewhere in the world that day would cheer her up. When she'd been proven wrong, she stood to turn off the TV, just catching a lead-in for the local news show. Before the tape stopped and the screen went blank, the lead-in promised a report on another fire at Omega Oil's refinery near the Mississippi River north of New Orleans. She dropped back to the sofa.

She had thought of Sam often in the past week. She had thought about his reluctance to get involved with her, her desire to get involved with him, the final scene that had been played out in this room. She had wondered what was wrong with her that she couldn't give herself to a man without having her gift shoved back in her face, and she had wondered why she had twice chosen men who had nothing to give her except heartache. But in all her thoughts, in all her emotional wanderings, she had not once thought about the reason she and Sam had come together in the first place.

She had promised him that she would draw up a profile of the arsonist. True, she had very little to go on, but at this point even very little was something. She had been wallowing in her own feelings while the arsonist had plotted another fire. She wasn't conceited enough to feel guilty; she doubted seriously that anything she could have done would have made a difference. But she was ashamed that she had not followed through on something she had promised. Even if that promise had been to Sam.

Tootsie came up and laid her head in Antoinette's lap, as if to say, "I'm here. It's going to be all right." Absentmindedly Antoinette scratched the dog's ears, wondering what other responsibilities she had forgotten. She had stopped eating properly, stopped sleeping normally, stopped feeling anything except exhaustion. She had to take herself in hand quickly or she was going to end up in a hospital bed herself.

She would come through this fine if she made an effort. She would do the profile, take it right to Sam's office and drop it in his lap. She would be polite, disinterested and, best of all, finished with him. She would shake her depression, throw away the unopened package of cigarettes she'd bought that morning and get on with her life.

And if there was a small part of her that still wished things were different, then that was to be expected. She was, after everything, just a human being. Understanding motivations and drives, feelings and needs, was one thing. Coping with them was another.

She stood, flipped off the TV, and headed to the bathroom for a long, hot shower. There was plenty of work to do to keep her mind occupied for the rest of the evening. She would finish the profile before morning. Tomorrow she would present it to Sergeant Sam Long.

Sam stared unseeingly at the mounds of paper on his desk. Paperwork was the thing he liked least about being a cop. No, that wasn't quite true. The thing he liked least about being a cop was the inevitable phone call reporting a need for his services. He'd like to wake up one day and find out he was out of a job. He wouldn't mind living in a world where enforcing the law was obsolete.

The papers blurred in front of his eyes. He'd been working around the clock. His other duties had been temporarily suspended, and he, along with two other investigators, was now working full-time on the Omega Oil case. The refinery fire had been a blow, proving, among other things, that Howard Fauvier, who was safely behind the locked doors of a psychiatric ward, had probably never had anything to do with the campaign of sabotage. It had been one more dead end, but there was hope for more leads in the next week. The corruption in Omega's management was more deep-seated than anyone had guessed. The investigation was beginning to point to a small group of executives who had more to gain from Omega's demise than they had to lose.

He did not feel the thrill of the hunter closing in on his prey. He was too tired to feel much of anything. Those things he did feel, he tried to push to the back of his mind, fully aware of what he was doing. When the exhaustion seeped past his defenses, he saw vulnerable blue eyes and felt the softness of a female form melting against his body. He smelled the scent of sweet olive and heard the deep, throaty laugh of a woman—right before he hurt her again.

He hadn't wanted it to end the way it had. He had wanted to make love to Antoinette, wanted to take his fill and leave her filled, too. He had wanted to part friends as he had so many times in the past with other women. He knew now that he'd been wrong to let things go so far. He'd sensed the differences between Antoinette and the other women he'd known, right from the beginning. Even more important, he'd sensed the differences in himself.

There was no place in his life, in this life, for a real relationship. His job was his life. He'd been on the streets himself, he knew what went on out there. He was a good cop, a dedicated cop. He was also chronically in danger. There was one way to stay ahead, one way to stay alive. His concentration had to be single-minded. And he was happy that way. He wanted nothing better, nothing different.

He wanted her.

Sam put his head in his hands and stared at his desk. The room was filled with other desks, but short of taking out a gun and firing a shot into the air, no one would notice what he did. This was a police station, not an IBM executive suite. Phones were ringing, people were being booked, statements were being taken. No one would notice if one cop went quietly crazy from exhaustion and gut-wrenching loneliness.

"Sam?"

The voice was soft, musical and unmistakably hers. For a moment he was sure he'd imagined it. Sam lifted his head and stared at the woman standing in front of him. She looked exactly like he felt. "What are you doing here?"

Antoinette had dressed with care, selecting a prim navy blazer and taupe skirt that proclaimed her a professional. Her hair was parted precisely in the middle and pulled back in a perfect chignon. Her expression was equally proper. Unfortunately, she had a suspicion that the circles under her eyes, which had refused to relent to a skilled application of makeup, gave away her state of mind.

"I brought you the profile I promised. I'm sorry I didn't finish it sooner."

He blinked, flooded with the realization that he was being given a second chance. Or a third chance. Hell, he'd lost count of the times he'd rejected her. He wondered if she had. He stood, pulling an extra chair from the neighboring desk and bringing it alongside his own. "Please sit down."

"No, thank you." She was proud of the calm sound of her voice and not so proud that her hands were about to twist the handle off her purse. She forced them to relax. There were times when having the skills of a debutante was an advantage. "I've got to get back to my office."

"At least let me look this over before you go. I might have questions." He tried to hook her gaze, but he knew she was looking just a little to the right on purpose. It gave him time to examine every one of her features, like a man who has been without the gift of sight for years only to have it returned for one glorious moment.

"You have my number at the office," she said pleasantly. "I'll be glad to answer anything, and I'll be free between three and four today. I hope this is helpful."

"Antoinette, I'm sorry." He walked around the desk and sat on the edge in front of her.

"For what, Sam?" she asked evenly. She hesitated for a moment, realizing that she was playing a game. She knew exactly what he'd meant. "You did us both a favor."

He wondered if she practiced telepathy as well as hypnosis. He'd repeated that line to himself so many times in the past week that it had become his life's motto. He'd thought about having it emblazoned on his shirts. "Did I?" he asked quietly. "Usually when I do myself a favor, I feel happy. I've felt lots of things this week, but happiness wasn't one of them."

The perfect facade seemed to crack as he watched. He remembered only too well the vulnerable, aching expression now in her eyes. "Don't start this again," she said huskily.

"Starting is much better than ending."

"You should know—you're quite adept at both." Her words lacked the force to be truly sarcastic. They were merely tired.

There was no chance that they would ever be friends, no chance that she would believe him if he told her he wanted to try again. He knew he was still ambivalent. He wanted her, but he wanted no ties. He wanted to hold her, but he wanted none of the commitments that holding brings. He wanted to love her, but he wasn't sure that there was room inside him for love.

He couldn't lie. He couldn't make her think he'd come full circle and was ready to give all the things he couldn't. There was only one weapon he had that might bring them back together to deal with their future. The truth. The truth and a reaching out, a visible sign that he wanted more than the sadness that being away from her was bringing them both.

"I'm going down to my uncle's place on Bayou Midnight tomorrow," he said, reaching for her hand. "Come with me."

"No." She tried to pull away from him, but his fingers clasped hers in a grip that she knew she couldn't break.

"I have a place down there, too," he continued. "It's not much, a fish camp in the middle of a swamp, but it's mine and it's private. We can have the whole weekend together."

"What for? So you can decide you don't want me at the last minute and we can spend a whole weekend in miserable frustration?"

His free hand reached up to caress her cheek. "Oh, lady," he said softly, "it was never that I didn't want you. Don't you understand? I wanted you too much."

She was rooted to the spot by the emotion in his voice and the fact that he would tell her such a thing in front of his colleagues. True, no one was watching them, and no one was listening. But she suspected that Sam valued his professionalism more than he valued anything in his life. It was a sign of how deeply he felt that he would say something so personal in the middle of the police station.

"And now?" she asked finally. "Do you want me less, so it's all right to have me? Or do you want me more, so you don't care anymore? Or do you...?"

His fingertips touched her lips. "No answers. I have no answers. And no promises. And no plans beyond the weekend." He hesitated. "And no lies, Antoinette. Let's both just take a chance and try to forget everything else out there for a change. Come with me. Sleep the nights with me. Let me show you where I really grew up. Just be with me, and let it be enough for now."

Sleep the nights with me.

She heard what he was offering. Her pride and her common sense told her it was not enough. But she also knew how little life was offering without him. She wanted to know him better; she wanted to understand what drove him. She wanted to be with him during the day and asleep in his arms at night. He knew just how to make it impossible to refuse him.

"I'm not very courageous," she said finally. "And you're going to hurt me again."

"I've been trying not to hurt you."

She nodded and turned her face to kiss the fingertips that still lingered on her jaw. "Obviously I've gone crazy, but I'll come."

He understood the true depth of his desire for her when her answer brought him no satisfaction. He had a whole day to get through before they could be together. He wondered how he was going to manage it.

"Good." His fingers slid through her hair to the chignon, and he pulled her mouth to his for a brief, hard kiss. He heard the polite cough at the next desk. It didn't faze him. He knew he'd pay the price when Antoinette was gone. "I couldn't interest you in a preliminary run-through tonight, could I?'' he asked in a voice that reached her ears only.

"Let me put this in perspective, Sam," she said.

"Not in too much perspective," he warned. "Don't take the edge off it."

"I think that would be impossible."

She pulled away from him, and he saw that her cheeks were rosy. He laughed, squeezing her hand before he let her pull it from his. "I'll pick you up tomorrow morning at six."

"Six? I haven't been getting much sleep...." Her voice trailed off.

"Neither have I." His eyes narrowed, and the corner of his lips turned up in a half smile. "And I don't intend to get much this weekend. So go to bed early."

Her answer was a look that could have heated the water in the station cooler. He sat on the edge of his desk and watched her wend her way between desks and out the door. He paid no attention to the laughter of the men around him when she was gone.

Packing for a love affair in the middle of the swamps took ingenuity. Antoinette wondered if the alligators and mosquitoes expected more formal attire than jeans and casual shirts. She wasn't about to tell Sam, but like many other citizens of the City That Care Forgot, her definition of rural Louisiana had always been the sprawling suburbs that stretched on either side of New Orleans. The times she had traveled elsewhere had been as an adult in an airplane going to another big city for professional conferences or as a child going to one of the socially approved summer camps in the North Carolina mountains.

She knew the history of the Acadian people who had settled the bayous in the south. She had watched with interest as Cajun cuisine and lore had surged in popularity in the past years. She loved the spicy food, the wail of accordions, fiddles and mournful French lyrics that was Cajun music, the folktales and the pride in a culture that had not quite melted into the old melting pot. She had promised herself often enough that she would take a weekend and explore southern Louisiana someday.

She had not expected to explore it with Sam.

Antoinette stopped dropping clothes into her suitcase and wondered if she really had lost her mind. She was expecting Sam any minute. She was repacking a suitcase that had been packed the night before, just to give herself something to do. The bottom line, the absolute truth, was that she didn't believe he was coming. She'd been up since five doing busywork to force that thought out of her mind, but it was relentless. She was, quite simply, waiting for Sam to reject her again.

The pounding on her front door and Tootsie's alert barking assured her that, if he was going to reject her, he was going to do it in person. She snapped the suitcase shut and went to open the door. The look on Sam's face assured her that she'd been worrying for nothing. She was so relieved that she went straight into his arms.

"I thought you might not come." Antoinette linked her fingers behind his neck and stared into his eyes, trying to read any hidden signs of hesitancy.

"I thought you might not want me to."

"I've packed twice, just to keep busy."

"I've been ready since five." Sam traced the outline of her face in gentle kisses, ending finally at her mouth where the kiss wasn't gentle at all. "I've been ready since yesterday," he amended when he pulled away.

"Why is this so difficult?"

"Because I'm a difficult person." Sam held her face tilted up to his, wanting her to understand. "I'm exactly the kind of man I'd warn any woman not to get involved with."

"When I was a child, the only times I ever got into trouble were when someone dared me to do something. I could never resist a dare. I feel an attack of that coming on now."

He laughed, and the serious expression on his face dissolved, giving her a picture of a younger, happier man. "I'm beyond trying to talk you out of it. Let's go."

"Let me check to be sure Tootsie's got enough food until my neighbor can get over to check on her."

Sam bent to scratch Tootsie's head. "Do you want to come with us, Toots?"

The wiggling stump of Tootsie's tail was answer enough.

Antoinette was surprised and touched by his offer. "Are you sure?"

"My place doesn't have enough solid ground this time of year to interest her, but my uncle has a dog and more cats than I can count. She can stay there."

"She'll love it."

The drive out of New Orleans took them into the swamps and marshes almost immediately. There were long stretches of elevated interstate with nothing below them except miles of waving grass laced with narrow, winding waterways. There were cabins on stilts and boats with early-morning fishermen aboard. They passed a cypress swamp, eerie in its misty beauty. As untouched as it seemed, Sam told her that more than one of his cases had come to an end in that very place.

"There are places in there even the most experienced swampers haven't seen. The swamp has a habit of taking what it's given and devouring it until there's no sign it was ever there."

Antoinette shivered. "Are you talking about bodies?"

He smiled a little at the expression on her face and wished his car didn't have bucket seats. "I was trying to be poetic. Yes, I mean bodies. That swamp's a convenient dumping ground."

"How awful."

"Murder usually is."

The lead-in was too perfect to miss. Antoinette watched Sam instead of the scenery. "You haven't said anything about the profile I gave you."

"I'm still trying to digest it. Has anyone ever told you you're a perceptive, intelligent lady?"

She was warmed by the compliment. "No one whose opinion mattered quite so much."

He rested his hand on her shoulder for a moment in answer. "I realize you had very little to go on and that most of what you said was nothing more than intuition. But I think your ideas have merit. Right now, though, we're looking at Omega's top echelon for answers. Your profile seems to lead in the direction of someone at the bottom.''

She nodded. "A loner, or maybe someone who's teamed up with one or two others who are equally dissatisfied. Someone who feels alienated from the mainstream of decision making and has no other alternative than to strike out in the only way he can.''

"Do you think Howard Fauvier could have been part of a plot?''

That was one thing Antoinette was sure of. "No. Howard would have told somebody by now. His defenses are down. I know he couldn't hide anything that serious.''

"Your profile was strongly affected by Laurie's story. You have to realize that we don't know if our mysterious heroic Cajun was the arsonist. It's only a theory.''

"It's a theory that seems to make sense.''

"Especially to someone who wants to believe that all bad people are really good deep down inside.''

She laughed because his words had been said with no malice. Their jobs gave them different outlooks on human nature. Somewhere along the way they had agreed to disagree with humor.

They turned off the interstate and followed a road along the Mississippi, passing several old plantation homes and many more factories. There were fields of sugarcane and huge cane-processing plants. Tiny bayous with murky brown water were populated by fishermen, some with poles and patience, others with basketball-hoop-size crab traps.

"This is civilization," Sam warned her. "Where we're going is one of the most isolated spots in the Atchafalaya Basin. If you ever wanted to know how the Cajuns lived fifty or a hundred years ago, you're about to find out.''

"This is all new to me. What's unusual about the way your family lives?''

Sam relished telling the story. "Even as late as the twenties, there were lots of people living in these swamps, fishing, trapping, selling what they could and living off the land. Then there was a big flood, and the Corps of Engineers put up protection levees that raised the water level in the basin. Some people stayed, living in camp boats, but most moved to surrounding towns where they wouldn't be flooded out each year. Outboard motors made it easy to live along the edges and zip in and out to their trotlines or their traps and be back before supper. People got used to the comforts of electricity and running water. Life changed.''

"Your family didn't move?''

"They did, for a time. My mother told me stories about the little town where they all her relatives went. They'd all gotten along fine until they started crowding in on each other. My uncle Claude decided he couldn't stand it anymore. He loved the swamps and he hated the town where they were living. So one day after a particularly good day of fishing, he decided his catch was an omen. He refused to go back home. He lived in an old duck blind for six months while he scouted out a place to put together a house.''

"Did it flood?''

"Every year, like clockwork. But he was only sixteen—he had a lot to learn. By the time he was twenty, he knew exactly where and how to build. That cabin is still standing. It's mine now. You'll see why it's floodproof when we get there.''

Antoinette enjoyed the sound of pride in Sam's voice. The closer they got to Bayou Midnight, the more relaxed he seemed. "And where does your uncle live?''

"He's built a home on the banks of the bayou, about two miles from my place. There's a little settlement there now, although Uncle Claude's house and Leonce's are off by themselves. They have electricity and water and Leonce even has a telephone. But compared to most people's, their places are primitive.''

"Leonce?''

"My cousin, Uncle Claude's son. He's married to Didi, who's actually a distant cousin, too. My other first cousin, Martin, lives with Uncle Claude.''

"I'm not sure I've got this straight.''

He flashed her a smile that told her it didn't matter. "That's only the bare bones. You'll find that Cajuns are more family-oriented than almost any other group of people. Everyone has his nose in everyone else's business. And everyone is related to everyone else. Uncle Claude's more reticent than most. He won't overwhelm you. You'll like Didi and Leonce. Leonce works on an Omega Oil rig and fishes and traps when he's not there. Didi's the best cook in the bayous.

"Martin's hard to get to know," Sam continued. "He doesn't talk much. The swamps and the marshes are his whole life. He supports himself by fishing and trapping, wouldn't be caught dead working for an oil company. He served in Nam and came back quieter, even more set in his ways. But he's a good man. I owe him a lot."

"Why is that?"

"He took me under his wing when I was sent down here in disgrace. He's the one who taught me about the beauty of the swamp and about listening and waiting."

Antoinette was surprised at how much Sam had revealed in such a short time. Away from the city he was a different person. She settled back to watch the scenery pass with Tootsie's head hanging over her shoulder from the back seat. If she'd had any doubts about spending a weekend in the middle of a place that couldn't decide if it was land or water, she no longer had them. There was something special here, something that made Sam more alive, more relaxed. Whatever it was, she wanted to share it with him.

They stopped for breakfast at a little café with a sign advertising homemade doughnuts and crawfish stew. The coffee was as black as the bayou flowing beside the café, the doughnuts as fresh as the spring-scented air. They ate platters of sausage and scrambled eggs and listened to the lilting accents of the other customers.

There were some with the Deep South cadence of northern Louisiana and Mississippi; there were others whose word sequences had the feel of France. Sam explained that there were still people along the bayous who spoke Cajun French exclusively but more that only used phrases here and there. Sadly, Cajun French had been nearly extinguished by a government and school system that had, years before, ar-

bitrarily decided it was harmful. Now, even with official
attempts to cultivate it, much of the language had been lost
except in the most isolated parts of the state.

The rest of the trip passed in comfortable silences and
official tour-guide rhetoric. The farther they went, the
wilder the countryside. They left the paved road and began
to drive along a winding, clamshell path that followed a
bayou choked with water hyacinth and duckweed. The road
twisted and turned, leaving the banks of the bayou, only to
dip back again and again. Eventually it was nothing except
tire ruts and trampled weeds.

"Is this Bayou Midnight?" Antoinette wanted to know.
They had long ago left behind anything resembling civilization. There were boats dotting the bayou, but there had
been no houses for close to a mile.

"Not yet. The road has to get rougher, the water blacker."

Privately Antoinette wondered if either of those things
was possible. Twenty minutes later she no longer wondered. Just as she was sure that Sam had brought her into
the middle of this wilderness to make some esoteric point,
they made a sharp turn and pulled up in back of a house
built on the banks of a natural levee bordering a wide, inky
waterway.

"We're home."

Antoinette was touched by the simple words. It wasn't
their content but the way they were said that tugged at her
heart. He might as well have added that this was the place
where Sam Long belonged, where he could laugh and love,
where he could be the man he truly was. She felt an overwhelming wave of relief sweep over her. Had she wondered
all this time what she saw in the man sitting beside her? Had
she really wondered if she was imagining all the qualities she
had sensed just because she needed and wanted a man with
them? There was no reason to wonder any longer. Here, in
this place, Sam had no defenses. When he turned to her, the
warmth in his eyes was the only answer she would ever need.

"It's beautiful, Sam."

The house itself was small, made of wide, sun-bleached cypress boards raised yards off the ground by pilings. The roof was gleaming tin, built at a steep pitch to facilitate drainage and probably, at one time, to help provide drinking water with the addition of a cistern. To the side of the house and closer to the water was a shed with a small dock built off it. There were huge old trees shading the house with Spanish moss draped from their limbs like ghostly beards. The only movement was the breeze that swayed the very tops of the trees and the approach of a spotted hound in no particular hurry to examine them.

"I don't see Nonc Claude's car. He's off somewhere."

"Are we going to drive to your place and wait till he comes back?" Antoinette asked.

"We don't *drive* to my place. We canoe or take Martin's pirogue. In the springtime my place resembles a boat more than a house." Sam got out and came around to get Antoinette. Tootsie bounded out and immediately made friends with the hound, disappearing around the side of the house to investigate her new surroundings.

Hand in hand, Antoinette and Sam circled the house, stepping up onto a wide porch shaded by the overhang of the tin roof. Antoinette was enchanted. "Oh, look, Sam. There on the bank. Look at those spider lilies, growing practically in the water." She pointed, still holding his hand so that she carried it with her. "And there's a heron. What a magnificent bird."

Sam had expected her to be a good sport, but he hadn't expected this genuine enthusiasm.

"We've got all the fish you'd ever want to catch, all the birds and flowers you'd ever want to see . . ." He hesitated a moment and then added a postscript to test her reaction. "And all the gators and moccasins you'll ever have a yen for."

Her eyes widened but so did her smile. "I'm not leaving until I get to see a gator. The moccasins I can do without."

"Have you ever eaten gator?"

Antoinette sensed the dare in his voice. She responded by stiffening her spine. "Alligator sauce piquante. At Antoine's, if you must know. And I enjoyed it thoroughly."

"Good. Didi's cooking a feast for us tonight. She makes a gator sausage you'll love."

"Sounds wonderful." She gave him a radiant smile. "What else can I look forward to?"

"Swamp rabbit." Sam looked away, but his expression was too relentlessly nonchalant to fool Antoinette. She loved this side of him, and she was happy to play along.

"I love rabbit."

"Swamp rabbit," he said, emphasizing the first word.

"All right," she conceded. "What is it?"

"Fried muskrat."

Antoinette stared at the water, counting three more jumping fish before she answered him. "I'm always glad to have new experiences."

"Then there's nutria stew."

Antoinette had seen enough nutrias in her time to be completely revolted by the thought of the big orange-toothed rats on her dinner table. "I will not eat nutrias!"

"Good, neither will any of the rest of us."

She faced him, hands on hips, but her mock anger disappeared abruptly at the tender expression on Sam's face. He cupped her chin with his hands and bent for a long, slow kiss.

"I don't know about you," he said finally, pulling away, "but I'm ready to go to my place. Are you?"

She wondered if there was any place at all where she wouldn't follow him. She nodded, waiting on the porch while he scribbled a note to his uncle about their arrival and about Tootsie. Then, arms around each other's waist, they walked out to the bank of the bayou to find Sam's canoe.

Chapter 9

"I never would have expected you to know how to canoe."

"I never would have expected to use what I learned at Camp Winitonka in the middle of a cypress swamp." Antoinette ducked, avoiding a long strand of moss hanging from a branch overhead. The waterway they were traveling was so narrow that the branches of the willow and cypress trees on either side of them met in the middle and tangled over their heads. The moss seemed to bind them together.

Sam watched from the back of the canoe as Antoinette instinctively stopped paddling to let him guide them around one of the countless cypress stumps blocking their path. Her paddle dipped into the water once again with a clean, straight stroke, and he silently admired the inherent grace present in that simple movement.

"In the winter this gets so low it takes a pirogue to get through. Nonc Claude and Martin build their own. Martin always says Nonc Claude's pirogues can ride the dew."

"I had no idea this would be so beautiful." Antoinette's voice was reverent. "It's not beautiful like the endless views of the ocean or the mountains. Some of it's plain, almost dull. Then you see a picture, one still, glorious picture like that old dead cypress there against the bank or that clump of willow trees with the sky behind it, and you realize just how breathtaking it is.''

Sam smiled to himself and wondered if Antoinette realized how much pleasure her words gave him.

"No one else has ever been here," she continued. "No one. I'm sure of it."

He could have pointed out numerous signs of civilization: the Styrofoam markers leading to hidden traps and trotlines, the cleanly cut stumps of century-old trees, the gris-gris bag hung by a superstitious bayou dweller who was using his special brand of voodoo to scare off predators. He pointed out none of them, sure that Antoinette would rather pretend. He found he liked the fantasy himself.

They startled an egret, which rose, its magnificent white wings spread like the snowy sails of a three-masted schooner before it disappeared into the jungle beside them. A garfish swam to the surface close enough for Antoinette to examine it. It was at least six feet long but less than a foot wide, with the head of an alligator and the body of a fish. Sam quickly explained that the fish's rows of teeth were sharp enough to rip a large bass in two when he saw Antoinette drag her fingertips through the water.

"There's so much life here," Antoinette said softly, wiping her hand on her jeans. "I can feel it fermenting all around me, just out of my sight. It's like . . . it's like this is where everything started, primal and wild and fertile."

"We're almost to my place."

"Sam, how can there be a house here? There's no land."

"Remember, the water level's usually much lower."

They traveled the rest of the way in silence, neither of them wanting to break the stillness of the swamp. They were almost on top of Sam's cabin before Antoinette saw it.

She had been prepared for another house on pilings, perhaps on stilts. What she saw instead was a cypress cabin, a smaller version of Sam's uncle's, on a flat-bottomed barge. It was anchored at a short dock leading to a rise of land—or almost-land—beyond them. The area was so remote and the cabin so well concealed behind the clusters of trees that she had to blink to be sure it was real.

The sky had darkened as they'd canoed the last mile. In response the frogs had begun a symphony as if they'd been fooled into believing that night was coming. The wind had picked up, necessitating deeper, stronger strokes to guide the canoe, and Antoinette realized she was about to experience her first bayou storm.

"Sam, thank you."

He realized his eyes had shut at her simple, heartfelt gratitude. He opened them, trying to put the words in perspective, but control remained just out of his reach. There was nothing he could do except let himself be moved by the emotion in her voice. If he had hoped she would be a different person here, a person he could easily walk away from, he realized his hopes were for nothing. If anything, she was more herself, more the woman he could fall in love with.

"There's a storm coming," he said finally. "We'd better get inside." He guided the canoe expertly through the trees and beside the barge. The house had been built on the back two-thirds of the deck, leaving room at the front for the canoe. "Hold on to the barge while I get out so we don't tip, and then I'll help you up."

He was out of the canoe and reaching for her hand before Antoinette had a chance to think about his words. She was beside him and the canoe was on the deck before she could murmur "All right."

She straightened, arms spread wide to encompass it all—the swamp, the cabin, the man. "It's wonderful. Perfect."

He tried to see it through her eyes. He saw a weather-beaten one-room cabin on a rusting steel barge, secreted behind a stand of waterlogged cypress. He slapped lazily at a deerfly and admired the childlike delight on her face. "When you were a child, did you ever have a special place all your own?"

She stepped closer, touching her fingers to his lips. "If I tell you, will you promise not to laugh?"

He nodded solemnly, grasping her fingers and keeping them where she had placed them.

"Mignon and I had a French governess the year I was nine. Charlotte was a child at heart, a Gallic Mary Poppins. She'd nod and murmur polite French phrases whenever my mother told her what to do, then as soon as Mother was out of earshot, she did whatever she thought was best."

Sam was glad to hear her childhood hadn't been all formality and fussiness. "And your special place?" He kissed her fingertips.

Antoinette lowered her eyes to his mouth. "There was a shed where the gardener was supposed to keep his tools. He was a mean old man, but Charlotte found out that he was making a real dent in my father's liquor supply. In exchange for not telling my father, she got him to clean his tools out of the shed, and, with her help, we transformed it into our secret hideaway. We could be ourselves there, laugh as loud as we wanted, call each other nasty names if we were mad, read comic books, chew gum. We could even invite some of the kids in the neighborhood who we weren't allowed to play with." She smiled at the memory, glad to be sharing it with Sam. Then she continued.

"One day my parents discovered what had been going on. The tools went back into the shed, Charlotte went back to France and my mother went to an architect to have him design the perfect little playhouse for us. I think I played there exactly twice. Mignon wouldn't even set foot in it."

She smoothed her fingers over his lips. "So you see, I'm a soft touch for secret places. And obviously you are, too."

Thunder rumbled in the distance, and Sam put his arm around her shoulders, guiding her toward the cabin. He felt distinctly protective, a feeling he had reserved for only a few people in his life. "You're going to feel right at home. This isn't much fancier than a toolshed."

But it was. The barge was wide and long, large enough to accommodate a substantial dwelling. The cabin had been put together with love and skill, each board fitting precisely against its neighbor to discourage the one thousand and one species of Louisiana insects from setting up residence. There were large windows on three walls, each graced with a fine mesh screen and placed to encourage the free flow of air. But the best surprise was at the back, where a row of doors opened onto a screened-in porch that could only be reached from the inside of the cabin.

The cabin was sparsely furnished, but Antoinette suspected that each item had been chosen carefully. There were oval rag rugs on the floor, chairs and a cable spool table that looked as if it'd been transformed by a local craftsman, a cast-iron wood stove for heat and a propane stove in the corner for cooking. There were shelves with neatly stacked canned goods and perishable items in jars. Pots and pans and other necessities hung from nails over a counter that was half taken up by an old-fashioned water pump. The effect was primitive but comfortable. There was only one major furnishing that was missing. A bed.

"Come see the porch," Sam invited.

The bed was on the porch. It sat in the middle, overlooking a view of sky and water and wildlife that Antoinette was sure couldn't be topped anywhere in the world.

Sam put his arm around her and pulled her closer. "I moved to the porch last time I was here. I'll leave the bed here until fall, then take it back inside."

Antoinette was staring at the flowered sheets. The mattress was wide enough for two, although just barely, and it resembled a gigantic pillow more than a Sealy Posturepedic. Somehow she felt reassured. If it had been a narrow, single bed, she would have wondered about Sam's intentions. If it had been a standard double or, worse yet, a king-size bed, she would have wondered about all the women who had shared it with him in the past. As it was, it was large enough for them both if they stayed entwined through the night. And that was just fine with her.

"Have you ever slept on Spanish moss?" he asked, running his fingers through the hair draped across her shoulder.

"Sounds itchy."

He laughed, pleased by the matter-of-fact tone of her voice. "Gathering moss was a big industry back in these swamps. Now only a few people still do it, to sell to hatcheries. But years ago, it was used to stuff furniture and mat-

tresses. Didi stuffed this one for me. I'm afraid she got a bi
carried away and mixed a few other things in with th
moss."

"What things?"

"You'd have to ask Didi. I only know it smells wonder
ful. I wouldn't be surprised if it's some kind of Cajur
charm. Her father was a *traiteur.*"

"The one who taught you to take away headaches?"

"The same."

She turned, drawing his arm tighter around her shoulde
as she did. "What kind of charm do you suppose it is?"

"A love charm, knowing Didi. She's been after me to ge
married for years."

"Married to whom?"

"You don' know her yet, *cher*—" he mimicked the mu
sical cadences of a Cajun woman "—but you will, and whe
you do, she'll take your heart and bend it in half that one
and you'll be left wit' no thought of tomorrow, heh?"

"I think I'm going to like Didi."

"You will," he conceded. "And my family'll like you
You fit here. I've never met anyone else who did, but thi
suits you somehow, and it doesn't make sense that i
should."

Antoinette didn't know what to say. She could tell hin
that she already felt at home on Bayou Midnight, that th
little cabin in the middle of nowhere seemed like the perfec
place to be, that she had a strong sense of everything com
ing together for the first time in her life. But she had learne
to be cautious, and instead she just smiled and pulled awa
to wander to the edge of the porch to watch the storm com
across the swamp.

"I can smell it coming." She took a deep breath and fille
her lungs with the sweet scent of clean air and ozone. Th
trees were swaying as the wind continued to pick up, and a
she watched, a flock of brown birds lifted themselves to th
sky as if to meet the storm halfway.

"Lie here with me and watch it happen." Sam was be
side her again. They were doing a graceful, time-honore
dance. Advance, retreat, advance, retreat. She wasn't ner

vous; he sensed no last-minute virginal regrets. It was more that she seemed uncertain that he still wanted her.

It was funny because he had never wanted her more.

He turned her slightly, burying his hands in the hair falling around her face. He kissed her forehead, her eyelids, the tip of her nose. Her lips parted before he reached them, soft and warm and ready for his kiss. Her arms came around his neck, and the fragrance of sweet olive mixed with the smell of the storm.

"Which storm am I supposed to watch?" she asked against his lips.

"Whichever one you want." He hugged her tight, swinging her feet off the floor.

She was on the bed, and he was beside her. She didn't even question how it had happened. They were facing each other, their bodies not quite touching now, and she was trying to read the expression on his face. Outside, the wind was beginning to moan a love song.

"This bed has clean sheets." She turned her face into the mattress and inhaled. "And you were right. It does smell wonderful."

"Didi was obviously here this morning. I've never seen the place so clean, and the sheets aren't mine."

"You have Didi, and I have Rosy."

"Rosy changes your sheets?"

She laughed, turning her face back to his. "Rosy wants to take care of me. For that matter, so does my friend Daffy. If I'd told either of them about this weekend, they'd have broken into my house to sneak a black negligee into my suitcase." She wanted to touch him, to begin the passion that would rival the peaking fury of the wind, but she couldn't. Her hands, her whole body, were heavy with a new lethargy.

"Next time I'll tell them."

She smiled, wondering if he realized that his joke had been about their future.

Sam couldn't make himself begin. He knew that one touch, one kiss, would start something that would finish in a burst of sensation he might never recover from. He savored the feelings building inside him just from lying so close to her. Her warmth seemed to seep across the inches separating them, his fingertips could remember the texture of her skin, his memory could replay the soft, sweet noises she made when he kissed her.

Antoinette shut her eyes for a moment, as if seeing something in her memory. "Do you know I hadn't thought of it for years, but I just realized why it feels so right to be lying here beside you with the storm coming in on us."

He propped his head on his hand to see her better. "Why?"

She opened her eyes, and her expression was faintly embarrassed. "It's another childhood story."

"I don't mind."

"Mignon was afraid of storms. Terribly afraid. Whenever we had one, she'd sneak down the hall past my parents' room and crawl into bed with me. I used to wait for the storms, hope we'd have one...."

He saw her hesitation and it puzzled him. He raised his hand to her hair and began to stroke it. "You liked the storms?"

She smiled sadly. "No. I liked having Mignon sleep with me. It's one of my few memories of having someone's arms around me. We weren't a family who believed in touching."

He felt a pang of sadness for the little girl who'd been raised by the emotionless robots in the Garden District Victorian mansion. He also understood why reaching out to others was so important to her. Her casual touches weren't really casual at all. "I can see why you married so young."

"Yes?" She laughed at herself. "Well, I married a man who didn't like touching, either. At least, he didn't like touching me. I was a china doll, the kind you get for Christmas and put in a glass display case. I was someone to dress up and have on his arm at the appropriate social functions."

"Antoinette..."

She sensed his concern and drew herself back to the present. He had pulled her closer, and she rested her head against his shoulder. "It's all right," she reassured him. "It took me a while, but one day I finally understood it wasn't me at all."

"How could you have believed it was?"

"Because I may be a psychologist, but inside I'm just like everyone else. Same needs, same fears." She took a deep breath. "Same desires."

His hands left her hair, smoothing its way to her neck, then to her back. At her waist he stopped to pull her body completely against his. "Don't you know what you do to men?" he asked in a half whisper. "They look at you and all they can think about is touching you."

"I want someone to *really* touch me. Do you understand the difference?"

He could feel her breath against his neck, and he shuddered. "Are you talking about love?"

"I don't know."

"You are."

"I'm talking about someone wanting me because I'm me. Not because I'm beautiful, not because I'm rich. Because I'm me." She didn't want to sound self-pitying. She tried to lighten her words. "You must know what that's like, Sam. Haven't you ever wondered if the women in your life saw beyond your body and face?"

"Frankly, I've never cared why a woman wanted me as long as she did." He hugged her hard, feeling the softness of her body against his. "Not until now."

They both stopped short at his words. He was as surprised by them as she was. Antoinette felt Sam stiffen, and she realized that he wasn't really ready to make such a declaration of his feelings. She smiled, her lips grazing his neck as she did. "Don't worry," she teased, "I know that wasn't a proposal."

"I propose we stop talking." He rolled her over until he was half on top of her, looking down at the face that was so often in his thoughts now.

She let her eyes signal her desire for the same thing. She reached up to savor the feel of his hair between her fingers as he bent to kiss her. He tasted like the storm, wild and heady. His body over hers held the same leashed passion, and while she admired his control, at the same time she determined to break it quickly.

She pulled his shirttail from his jeans as his mouth moved over hers, finding the heat of his flesh and raking her nails lightly up his back as she parted her lips for the entrance of his tongue. His skin was smooth, the muscles beneath unyielding. She knew he kept himself fit for his job—if for no other reason—but the breadth of his shoulders, the perfect symmetry of his body, were a gift he'd been given. He would age the same way, straight and strong.

She felt his body contract as she continued to explore. He pushed himself up on his elbows, and she smoothed her hands around his rib cage, seeking his chest. She kept one hand there as the other began to unbutton his shirt. His chest was sprinkled with golden hair, a sensuous contrast to his tanned skin. She traced the spot where the golden V disappeared into the waistband of his jeans.

"You're not the only one who needs to be touched," he said ruefully. Antoinette watched his eyes close as she smoothed her hands over his chest in light, circular motions. He sat up momentarily to discard the shirt, coming back to rest across her as his hands began a similar path along the buttons of her blouse. She lifted slightly as he slipped the blouse from beneath her. She watched the expression on his face as he unhooked her bra and dropped it to the floor along with the blouse.

She waited for his reassurance, dreading a response that would make her feel like a thing instead of the person she was. She didn't want to be told how perfectly her body was shaped or that he'd never seen anyone more beautiful.

Sam leaned over her, his green-gold eyes half-closed. "Just promise me that you'll drag me off this bed someday," he said, his voice husky. "Because I'm never going to want to leave."

She laughed happily, sitting up a little to pull him tightly against her.

The sound of her laughter was all he needed. The feel of her breasts against his chest was sending signals to the rest of his body, a body that was only too willing to comply with his plans for it. He unsnapped her jeans, smoothing them down over her hips along with the wisp of silk beneath them.

Antoinette laughed again, and her laughter cleared away any cobwebs of doubt or caution. "Sam," she reminded him, "you forgot my shoes. My jeans'll never come off that way."

His curse was succinct and to the point. He leaped off the bed and settled at her feet, ripping off her sneakers and tossing them at the foot of the bed. With none too gentle hands he finished stripping off the rest of her clothes.

Then, standing above her, he finished undressing himself.

Antoinette's laughter caught in her throat. He was all the things she hadn't wanted him to say about her. Perfect. The most beautiful thing she'd ever seen. She tried to think of a response. She could settle on nothing original. She only held out her arms and said with a quaver in her voice, "I can't believe how much I want you."

How much he wanted *her* was obvious when he lay back down on the bed. The gathering storm poised over the little cabin, withholding rain but charging the air with bolts of silver lightning. Sam's body covered Antoinette's, his mouth settling on at first one breast, then the other as she moved with him, laughter, insecurity, everything gone except the feeling of this man against her.

She was not content to lie still and accept the splendid pleasure of his mouth and hands. She touched him, too, exploring every part of him that she could reach, learning to know him with her fingertips and mouth and tongue. With Sam she knew there would be no rules, no passion too heartfelt, no barriers she couldn't go beyond. He wanted her as she wanted him. He told her so with every move he made, with every kiss, with every caress.

She felt his mouth slide to her navel and below. Her legs were spread and his mouth was warm, touching her in just one of the places where she had longed for contact. She had known it would take little to build her response, but when the first waves threatened to sweep her away, it surprised even her.

She gasped and tried to move away from Sam's caress. There was no place to go. He was everywhere, everything, and she could not bring herself to leave him. Instead, she tunneled her hands through his hair and held him away.

"Not yet," she pleaded. "Sam, not yet. I'm not ready."

But she was, and he knew it. He lifted himself over her and plunged inside, only to feel the ripples begin. He withdrew and watched her go wild; he felt his own control snap.

On the tin roof above them, he heard the first sounds of rain. There was nothing gentle about the drops beating down. It was a real bayou storm, full of fury and passion and release. He held Antoinette, soothing her, waiting for the moment when he could begin the whole experience again.

"Where are you?" she asked, her voice breaking. "I want you."

"You have me. You have me now." He pushed her down against the mattress, his hands beginning to build her pleasure again.

"Why did you leave me?" she mourned. "It won't be like that for me again."

"No? Don't you think so?" His teeth nipped at her lower lip, forcing her to open for him. His tongue found hers, caressing, coaxing. He could feel her tension and knew that tears were just below the surface. He suspected she had a lot to learn about what her body could do if given the chance.

His hand found her breasts, drawing lazy circles around each rose-tipped nipple. She gasped a little as he drew them out with his thumb and forefinger until they were hard peaks once more. He took his time following the path of his fingers with his mouth. When he did, she gasped again.

Antoinette couldn't believe the sensations flooding her body. He was demanding a response she hadn't believed she could give twice. She was beginning to believe in spite of herself.

She heard the storm break wide open, the relentless drill of rain on the metal roof above them. She felt Sam poised above her again, and she reached to bring him down on top of her. Lightning flashed, and he was inside her. They were falling through the sky together, rain and lightning and the explosion of thunder. She rose to meet him, retreated, felt the unavoidable sting of tears. She held him tight, following the pace he set, setting her own pace, when miraculously she realized he had been right.

Sam heard her cries and fell against her, giving way to the storm inside him and the profound joy of becoming one with Antoinette. Perhaps he had understood more about the act of love than she, but he knew, even though he didn't want to know it, that he had never performed the act of love before that afternoon.

It was much later before she stirred. He had reluctantly moved just enough to give her breathing space, but he hadn't been able to force himself to put emotional space between them, too. He had never liked sleeping with a woman, never liked the feel of a body pressed against his, smothering him with unspoken demands. Now he couldn't seem to get as close as he wanted. He wanted to be inside her again. He wanted to feel whole.

Antoinette looked up at the man who still held her in his arms. His eyes were closed, his face as peaceful as she'd ever seen it. She wondered what it would take to smooth away all the lines of tension. She doubted it was possible.

The rain was still falling, but gently now, a flourish-filled cadenza after the fury of the storm. The thunder and lightning had moved far away, taking the wind with them. Antoinette stretched a little and felt muscles she'd never felt before.

"If it's really been six years, I'd better give you a pillow for your seat in the canoe," Sam mumbled.

"I was just making that up to impress you with my chastity," she said smugly. "I do this at least once a week. Especially if I can get a cop to take me to his cabin in a swamp."

"A sucker for a badge and cypress trees."

She stretched again, wrapping her arms behind him and turning to her side. "Actually, I may need that pillow."

"Actually, I have no intention of letting you get in a canoe."

"What about Didi's dinner?"

He brushed a strand of hair off her forehead and kissed the spot where it had been. "I have a feeling Didi would understand."

"I am definitely going to like Didi."

"I want you again."

"As long as you have two pillows."

"That can be arranged."

Antoinette sat up, aware of the empty space beside her. She noticed that the rain had finally stopped. Pushing her hair behind her ears, she watched the man standing at the porch windows stare out at the late-afternoon sunlight that was just beginning to break through the clouds.

He had covered her with an afghan, which in no way made up for the loss of his warmth, and she pulled it around her before she spoke.

"Hello, Sergeant Long."

Sam faced her, smiling a little at the picture she made. "Hello yourself."

He had pulled on his jeans, but his chest and feet were bare, and Antoinette wondered idly how she could find him so sexy and feel so lavishly depleted at the same time. "Is it time for dinner?"

"Do you want to go?"

She weighed a whole evening with just the two of them against the pleasures of meeting his family. Her face puckered in a frown. She felt like a child being given a choice between ice cream and chocolate cake for dessert.

"We'll go. Tomorrow night we'll stay here." Sam made the decision for her.

She brightened. She could have it all. Ice cream and cake in the company of the man she was falling in love with.

He saw her easy smile, read her thoughts with no difficulty. He wanted to tell her to go slowly, to keep a part of her from him because he couldn't bear to expose her to certain pain. He'd known from the beginning that he was wrong to let their relationship grow. And yet still, with the proof staring him in the face, he could feel nothing except the satiation of his body and the power of her smile.

Sam tried to keep his voice light. "You know, if you keep looking at me like that, we aren't going to make it out the door."

Antoinette pulled the afghan tighter around her and slid her feet to the floor. In a minute she was by his side. "Am I allowed to tell you it's been a beautiful day?"

He tugged the afghan from her fingers and it fell at their feet, a useless tumble of green and turquoise. "You can say anything you want, but I won't guarantee you'll always get the response you'd like."

"I've never wanted anyone to tell me lies."

His hands drifted over the slender curves of her body, a body that was now achingly familiar and even more provocative. "Thank you," he said.

She didn't ask for what. She just let him pull her against him, and they stood as close together as two people can and watched the sun play over the water.

Chapter 10

Claude LeBeaud squatted at the end of the dock stretching into Bayou Midnight, his grizzled head bent as, with sparing, practiced movements, he worked over a large fish. Behind him the sky was an explosion of colors Antoinette was sure she had never seen before. She knew she would remember this moment always—the old man, the sky, the feeling that she was exactly where she was supposed to be.

Sam's uncle didn't lift his head as their canoe glided through the black water to the dock, but as Sam turned the canoe toward a tiny landing on the shore, Claude nodded in satisfaction.

"Don' let nuthin' stop you from eatin' Didi's cookin', do you, Sam-son? Not even *une belle femme?*"

"We could smell her cooking all the way across the bayou, Nonc Claude. Didn't want to disappoint Didi."

"When M'sieu Gator, he learns to fly, that's when Didi'd forgive you for missin' dinner," Claude agreed.

Sam turned the canoe so that his portion slid into the landing. He got out to pull it onto land. When it was secure, he offered his hand to Antoinette. In a moment she was standing beside him. She followed him to the end of the dock to meet his uncle.

Claude stood as they approached, wiping his hands on a rag. "I won' shake. Lookit me, ma hands covered wit' fish."

"That's all right, Mr. LeBeaud," Antoinette reassured him. "My hands are blistered from all the canoeing your nephew's made me do anyway."

Sam's laughter was warm, and for her alone. "Don't let her fool you. She made me come back here the long way so she could see more of the bayou. Nonc Claude, this is Antoinette Deveraux. Antoinette, my uncle, Claude LeBeaud."

"Deveraux. Good French name. Not Cajun, but—" He shrugged.

"Will I be forgiven?"

"*Mais* yeah, *chere.* Las' thing I knowed, not bein' Cajun wasn' no sin."

"Is everyone else inside?" Sam asked.

"Everybody. Even Martin."

Antoinette and Sam followed his uncle off the dock and up onto the porch. Tootsie waited there to greet her, giving Antoinette a lick and a fond wiggle before disappearing once more in the company of Claude's hound. Sniffing appreciatively, Antoinette decided that Sam was right. Some of the wonderful smells she had experienced paddling down Bayou Midnight were coming from the house. Her mouth began to water.

The inside of Claude LeBeaud's Acadian-style cottage proclaimed the fact that two bachelors lived there, bachelors who lived outdoors more than they lived in. Sam had explained that Leonce and Didi lived on a nearby inlet of Bayou Midnight, and Antoinette wondered how their house compared with this one.

There was nothing inside this house that could be considered an adornment unless it was the fine set of deer antlers that were being used for a hat rack. One wall was decorated with tar paper to keep out the wind; the others were the same weathered gray of the exterior.

To say that the furnishings were simple was an understatement. Antoinette was reminded of the proverb "waste not, want not," and wondered silently if it had originated with the Acadians. There was something soothing about the simplicity, though. Everything was immaculately clean and in good repair. And the view from the front windows overlooking the bayou was all the beauty anyone would ever need.

Two men who were stockier, dark-haired versions of Sam sat on straight-back chairs watching a small black-and-white television set. They stood when Antoinette entered the room, both thoroughly assessing her, although the shorter of the two let his eyes flicker back to the television screen once while the introductions were made.

Martin was the taller of the pair. His hair was shiny black, and his features were even, with the aquiline nose of his blond cousin. There was something about the way he held himself that reminded Antoinette of Sam, and something about the guarded expression on his face that emphasized their similarities, too. Martin followed his gruff greeting in English with several staccato sentences of Cajun French that went right over her head. She could only nod, hoping she would catch on quickly.

Leonce was all smiles. He had Sam's nose and a similar cleft in his chin. His face was rounder and almost beatific, his potbelly a testament to his wife's artistry in the kitchen. Although it was still tinged with music, his greeting was in English, without the extremities of accent as in his father's speech.

"Didya ever hear of such a thing? I'm doin' all the work in somebody else's kitchen, and nobody tells me she's here!" A blond and blue-eyed dynamo marched in from the hallway, a spotless white apron covering her blue-checked dress. "Always the last to know!"

Sam swooped the petite young woman off her feet and gave her a hearty kiss on the cheek, setting her down in the midst of them. "Antoinette, meet Didi. Didi, Antoinette."

"I'm just glad these bums they didn't scare you off."

"I wouldn't let them." Antoinette got a definite feeling that she had an ally, whether she needed one or not. Didi was measuring her and Sam simultaneously, as if to figure out how to make the bond between them a permanent one.

"*Eh bien,* I've got fish to fry. Make them give you the comfortable chair. That one there," she said, pointing at her husband, "he'll forget he's breathin' if the TV's on."

"Spoils you, doesn't she?" Sam asked Leonce.

"Who?" Leonce asked, his eyes flickering back to the set.

Didi threw her hands up in the air and marched out of the room.

"I think I'm going to see if I can help," Antoinette told Sam, turning to follow Didi through the hallway. She came to a halt in the kitchen, half a minute behind Didi, who seemed to do everything at the speed of light.

If it was true that the kitchen was the heart of every home, this kitchen said everything about the LeBeauds. Simplicity did not reign here. The kitchen was huge. In the center was a table large enough to seat the inhabitants of a small town; along two walls were shelves filled to overflowing with food, pots and pans, dishes and a sizable collection of beautifully carved duck decoys. Strings of herbs hung from the curtain rod over the kitchen sink, and a thick length of braided onions and red peppers twined around another window. Like everything else in the house, the kitchen sparkled with cleanliness.

"I'm gonna shoot that Claude. I tell him not to mess with my gumbo, and he pours in the peppers when he thinks I'm not watchin'."

Antoinette's eyes watered just thinking about it. "What kind of gumbo is it?"

"Every kind. Got everythin' in it gumbo can have."

"Didi, the food smells delicious. Sam says you're the best cook on the bayou."

"That Sam-son, he wants to eat, that's why he say that. The man needs a woman to cook for him. Claude, now, he don't need anyone to cook for him. Claude can cook circles around a fancy French chef if he want. *Mais non,* he never want if I'm here to do it." Didi flicked some water into a cast-iron skillet filled with oil and listened to it pop. "We can eat, soon's I fry the fish."

"What can I do?"

"Git out the Evangeline Maid and put it on that plate for me," Didi told her, gesturing to a blue willow platter.

Antoinette discovered that Evangeline Maid was a Cajun version of Wonder Bread and began to take slices from the bag to stack them on the platter. "Why does everyone here call Sam Sam-son?"

"Claude, he started it. S'got nuthin' to do with bein' strong. Claude says Sam is as good a son as any he got naturally. So he calls him Sam-son. He's just one of Claude's boys."

Antoinette liked the history behind the nickname. It said a lot about the love in Sam's family. "It's beautiful here. I like to think of Sam growing up with his uncle and cousins in this place."

"Only thing not beautiful 'bout it's the lack of a woman. All those men livin' here without a woman to make them behave. Leonce was almost beyond hope till I took him over."

Antoinette smiled at the thought of tiny Didi leading Leonce and the others around by their noses. "Sam said you were a cousin of his, too."

"Cousin way, way back." Didi rolled tiny balls of fish in a mixture that looked like cornmeal and herbs. "You, you're not Cajun, are you?"

"No. My family was from a different part of France."

"Good. This family needs new blood. Even better if it's new French blood."

"Didi, Sam and I are just getting to know each other. This is all very casual."

"*Sa va bien.* Things, they're going well. He don't take you to his cabin if he just want to get to know you. Sam-son never takes anybody there." Didi began to fry the fish, pushing blond curls off her forehead with her forearm as if she was already hot from the work yet to do. "I'm the only woman's ever been through the door, and I just git to clean it up."

Antoinette decided she'd better change the subject. "Tell me about you and the rest of Sam's family. Have you always lived here?"

"Me, I'm from Pierre Part. Claude and the boys, they live here in the summer and fall, down in the marshes from November to spring. I met Leonce at a fais-do-do the summer I was sixteen."

"Fais-do-do?"

"A dance. Anyhow, my parents and Claude said we could git married, so we did."

Antoinette wondered if it had all been as simple as it sounded. "Sam says Leonce works for Omega Oil."

"Leonce loves the machines. Makes okay money for a boy from the swamps. Martin, now, he hates anything been built in the last two centuries. If *le Bon Dieu* didn't put it here, Martin, he don't want it messin' up the place."

Antoinette began to wash the few dishes that Didi had allowed to accumulate as she'd cooked. "Sam told me that Martin was the one who taught him about the swamps."

Didi giggled, a sweet, tinkling sound that was very much at odds with her no-nonsense speech. "I hear he'd drag Sam into a pirogue and threaten to drop him somewhere if he didn' shape up. Woulda done it, too. Talk about!"

"Are you planning to feed us, Didi?" Sam stood in the doorway. Antoinette wondered how long he'd been there.

"Lookit that! Sam-son's almost in the kitchen. Come a step closer, Sam-son, and I'll teach you to fry garfish balls."

"Didi's been trying to take me in hand for the last eight years," Sam said fondly.

"I git you yet, Sam-son. You won't die not knowin' how to cook." Didi bustled past him to inform the LeBeaud men it was time for dinner.

"If you don't know how to cook," Antoinette said, wiping her hands on a dish towel, "how do you eat?"

"I cook. Didi just doesn't see it that way."

"He don't cook, he turns on his oven, that one, and he warms up chicken no Cajun would feed a crawfish." Didi passed Sam on the way back through the kitchen, stopping for a quick kiss on the cheek as she did. "Needs a good woman, that one." She stopped in front of Antoinette. "You. Do you cook?"

Antoinette met Sam's eyes and smiled lazily. "I sure do," she told Didi. "You and I'll have to trade recipes."

Didi's grin was wide enough to swallow Bayou Midnight.

The meal surpassed anything Antoinette had believed possible about food. Everything was absolutely fresh and bursting with flavor. The raw oysters were plump with just the hint of saltwater that made them the most sought-after kind. The gumbo, which was more of a stew than a soup, was redolent with spices and every variety of seafood Antoinette could think of. The fried garfish balls were surprisingly good considering what the fish itself looked like, and there was a crawfish jambalaya made with rice and tomatoes that was a meal in itself. It was hard to believe that the men wanted dessert, but when all the plates had been cleared away, they sat expectantly while Didi brought them each a square of bread pudding so rich with eggs, cream and a potent whiskey sauce that inhaling the aroma would add pounds to a dieter.

"You have to eat it," Sam told Antoinette. "Didi will think you don't like her cooking."

"I love the cooking. It's the fact that I don't have room for it that I don't love."

"Don' think nuthin' about it," Claude assured her. "Jus' eat what you want. Didi feeds us all like we are gonna run outa food tomorrow. Leonce, he used to be skinny, like me." Claude patted his lean waistline. "Now he looks like one of the rats I catch on a good day. Fat, sleek and full of sass."

"Nonc Claude traps for nutria and muskrat down in the marshes part of each year," Sam explained. "He and Martin have a camp down there."

"Mink and otter, too," Didi added, not at all offended by Claude's teasing. Silently she passed him another square of pudding, which he accepted with a nod.

Martin pushed his chair back from the table with a sharp scrape. "Won't be goin' this year."

Sam frowned. "Why not? You always go."

Martin's face showed his disgust. "Omega Oil."

Sam was instantly alert. "What does Omega have to do with your going down to the marshes?"

Claude answered, his voice more philosophical than his son's. "Our camp's on Omega land. The company, she don' wanna lease her marsh no more. *C'est tout.*"

"That's one I haven't heard." Sam pushed his chair back, too. "Omega seems to be in business to make enemies."

"Swampers don' like Omega, I kin tell you that. The other companies, they messin' up the swamp, too. But not so fast as Omega. Omega, she goes in and chug chugs. Nex' thing you know, no more swamp. Jus' a big *trainasse* where there used a be trees." Claude shook his head. "Omega don' care about the swamp, she don' care about the swampers."

"*Trainasse?*" Antoinette asked.

"An artificial channel. What do you think, Martin?" Sam asked his cousin, who was still scowling.

"I been trappin' that land since I was eight years old. It's my land, not Omega's."

"When the rats run over the marsh an' eat it down to nuthin', then the company, she'll let us back in," Claude said, more to Martin than anyone else. "Meantime, we stay here and fish. Fish'll keep us jumpin'."

Martin's answer was unintelligible to Antoinette, but obviously not to everyone else at the table. She had realized as the meal progressed that the family was conversing in English when normally they would probably fall back into the peculiar mixture of English and French that was so typically Cajun. Now Martin's answer, whatever it was, was totally French and totally—she was certain—profane.

"How many people down here feel this way about Omega?" Sam asked.

Didi was the first to answer. "You git in that canoe of yours, Sam-son, and you paddle up and down Bayou Midnight. Then paddle anywhere else in this basin. You stop and talk to anyone you see and ask how they like Omega Oil. My man, he's an Omega man. Their men, they'll be Omega men, too. Ask anybody about Omega. They'll tell you, them, that Omega oughta be shot for what they do down here. An' that's the truth.''

Sam shook his head wearily, watching as Leonce got up and left the room silently. "If it's any consolation, there are people all over the state who feel the same way."

Martin stood, jamming his hands in his pockets, and left the room, too.

Claude watched his sons' departures, his eyes sorrowful. "Martin and the swamp and marsh, they're one. He don' know nuthin' else. He'd a been better born a hundred years afore this. This world's got no place for Martin in it. No place at all.''

The trip back to Sam's cabin was made in silence. The canoe glided through the moonlit water without making a sound, and neither Antoinette nor Sam felt like interrupting the croaking concerto provided by the bullfrogs. Once, she saw movement in the water and watched as the majestic head of an alligator broke the surface before disappearing once again into the ebony water of the bayou. The night had turned cool, and as soon as they had gotten out into the water, even the mosquitoes had ignored them. Antoinette had never felt more filled with peace.

At the cabin Sam set her suitcase on the deck before Antoinette helped him pull the canoe up for the night. Inside the cabin he lit a kerosene lantern to supplement the moonlight pouring through the windows. Together they filled a basin with water from the pump on the counter. Sam wandered out to the porch as Antoinette used the water for a lick-and-a-promise bath and for brushing her teeth. She changed into the ivory silk nightgown she had bought herself the day he'd asked her to go to the bayou.

"Your turn." Antoinette joined Sam at the porch windows. He put his arms around her, resting his cheek against her head.

"The best thing about that nightgown is that it's going to be off you soon."

"Think so?"

"As soon as I get back." He pulled away and disappeared into the cabin.

Antoinette stretched out on the bed and waited for Sam to join her. A light breeze blew through the windows, and although she doubted it was really possible, she imagined she could feel the gentle rise and fall of the barge beneath them. The unaccustomed physical activity of the day took its toll. She was asleep before Sam had finished bathing.

Much later she awoke to find herself naked in his arms. Sam was asleep, and she listened to the quiet rhythm of his breathing, sorry that they'd missed an opportunity to make love. During the day she had successfully put the complexities of their relationship out of her mind, but with half the weekend behind them now, it was hard to forget that, when they returned to the city early Monday morning, Sam might erect new barriers that she'd never be able to get past.

She understood him better now. Being with his family had taught her more than she'd expected to learn. Perhaps Didi had said it best when she'd said that the four men, living without a woman to take them in hand, had almost been beyond hope. From what Antoinette had seen and from what Sam had told her about his childhood in New Orleans, it was apparent that he had never benefited from the softening influence of a woman in his life. His mother had been too busy; he had lived the remainder of his life away from women. Even the job he had chosen to do was essentially done in a male world, although that was changing with the addition of more women to the police force.

Sam saw no need for what he'd never had. Depending on a woman for emotional support, for companionship, for love, was foreign to his background. She snuggled into his arms and wished that she could give him what she knew he needed. Sadly, she was a good enough psychologist to know that people have to make their own choices and their own mistakes.

"So you're awake."

She smiled against his chest. The night wasn't going to be wasted, after all. "I wish you'd shaken me or something when you came to bed."

"I undressed you. I covered your sleeping body with kisses. I finally gave up."

He smelled like the soap she had used, too, and she tasted his skin to see if it tasted the same way. "I guess I'm a sound sleeper."

"But you're not asleep now."

"I'm certainly not." Antoinette allowed Sam to roll her onto her back, cherishing the feel of his body stretched over hers.

"I wore you out today, didn't I?"

"Absolutely."

"I probably ought to let you get a good night's sleep."

"You probably should."

"I'm not going to."

"You'd better not."

His laugh rumbled through her, and Antoinette gave herself up to the feel of his hands and lips and to the knowledge that they had another twenty-four hours before life intruded once more.

The next time she awoke, sunlight was streaming through the windows, and Sam was nowhere in sight. She sat up and stretched, wondering why people slept on anything except Spanish moss. Certainly she'd had the best night of her life on the fragrant mattress. Her nightgown was on the floor beside the bed, and she slipped it over her sleep-flushed body before she went to look for Sam.

He was on the deck, a cup of coffee forgotten in one hand as he watched a blue heron poised on the shore only yards away. Antoinette slipped her arms around his waist and felt how completely relaxed he was. She was good for him; she knew she was. And he was certainly good for her.

"There's coffee in the kitchen. I didn't know when you'd wake up."

"I'll pass, I think."

He ruffled her hair affectionately. "Do you think I make it with bayou water?"

"I wondered."

"I bring in spring water for drinking and cooking. It's stored underneath the sink in gallon jugs."

"I'll be back."

When she returned with her coffee, Sam was arranging crates for them to sit on. "Not exactly deluxe accommodations."

"I'm very satisfied."

She made such a lovely picture. The mists of the swamp around them painted the morning in the style of one of the French Impressionists. Antoinette in the filmy nightgown, with her black hair falling over her shoulders and her feet delightfully bare, was a creature of the mists, too ethereal to be real. Sam doubted that he would ever stand on this deck again without thinking of her.

"What would you like to do today?" he asked, determined to break the spell.

"I want to see everything."

"What is everything?"

"The bayou, the swamp. How far away is the closest marsh?"

"Too far away to canoe. It's down toward the Gulf. Don't you know anything about Louisiana geography?"

"I know more than I did yesterday at this time."

"What else do you want to see?" Sam sipped the coffee that had turned cold as he'd watched her.

"A fais-do-do, Pierre Part, the rest of your family, a Cajun *traiteur* at work, an oil rig, Claude fishing for catfish."

"You forgot the Evangeline oak and the blessing of the fleet," Sam said dryly. "You really like this, don't you?"

"I really do." She stood, wandering to the edge of the deck. There was so much to see. Everywhere she looked, something new caught her eye. The bayou and the swamp changed momentarily. Now she watched a snake, dark and menacing, on a tree root on the shore. "I like your family, too."

"Real people?"

For a moment she wondered if she'd imagined the sting in his words. Then she knew she hadn't. "I'm not slumming, Sam," she said finally. "And I resent your thinking I am."

It was the second time he'd had to apologize for the same
slight. He remembered the day he'd accused her of living
where she did just to rub shoulders with the common folk.
"I'm sorry."

"Don't push distance between us yet." She didn't turn.
She just stood quietly sipping her coffee and watching the
snake slither into the water. Then she shuddered. "We have
the rest of this day and tonight. At least give us both that
much before you put up your walls again."

He had gone inside the cabin when she finally finished her
coffee and decided to dress to meet the new day. She passed
him on her way to the porch to change. His arms shot out,
and his hug was hard and oddly comforting. "I'll show you
everything I can today," he murmured, his lips close to her
ear.

She treated it as lightly as she could. "Well, tell me how
to dress, then, if I'm going to see everything."

"Comfortably."

"I'm comfortable now."

"But if you stay dressed like that, you'll be undressed very
quickly, and we won't be going anywhere."

"Shorts and a shirt," she said decisively. "And a long
evening here, alone."

"After we eat dinner with Didi and Leonce," Sam said,
his voice distinctly apologetic. "But we'll eat early."

"Didi wants to cook for us again?"

"Didi wants to bend my ear about Martin. She thinks it's
her job to make sure the LeBeaud men live up to her expectations. If Didi had her way, Martin would have a steady
job, find a good woman and settle down to wedded bliss like
his brother."

"That Didi," Antoinette said, tongue-in-cheek. "Where
does she get those crazy ideas?"

Sam laughed and hugged her again before he pushed her
toward the porch. "The bayou tour leaves in exactly fifteen
minutes. Since you're such a prize tourist, I'll show you a
place that's not even in the guidebooks."

"Another secret place?"

"Another secret place."

"Make it five minutes," she said happily. "I don't want to waste even one precious moment of this day."

Chapter 11

Antoinette eyed the supplies that Sam was bringing with them on his grand tour of the bayou and wondered exactly what he had in mind. "Hip boots?"

"I told you we were eating with Didi and Leonce tonight. I just forgot to mention that we're providing the main course."

"I've heard of desperate survivors of plane crashes eating boots, Sam, but I don't think even they ate rubber boots."

Sam just smiled and added more paraphernalia to what was already in the bottom of the canoe. "We can get whatever else we need at Nonc Claude's. I'm going to trade my canoe for his skiff. The place I want to take you is too far to paddle."

Antoinette tried to sound nonchalant. "I'm intrigued. What are those squares of mesh for, and those wires?"

"You'll see."

Claude and Martin were both gone when they arrived at the house. Tootsie was sitting patiently on the dock as if she'd expected them. She followed their progress to the landing, leaping up to cover Antoinette's arms with big licks when she disembarked. Antoinette played with Tootsie while Sam checked the skiff, which was tied to the dock. He made several mysterious trips into the house, loading the skiff with more supplies before he ushered Antoinette into it. Tootsie, obviously resigned to being left again, trotted up to the house and flopped down on the porch, watching as her mistress disappeared from sight.

It was warm enough for Antoinette to be glad she'd worn shorts and a short-sleeved blouse. The sun sparkled on the water, and the early-morning mists had burned off to leave the air clear and fresh. Without any responsibilities for propelling the boat, she could enjoy the passing scenery. She counted birds: ever-present crows, red-winged blackbirds and wrens, plus water birds she couldn't identify, along with the great egret and the blue heron which she could.

She watched Sam, too, who was busy guiding the boat through narrow channels and wider swampy areas. His shirt was unbuttoned halfway down his tanned chest, and the ragged denim cutoffs he wore exposed most of his nicely muscled thighs. With the wind blowing through his hair and the relaxed expression of a happy man on his face, Sam was the consummate outdoorsman. There seemed to be nothing more important to worry about than how many fish he would catch and whether there might be an afternoon thunderstorm.

"I'm lost. What direction are we going?" Antoinette asked after forty-five minutes of twists and turns that left her completely confused.

"Can't hear you," Sam said with a grin.

"Yes, you did. Why don't you want me to know?"

"Because this is a secret place. Once you see it, you'll want to tell everyone about it," he teased.

She grinned back at him, pleased with his silliness. This Sam was a new one, and one she was glad to be acquainted with. Lounging back with her hands grasping her knees, she watched as he took yet another turn, pulled close to shore and cut the motor.

"We're here."

Antoinette surveyed the surrounding landscape. They were in a small cove where firm ground lay just out of reach through yards of marshy-looking grasses. There were two moss-covered live oaks, which reminded her of the ones they'd picnicked under at City Park, and dozens of smaller hackberries. A wide strip of black-eyed Susans and mayweed decorated the immediate shore leading into the water. Antoinette turned her gaze to the bottom of the skiff and knew immediately what the hip boots were for.

"We're going to wade to shore." Silently she congratulated herself on sounding so wonderfully matter-of-fact. She pushed down thoughts of alligators and cottonmouths.

"It certainly looks that way, doesn't it?"

"Is this a test of my outdoor skills?" she asked politely.

"Questions, questions." Sam selected a pair of boots and tossed them her way.

"Sam, you have heard of quicksand, haven't you?" She worried out loud, still trying to sound matter-of-fact. "Are you sure that we won't sink into the mud and disappear?"

"I've never heard of anyone who did." He didn't smile, but his eyes were dancing. "'Course, they wouldn't have lived to tell stories, would they?"

Antoinette could feel her spine straighten. "Sam," she said, so sweetly she was afraid she might attract bees, "have you ever been to a Mardi Gras ball?"

He grimaced, showing by that one brief expression exactly what he thought of the idea.

"Well," she continued, sweeter still, "you'll be getting an invitation this year. Yes, you will. I'm going to have my mother see that you're invited to the oldest, stodgiest ball of all, and I'm going to be sure the chief of police knows you've been invited to represent the force."

"Good at assessing weak spots, aren't you?"

"One of the best." She leaned down to fasten the boots and tested their weight by lifting a foot. There was no question about it—she would sink as soon as she put one foot in the water.

"All right," he said grudgingly, "if you go under for the third time, I'll pull you back up."

"Promise?" Antoinette watched as Sam nimbly vaulted into the water and miraculously sank only to the top of his boots. He grasped the boat and began to pull it to shore. The skiff was through the weeds and anchored next to solid ground before Antoinette could step out. "Why am I wearing these boots?" she asked.

"Because you look so cute in them."

She made sure he caught her glare and bent to begin unfastening the boots.

"And because you're going to need them to set your nets," Sam continued.

Her hands fell to her sides. "The wires and cotton mesh?"

"City girl, those are crawfish nets. You and I are under orders to bring fifty pounds of mud bugs back to Didi's house tonight for a real Cajun crawfish boil."

The sun was higher in the sky, and the shade of the largest live oak had become a necessity. Antoinette lay on the blanket that Sam had packed and watched him check his nets. There were ten altogether, lined up in the tangles of weeds along the shore. They were baited with chicken necks and some part of a cow that Sam called "melts," refusing to identify it further. Four of the nets were hers, a generous gift from a man who wouldn't take no for an answer. Sam was catching more crawfish than Antoinette because he hopped up to check his nets and rebait more frequently than she did, but Antoinette was catching her share of the finger-length, bronze-colored "mud bugs." She was secretly bursting with pride over her success.

They had snacked all morning, first on cold squares of bread pudding left from their feast the night before, later on fruit. The Atchafalaya Basin was too generous not to offer them more, however, and Sam had set up several fishing poles before the nets had been secured, succeeding in capturing one large channel catfish almost immediately. The fish had been cleaned and filleted with a deftness that testified to his years on the bayou, and Sam, the man who supposedly didn't cook, had fried it over a small camp stove, slapped it between thick slices of French bread and presented it to Antoinette with a flourish. Even considering that she was the po'boy connoisseur of New Orleans, she rated it the best she'd ever had.

As delicious as it was, Sam's lunch couldn't take the edge off the anticipation of the dinner to come. The crawfish, which resembled miniature lobster, would be boiled with garlic, red peppers and spices. Corn on the cob, new potatoes, whole onions and pieces of spicy sausage would be cooked with them, and the whole meal would be eaten with no utensils as soon as it was cool enough to manage. A crawfish boil was a southern Louisiana feast, and even the most sophisticated gourmand in New Orleans responded to the thought of one by licking his lips.

"Do we have our fifty pounds yet?" Antoinette asked lazily when Sam returned to drop to her side.

"You're not finished yet, lady. Your nets need checking."

"You don't understand my strategy." She ran the tip of her finger down his nose. "See, I'm a great believer in Darwin's theory of natural selection. Only the strongest shall survive and all that? Well, if a crawfish gets in my net, I have to give him the chance to get back out. Otherwise, I'll catch some of the best crawfish in this bayou. Then the gene pool will be substantially weakened—ouch!" She exhaled sharply. Sam was stretched out on top of her, their noses almost touching.

"No Cajun man allows his woman to talk her way out of doing her job. And your job is to check those nets."

"I'm temporarily unable to," she pointed out, threading her fingers together behind his neck. "Have mercy, monsieur. Besides, you're only half Cajun."

Sam smoothed Antoinette's hair back from her forehead. Their mood had been light all morning, and it had suited him perfectly. It had been a revelation that he could spend such relaxing time with a woman. Antoinette had no pretenses, no expectations. She wanted to be with him; she thoroughly enjoyed every new experience. He sensed that she, like he, rarely took the time to have fun, and now that she was, she was making the most of it.

As the morning passed, he had found himself planning other trips, wondering how he could fit all the things he wanted to do with her into their hectic work schedules. He had realized it would take a lifetime. The thought had been sobering but only for a moment. She had excitedly pointed out a colorful turtle sunning itself on a nearby log, and once again he had been drawn into the web of enchantment she was spinning.

Jubilant little girl, sophisticated debutante, compassionate healer, enthusiastic, responsive lover. She was all the things a man could want in a woman. He'd never thought he wanted all those things, and he had never wanted any of them on a permanent basis. Now he realized how little he'd understood about himself.

He didn't even realize how his thoughts showed in his face.

"Sam," Antoinette said softly, their teasing forgotten, "it can't be as bad as all that."

It was much worse, but there was no way to explain that to her, no way to let her know just how she could shatter his life if he let her.

"Make love to me," she whispered, wanting desperately to destroy the sudden shadows in the eyes that had danced all morning. "We're hidden from the water."

He knew what a bad idea it was even as he began to caress her. She fit him too perfectly, melted into him in a way that left him wondering if he would ever be free of her. She was all the complications he didn't need. And at that moment she was everything he wanted.

They undressed hurriedly, helping each other so that they wouldn't have to be separated. There were no leisurely explorations, no chances for building passion. It had arrived full-blown, making its own demands with no apologies. They gave in to it gladly, racing to the peak together.

Afterward they lay entwined in the shade, letting the faint breeze from the water cool their sweat-slick bodies. When they rose to dress and check their nets one more time, they held hands as they trudged through the alligator weeds and water primrose.

Sam took a different way back. He pointed out a channel that led to an egret rookery in a back-hole cypress swamp he had discovered as a teenager. He told her stories of the egret rookeries farther south in the marshes and on Avery Island to the west of them. He shared stories of his family and exploits of his youth. She listened with rapt attention, aware that moments of sharing this way were few and far between in his life.

About a mile from his cabin she realized she loved him.

Loving Sam wasn't wise. Perhaps it was no wiser than loving her former husband had been. Sam had never lied to her; she had known from the beginning what he wanted and what he didn't. What she hadn't known was how quickly she would grow to love him. She had believed she could control her feelings. She had even told Daffy as much. It was no longer a question of a short affair that might leave her emotionally bruised but still whole. She had done the unthinkable. She had kept nothing back; she had not waited to see if Sam might learn to love her, too.

When he spoke again, the sound was a surprise. "Why don't you go change? I've got to find a place for the crawfish."

Antoinette realized they were at the cabin. She smiled mechanically and stepped out onto the deck, going inside without a word. She pumped some water and washed up quickly, changing into khaki pants and a red knit shirt with the same lack of enthusiasm. She waited on the deck while Sam changed, and then got back into the skiff for the trip to Didi's.

"You've been very quiet. Did I talk too much?" Sam asked as he guided the skiff toward Bayou Midnight.

"I loved it," she said and meant it. "And I've loved the day." And I've found I love you, she added silently. And that was the reason I was quiet.

"Next time I'll take you down to the marshes. We'll get Martin's airboat and take off at dawn."

She schooled herself not to respond with the surge of emotion his words invoked. *Next time.* "I'd like that," she said simply. "I'd like that a lot. Just let me know in time so I can buy hip boots that fit." She watched the waves billowing out behind them, not risking a glance at his face. If there was ambivalence there, she didn't want to see it. She wanted only to savor the two words, "next time," and believe in possibilities.

Didi and Leonce's house sat on an inlet of Bayou Midnight about half a mile from Claude's. Antoinette could see the differences immediately. In design the house was very much like Sam's uncle's, but someone had painted this house white with a contrasting trim of light blue. Even from a distance Antoinette could see flowers hanging from the porch overhang and more flowers leading down a path to the water. To the side of the house was a large vegetable garden with a scarecrow whose raggedy arms were thrown open in a caricature of welcome.

"Looks like Martin's here, too," Sam said as he pulled the skiff to a short dock and secured it.

Now that they were closer, Antoinette could see Martin and Leonce standing together on the front porch. Martin was gesturing excitedly, and Leonce was standing far enough away to avoid being hit by his flailing arms. Words drifted down to the water, but the conversation was obviously in Cajun French, and once again Antoinette's limited French vocabulary was no help. Sam, however, was frowning.

"Would you like me to stay here?" she asked him. "Martin sounds angry, and I might be in the way."

"No, come on up. Martin's excitable, that's all. Leonce is the only person he ever lets go with. He'll calm down as soon as he realizes we're here."

Skeptical, Antoinette followed Sam, who was carrying the gunnysack of crawfish, up the path to the house. Sam had been right, however. As soon as the men caught sight of them, the conversation died.

"I've got dinner here." Sam set the sack down on the porch. "Where should I put them?"

"Didi got the washtub ready for 'em out back," Leonce told Sam, smiling a greeting to Antoinette at the same time. He kicked the bag with the toe of his worn boot. "Didya forget how to catch crawfish, Sam-son? Nuthin' in here."

"Then I guess one of us'll have to go hungry," Sam said seriously, poking his cousin's round belly. "Martin, you're staying, too, aren't you?"

"Nah." Martin turned on his heel and headed for the porch steps. He threw an unintelligible parting comment over his shoulder and headed for the water.

"You git my apologies for Martin," Leonce said to Antoinette. "He's havin' a bad time right now. He don't mean to be rude."

"That's all right," Antoinette assured him. "I can tell he's upset. I wasn't taking it personally."

"Didi's waitin' inside for you. Didi," he yelled, as if to make his point, "'Toinette's here."

Antoinette smiled at the shortened version of her name and decided she liked it. The door flew open, and Didi dashed through it, coming to an instant halt in front of Antoinette. "Gladya here. Come see my house."

Antoinette followed her inside for a whirlwind tour. When it was finished, she was left with an impression of comfort, creativity and warmth. Leonce's income and Didi's ingenuity had obviously provided them with a standard of living any middle-class American would be happy with. Didi had decorated with good taste and a flair for color. In addition, the house showed her ability as a seamstress and homemaker. Leonce's preferences were apparent in the huge color television set in the living room and the video recorder on top of it. A satellite dish in the backyard ensured that he could get the very best reception.

"Now we got the pot heatin' outside," Didi said, rubbing her hands together as the two women headed for the kitchen. "I'm gonna let the men boil the crawfish. I put everything in the water for 'em. Even Sam-son couldn't mess it up."

"What can I do to help?"

"Sit and talk to me." In her usual down-to-earth fashion, Didi got right to the point. "Sam-son says you work with people who got troubles."

Antoinette nodded. Didi was bustling around the bright, attractive kitchen, and she looked absolutely in her glory. It was a joy to watch her while, with blond curls bouncing, she did three jobs at once and managed to carry on a conversation, too.

"Well, Martin, he's got troubles. And I'm the only one in this family who sees it."

Antoinette knew she was being drawn into a family squabble, but she wasn't sure how to avoid it without sounding rude. "You're worried about Martin," she said noncommittally.

"More than that. I think his mind's goin'. He don't take care of himself, don't eat good, don't seem to sleep. He goes out on the water, and half the time he don't come home. Claude don't know where he is most of the time."

"He is a grown man," Antoinette pointed out gently.

"Sure he is, but he don't do the things grown men do. He's got no friends, no women, no nuthin'. Just his traps and his fishin' and his boats. He don't talk to no one but Leonce, and then he yells. You heared him yellin' when you come up, didn'tya?"

"I did, Didi, but I couldn't understand what it was about."

"That's anuther thing. He don't speak English anymore hardly. Used to when he had to. Never liked it, but he was in the army. He had to speak English then. All of us, we speak French sometimes. But Martin, he acts like he's got a secret to keep. Don't want anyone who don't speak French to know it."

"Is it the thing about Omega Oil closing down the marshes that's making him so angry?"

Didi was shucking corn and washing potatoes now, and she looked up from the sink to shake her head. "Not just that. Things're changin'. He don't want no changes. Nuthin' ever stays the same, though, does it? He don't know that, might never know it. Leonce says Martin come back from

Vietnam wantin' the bayou to be just the same, like it oughta stay frozen while his world went crazy over there. Leonce says Vietnam did this to Martin. But Vietnam was a long time ago, heh?''

"Have you talked about this to Sam?"

"Sam-son won't listen." Didi momentarily stopped, turning to face Antoinette. The cessation of motion was all Antoinette needed to understand how serious Didi thought this was. "Sam-son, he's got a blind spot about his family. He thinks the sun and moon were invented on Bayou Midnight. No one here can do wrong. He don't see what's happening. He loves Martin, and when Sam-son loves somebody, he loves them all the way. He'd kill for Martin or Leonce or Claude without thinkin' twice, and I guess he'd kill for me, too. But he won't listen." The string of French phrases that followed would have sounded more appropriate from Martin, but Antoinette knew they said everything about Didi's frustration level.

"What are you afraid might happen?" Antoinette asked, wondering if Didi thought Martin might get violent.

"I don't know. I guess I think Martin's gonna go off in the swamp one day and forgit to come back."

Antoinette shuddered at the thought.

"I need the stuff to put in with them crawfish," Leonce said, wiping his feet on a mat at the back door and swinging the screen door open.

Didi silently handed him the basket she had just filled with corn and potatoes, and a previously prepared basin overflowing with bulbs of garlic, onions and big chunks of sausage.

"At least there'll be something to eat," Leonce teased good-naturedly. "The crawfish them two caught wouldn't fill one belly."

"Especially your belly," Didi retorted, drying her hands on a dish towel. "Didn't see you out crawfishin' today, Leonce."

"Martin went. Got about two hundred pounds, but the man he sells to said the price dropped. Martin opened the sacks and dumped them on his feet." Leonce tried to laugh, but the sound showed his discomfort with what his brother had done.

Didi caught Antoinette's eye and shook her head. "That don't make no sense. Nuthin' he does makes good sense anymore."

"Don't go fillin' 'Toinette's head with junk about Martin. He's a good man, different from most, but good. And he's my brother," Leonce said with an edge to his words that Antoinette couldn't miss.

"Crawfish are boilin'," Didi reminded him, no apology in her voice.

They ate outside near the water's edge on a picnic table covered with newspaper. The crawfish more than lived up to Antoinette's expectations, and even though Leonce continued to tease Sam about how few there were, there were still pounds left over when they had all eaten their fill.

The crawfish shells were thrown into the water, and a giant bass came to the surface to snap one between his powerful jaws. "That one, I hope he likes red pepper," Didi said with her tinkling giggle.

The conversation was pleasant. Didi seemed satisfied to have talked over her concerns with Antoinette, even though Antoinette had offered little in the way of guidance. Only once during the meal did she try to broach the subject of Martin to Sam, and when his reaction was similar to Leonce's, she just shrugged, agreeably changing the subject. Antoinette could see that, as worried as Didi was about Martin, she had realized there was little more that she could do than worry.

When it was time to go, the two women hugged goodbye, exchanging phone numbers and promises to keep in touch. Antoinette was still smiling when they took the skiff back to Claude's and traded it for Sam's canoe. The paddle back to his cabin was done in the glow of a subtle sunset and in silence. The sounds of a bayou evening serenaded them all the way home.

Much later, Antoinette lay in Sam's arms and listened to the deep bellow of a bull alligator somewhere outside the porch windows. She was satiated in every way and completely content except for the knowledge that tomorrow meant going back to the city and an uncertain relationship with the man beside her.

"I feel like I've been here for years," she said, unwilling to let Sam fall asleep while she lay awake listening to the night.

"Anxious to get back?"

"Not at all. Let's both call in and say we contracted swamp fever. Then we can stay another week or two."

Sam smiled in the darkness, aware that she was only half teasing. "You could move down here and start a practice. Gator psychologist."

"I might even find a person or two who could use my services." She had said the words lightly, but the image of Martin was between them both as soon as she had finished speaking.

"I gather Didi talked to you."

Sam hadn't moved away, but Antoinette felt him stiffen. "She did. She doesn't feel like she has any place to turn, and I was a handy listening ear."

"She thinks Martin's crazy."

"She's worried about him, Sam. And I think she has reason to be."

"You don't know Martin. Just because he's not like everyone else, you think he should change. Not everyone needs what Didi and Leonce have. Martin doesn't...."

And you don't. Antoinette silently finished the sentence for him. She hesitated to voice her fears, aware just how delicate this subject was, but in good conscience she couldn't stay silent. "It's not a question of everyone needing to conform. I appreciate the differences in people—that's what makes the world such a wonderful place to live. But, Sam, Martin is more than just a nonconformist. He's angry, his temper is difficult if not impossible to control."

"You can tell that after seeing the man exactly twice?"

Sam's sarcasm sliced right through her, but she continued in spite of it. "Of course I couldn't. I'm using what Didi told me tonight. Obviously I can't do anything for him. I'm not trying to recruit another client. I just think that some-day in the future you might regret not listening to Didi.''

"I brought you here to meet my family, not to criticize them or me."

Brick by brick the defenses were going back up. Antoi-nette was only surprised that for almost two days Sam had been open with her. She regretted the loss of it with all her heart.

"If I hadn't told you I was worried about Martin, what else would you have found to hold against me?" she asked, pulling herself out of his arms. The bed, which had been the perfect size, now seemed much too small.

"Don't psychoanalyze me, Antoinette."

"I'm not going to do anything," she promised, "be-cause it's perfectly apparent to me that anything I do or say is going to be used against me."

"Then be quiet and go to sleep."

She tried, holding back the tears that the most vulner-able part of her wanted to cry. They were both very still, not touching at all. Antoinette listened to the crickets and the frogs for long minutes. She jerked upright suddenly when the bull alligator bellowed again.

"Damn it!" Sam swore.

"I'm sorry," she said softly. "It startled me."

"I'm not swearing at you. Come here."

She felt his arms pull her down, and in a moment she was on top of him. The night was cloudy, and without the moon to illuminate the room, she could barely make out his fea-tures.

"Are you a good enough psychologist to see that Martin and I aren't much different?" he asked. "When you criti-cize him, you're criticizing me, too. When it comes right down to it, I feel the same way about my life as Martin feels about his. We're both happy. We don't need anyone inter-fering."

It was time to stop beating around the bush. Antoinette knew exactly what he was talking about. It had been be-tween them since the beginning of the conversation, since the beginning of their relationship.

"Are you happy?" She lifted herself on her elbows and framed his face with her hands. "Did you invite me here to show me how little you need my interference in your life? Because if you did, I misunderstood. Give us a chance, Sam. I'm not asking you to marry me. I'm not asking for all your free time. Just don't let a distorted fantasy of what a good cop is interfere with something very special."

"Has it ever occurred to you that I might know what I need better than you do? You and Didi are sisters under the skin, aren't you?"

"Every time I've trusted your feelings, you've come back to me. If you were so sure, you wouldn't have asked me to come this weekend. If you were so sure, you wouldn't have talked about taking me down to the marshes next time you come here." She put an end to the conversation by molding her mouth to his. His hands tangled roughly in her hair, and it was clear he was angry.

Antoinette knew that anger could be a powerful aphrodisiac. The bodies that had been so well sated responded to their argument with a new level of need. Tongue met tongue, hands traveled roughly over opposing bodies, and when Sam finally thrust into her, she was more than ready.

She fell asleep, half on top of him. It was a position she wouldn't have allowed herself if she'd been awake enough to consider it. It was possessive, intimate and loving, all the things Sam didn't want.

He lay awake after her breathing had slowed and deepened, wondering why she felt so right lying there.

Chapter 12

Dawn hadn't arrived when Antoinette heard Sam's movements in the next room. It was raining, a soft, formless rain that met the mists and joined them in a seemingly impenetrable cloud of moisture. She swung her legs over the bed and stood, dreading the canoe trip back to Claude's to get Sam's car, dreading the day.

Sam was standing at the sink shaving. She lingered in the doorway watching the wonderfully male ritual, but she denied herself the pleasure of walking across the room to wrap her arms around his waist for an early-morning hug. Their weekend was over. In a few short hours she would be back at work and so would he. She knew Sam well enough to know that there would be no sharing, no humor today. She knew him well enough to know that if she touched him, he wouldn't respond the way she wanted. Instead, she murmured a good-morning greeting, although she was sure Sam already knew she was there, and went to her suitcase to get her hairbrush.

Twenty minutes later they were in the canoe, covered with rain slickers that had seen better days. The cabin disappeared when they were no more than thirty feet from it, like

Brigadoon melting back into the mists. The swamp was foreboding in the darkness without even the faintest light from the moon to show them the way. Sam guided by instinct until the glow of predawn, which was just discernible through the rain, began to light the sky.

Antoinette dipped her paddle into the water again and again in a motion that had become second nature over the weekend. She watched the swamp become suffused with mist-shrouded light, and as they turned into Bayou Midnight, she watched the sun break over the horizon. She wanted to linger, even with the rain making uncomfortable puddles at her cold, bare feet, but Sam's strokes were strong and even, and Antoinette couldn't force herself to ask him to slow down.

Their progression up the bayou took on symbolic importance to her. The rain was still falling, but the mists were clearing, and slowly, carefully, the real world was becoming revealed in the light of day. She wanted to call back the mists, call back the weekend. She wanted to hold off all the forces that would make Sam forget or ignore what they had experienced together. Back in the real world he would find reasons to stop seeing her. Back in the real world she would let him, afraid to risk touching the remote policeman who claimed that his job was all the satisfaction from life he needed.

Their progression up the bayou had much the same effect on Sam. His arms had ached to hold Antoinette that morning. He had known she watched him as he shaved, known just how much she would welcome his arms around her. In the golden glow of the kerosene lamp, with her long hair tumbled around her face and her nightgown hinting at the sweet contours of her body, she had tempted him almost beyond reason. But reason had won out. Their time for loving was over. Now he watched her back as she stroked the water. She had not murmured one word of complaint as they maneuvered cypress stumps and stands of tupelo in the rain. He knew how uncomfortable she must be; he was that uncomfortable himself. It was like Antoinette to find enjoyment even in this. It would be one of the hardest things to forget about her.

Their progression up the bayou was watched by another. A man stood in the shadows of Claude LeBeaud's boathouse as the canoe glided toward its destination. He cursed softly, the musical syllables falling to earth with the rain. He had forgotten that Sam-son's car was there and that Samson and his lady friend would be returning to the city that morning.

Martin pulled himself farther into the shadows. He could be in plain sight, and then he could merge into nothingness. It was a trick that had served him well in the swamps and the marshes when he wanted to keep his presence a secret from the creatures there. It was a trick he had taught Sam-son. He knew enough about Sam-son's job to imagine that Sam-son had used this skill, this sleek, spare use of his body, to save his life more than once during his police career. It had saved Martin's life in Vietnam, too. It had saved it so that he could leave one swamp to come home to another. Saved it so that he could watch mankind destroy one part of the world, only to come home and watch society destroy another.

There had been a time when Martin could share his thoughts with Sam-son. That time had passed. There was nothing that he could share with anyone now. Not the burning rage that threatened to annihilate whatever sense he had left, not the terror that his family could be destroyed by his actions, not the sorrow for what he was being forced to do.

Martin heard the rustle of the water and the slide of the canoe onto dry ground. There was nothing he could do today about anything. And there was nothing he could tell Sam-son. Let him go home. Let him go back to the city and forget that Bayou Midnight existed. Martin would wait. He was good at waiting. He would move when it was time, and he would know when that time was right.

Sam stood on the shore, his body tensed and alert.

"Sam?" Antoinette hugged her arms around her for warmth. Now that they were on land once more, she wanted nothing so much as the rainproof interior of Sam's car.

He was silent for a full minute, the rain battering the old cap he was using for protection. "I thought I heard something," he said finally.

"You did. Thousands of raindrops."

"No. Something else. Someone else."

"Will it spoil your sleuthing if I go look for Tootsie?"

He shook his head, then turned to follow her. "I'll help you. We'd better get going, or we'll both be late for work."

Antoinette walked toward the house, calling for the big sheepdog while Sam did the same as he carried her suitcase to the car. She was rewarded almost instantly by the sounds of Tootsie bounding down off the porch to leap at her, spreading mud and love in her wake.

Antoinette held her off, scratching the dog's ears fondly as she did. "Toots, I don't know which of us needs a bath worse."

Tootsie followed her to the car, and Claude's hound meandered behind to say a tongue-lolling goodbye. Antoinette towel-dried Tootsie with an old rag before she loaded the dog inside. Then she stepped out of the slicker, shaking it and jumping into the car simultaneously while Sam did the same. With the slickers folded in the back seat and the windshield wipers working full blast, Sam pulled out of the yard. The road was potholed and muddy, but Sam maneuvered the car along it as if it were a perfectly maintained speedway. They were on the clamshell road that meandered beside the larger bayou feeding into Bayou Midnight before either of them broke the silence.

"It's over," Antoinette said with a sigh, leaning back against the comfortable seat with a posture that signaled her resignation. "It was a perfect weekend, but it's over."

Sam wasn't sure who she was trying to convince. And he wasn't sure if she was talking about more than the weekend. He didn't want to talk, and he didn't want to think about all the implications of her words.

"You're remarkably easy to please," he said finally because the silence had become uncomfortable.

"Do you think so?" she asked, hurt that he would make her pleasure in Bayou Midnight sound so childish. "Maybe I should be more discriminating."

"Antoinette, I don't want to fight with you." As soon as the words were out, Sam realized they were a lie. He did feel like a fight, although he wasn't sure why.

"I wasn't aware that we were fighting. I thought we were talking about the weekend."

"There's a fight brewing."

"You'd like that, wouldn't you?" She stared straight ahead, watching the windshield wipers. "If we fight, that'll be what you remember about this trip. It'll be easy to forget everything else."

The words lit the tinder of his temper. She had understood his motivations better than he had himself. "Do you know what it'd be like to be married to someone who constantly tore you apart and put you back together again like a specimen in some damned laboratory?" Sam slammed his hand down on the steering wheel in an uncharacteristic display of emotion. "You think you know more about me than I know. Take a hike, lady. I don't need your damned analysis."

"Who said anything about marriage?" Antoinette was stunned at his words.

"You don't have to say anything."

"Now who's reading whose mind?"

"I'm no fool. I don't believe for a second you saw any of this as a fleeting affair. You're a traditionalist to the core. You were taking a risk, but you were hoping that after one weekend together I'd change my mind about needing you in my life. And that means marriage."

"I wasn't thinking that far down the road," she denied.

"Be honest. Do you believe you'd ever be happy with less?"

"I've had much less for six years. I've been perfectly happy without a man in my life at all. Don't tell me you're one of these men who believes every woman in the world is trying to lead him to the altar?"

"No one has ever gotten close enough to lead me anywhere."

Until now. Antoinette heard the words, even though Sam didn't say them. He was angry because he didn't like what he was feeling. He didn't like knowing that she was becoming important to him. Well, he wasn't the only one who didn't like his feelings.

"I can't help what you think about women in general," she said, losing her temper. "But I don't like being put in categories where I don't belong. If you think I've set my heart on an obsessive-compulsive cop who's a misogynist to boot, you've got another think coming!"

There was absolute silence in the car for the next half hour until they pulled up in the parking lot of the café where they'd eaten breakfast on Saturday. Even after the engine was turned off, Sam sat gripping the steering wheel, and Antoinette wondered if she would have to pry him loose to get him inside.

"Obsessive-compulsive cop?" he said finally. "Misogynist?"

"I may have laid it on a little thick," she admitted.

"I don't like fighting with you. If I did it to put the weekend in a different perspective, I'm sorry."

Antoinette turned to watch him. She had wanted nothing more all morning than to touch him. Now she gave in to the desire. Her fingers stroked his hair, circling his ear to rest on the side of his face. "It was a wonderful weekend. And I know it was wonderful for you, too. No matter what happens now, I want to remember it just the way it was. I want the same for you."

"You understand me too well."

"I don't mean to analyze you."

"I don't like sharing that much of myself with anyone."

"It's only me, Sam. Just Antoinette. I'm not making any demands just because I know who you are."

He turned, bending toward her for the first kiss of the day. It was light and quick, and Antoinette thought it said a lot about what he was thinking. It was Monday morning, and he was afraid that even a kiss would trap him. "Let's go eat."

The rest of the trip was more pleasant. It was only when Sam put her suitcase on the front porch and waited as she unlocked her front door that the tension built again.

"Well, it looks like we'll both be able to make it to work on time," Antoinette said.

Sam checked his watch, even though they both knew what time it was. "I'll have to hurry."

"Yes. Thank you for everything."

He bent to brush her lips lightly, but at the first real taste he groaned and pulled her closer. Goodbye was momentarily forgotten as he took what he had desired all morning. Antoinette let her arms circle his body, holding tight for this one moment that was being given to her.

When he finally pulled away, she didn't even risk a smile. She went into the house without a backward glance and closed the door behind her.

Antoinette hummed one of her favorite songs, a soulful jazz ballad about missing New Orleans and dreaming of magnolias in June. She lifted her eyes to the fully blossomed magnolia tree that stood in the tiny yard of her office building and wondered if the person who had written the song had ever lived in the city or if he had just been overcome by the desire to rhyme June and tune. Magnolias in New Orleans were always open by May. This particular magnolia had been loaded with buds right before she'd gone down to Bayou Midnight with Sam. Now, two weeks later, it was fragrant with waxy ivory blossoms. It was the only thing in her life that had bloomed just as it was supposed to.

Antoinette realized that, if she was paying attention to the passage she'd been reading before she got distracted, she would have committed it to memory by now. She'd been over it at least six times, and she still didn't know what it said. At the sound of her office door opening, she looked up, grateful for the break.

"Still hasn't called?" Daffy came into the office and shut the door behind her. She was dressed in a brilliant blue leotard top and tights, with an orange plaid skirt that swirled around her calves when she walked. Her red curls were covered with a green paisley kerchief. Even the exuberant display of color didn't make Antoinette smile. She shook her head in answer to Daffy's question. There was no doubt who Daffy meant.

"Call him, then."

Antoinette sighed and shut the journal she'd been trying to read. In the two weeks since she'd last seen Sam, her ability to concentrate had been next to nothing. She had refused to give in to the other signs of depression. She had eaten regularly, tried to sleep the required number of hours, spent time with her friends. But there had been little she could do at moments like these to force her mind to stay on track. Daffy had seen it, and in her typical take-charge manner, she had determined to do something about it.

"You aren't going to let this go, are you?"

Daffy's face showed her concern. "I will if you really want me to."

"I do."

"All right." Daffy turned back to the door and reached for the knob.

"Wait." Antoinette stood and motioned to the sofa. The two women reached it together, dropping silently into opposite corners. "What would I say if I called him? Hello, Sam? Remember me?"

"You know, Antoinette," Daffy began, "times have changed, even for New Orleans debutantes. Women call men now. They ask them out, pay for dates, offer their body if the man they want is shy. It's a different world out there."

"I'm not different, though."

"You're tearing yourself to pieces, and there could be a perfectly rational reason why Sam hasn't called you."

"Oh, I'm sure the reason is rational. He doesn't want what I'm offering."

"Call him and make sure you've got the message straight, then. You of all people know how important communication is."

There was a knock on the door, and before Antoinette could answer, Rosy pushed it open and stuck her head through. "Still hasn't called?"

"My life is an open book." Antoinette shut her eyes and leaned her head back against the back of the sofa. She wished Sam were there to take away the headache that had nipped at her, just under the surface, all day. She wished she had a cigarette.

"Once, when I was between husbands, I was going out with a man who said he worshiped the ground I walked on." Rosy came in and shut the door behind her. Idly, Antoinette wondered who would be the next person to come in and give her advice.

"Then," Rosy continued, "he stopped calling. Just like that. I was so mad, I stuck my nose up in the air and minced around like one of Cinderella's stepsisters. Two weeks later I was reading the paper, and I glanced at the obituaries. John had been hit by a car, and they were having a memorial service for him that day. Here he was, deader than a doornail, and I'd been wasting all that energy getting mad at him. If I'd of known..." Rosy sniffed. "If I'd of known..." She sniffed again. "I could have been looking for someone new."

Antoinette swallowed twice, but she couldn't restrain the chuckle that finally erupted. "You made that up." She opened her eyes and glared at Rosy, but another chuckle took the edge off it. "Darn you, Rosy, you're trying to make me feel better!"

"Well, it's part true!" Rosy defended herself.

"Which part?"

"Well, he stopped calling. That part was true."

"And?"

"And I found out why from the newspaper."

"What did you find out?"

"That he skipped town with the payroll from the cafeteria where he was working. Guess he's still running."

"Enough!" Antoinette stood, but the smile on her face was the first real one that had been there in days. "I'll call Sam. I owe myself that much, I guess."

"If he's half the emotionless, repressed bastard I think he is, you're better off without him," Daffy said, standing to follow Rosy out of the office.

Antoinette knew exactly what Daffy was doing. If Sam made it clear he was finished with her, Daffy was giving her the ammunition she needed to get over him quickly. Sadly, Antoinette knew it wouldn't work. Sam was neither emotionless nor repressed. She might have been able to make herself believe it before the weekend they had spent together, but now she knew exactly who he was. A man with all the warm, human qualities she desired. A man too careful and too controlled, but a man whose loyalty and affection had already enriched many lives. The man she loved.

At her desk she looked up the station number, dialing it quickly before she could change her mind. She half expected not to have her call put through, but she was only on hold a few seconds before Sam answered.

"Sergeant Long."

She shouldn't have called. She sat down with a thump and cleared her throat. "Sam, it's Antoinette."

There was a silence, and Antoinette imagined the look on his face. He would not be pleased that she was on the line.

"Yes, Antoinette."

She used her free hand to torment a strand of hair, twisting it like a corkscrew. "Is this a bad time to talk?"

"It's all right."

"I've missed you."

More silence. "I've been very busy," he said finally.

She shut her eyes and cursed Daffy and Rosy, but the blame was hers for listening to them. "Yes, well, so have I." She heard her own words and realized she was pretending. Anger shot through her at being reduced to such adolescent behavior. She opened her eyes and sat up straighter. "And because we're both busy people," she continued, "I think I ought to lay my reason for calling on the line. I want to see you. You and I still have some unfinished business."

"The investigation is taking all my time," Sam said, and she knew he was going to use Omega Oil as an excuse for not seeing her.

"Then I won't demand much," she broke in. "Let's meet somewhere for a drink. We can say what needs to be said over one round."

"I don't have the time...."

Antoinette refused to argue; she just remained silent, waiting for him to be honest.

"I don't know what good this will do either of us," he said finally.

"You owe it to me."

"All right." He named a French Quarter hotel, and they agreed to meet that night after happy hour was over.

Antoinette replaced the receiver and reopened the journal she'd been reading before Daffy intruded. With determination that was purely intellectual, she completed the article.

Sam was late, and the psychologist in Antoinette wondered if it was passive-aggressive behavior because he was being forced to do something he didn't want to do, or just typical male reluctance when anticipating a scene. When he finally arrived, he took the seat across from her without a word of greeting. His suit was dark green and his tie curry colored. He was not the man she'd known on Bayou Midnight.

"Have you ordered?"

"I'm on my second round," she informed him. She lifted her hand, and the cocktail waitress came to take his order. Then they were alone.

Antoinette had promised that this would be quick. She had no intention of breaking that promise. "I won't ask how you've been or how the investigation is going," she began. "I'll get right to the point."

"How have *you* been?"

She tried to weigh his words. They had sounded genuinely concerned. But then, she shouldn't be too surprised by that. Sam had feelings for her; that had never been the issue. The issue had been whether he would let them grow and risk the possibility of a solid commitment.

"Actually, I haven't been doing too well. I've been waiting for the phone to ring for two weeks now, and the waiting has been difficult." She searched his eyes, but he was too good at hiding his feelings for her to fathom what they might be. "Sam, it's clear you've made a decision about us and that you've neglected to inform me what it was. I'd like you to spell it out."

"Why are you doing this?"

The waitress came with his drink, and Antoinette shook her head as he reached for his wallet. She nodded, and the young woman left.

"I'm doing it because I believe in people being up-front with each other. Obviously it's just one of the ways we differ." She folded her hands in front of her and realized her knuckles were white. She forced each finger to relax.

"I was up-front with you right from the start. I've never lied about the possibilities of a future for us."

Antoinette listened to the carefully neutral tone of Sam's voice. This was not the man she knew. This was not even a man she wanted to know. Determined to get this over quickly, she riveted her eyes on her fingers.

"What you've been is ambivalent. You want me, you don't want me. You want me, you don't want me. Let me hear it from you loud and clear for once, please. If we're really finished this time, please tell me. I'd like to get on with living."

"There's no place for a woman in my life."

She nodded, although the words had felt like daggers. But the words had only backed up what she'd already known. "There was a place for one two weekends ago. Did that meet all your needs for a while?"

"It wasn't like that."

"Wasn't it?"

"I didn't invite you down to my cabin just to work off my sexual appetite, if that's what you mean."

"Then why did you invite me?"

Sam had asked himself the same question, over and over, hoping each time for a new answer. But the truth was simple and insulting to both of them. He had invited her because he couldn't stop himself. He had picked up the telephone a dozen times since for the same reason. The calls had never been completed because now he knew he cared too much about her to hurt her anymore. He only wished he had cared that much before. He should never have taken her to Bayou Midnight, never made love to her, never let her into his life.

"Inviting you was a mistake." Sam finished half his drink in one swallow, but it was no fortification for what he knew he must say. "You're very vulnerable, very serious about the commitments you make. I knew that, but I was too selfish to let that guide me. I wanted you, even though I knew it couldn't last, and I took what I wanted. It was wrong, and I'm sorry. I'm not going to make it worse for either of us. This has to end, and it has to end now." He finished the rest of the drink before he finished his sentence. "Before you fall in love with me."

If he hadn't been so absolutely on target about her feelings, she would have laughed at the conceit in the last sentence. As it was, the only mistake he had made in his analysis was the timing. "You're too late," she said, looking up from her hands. "I'm already in love with you."

"Don't be!" His words were harsh and to the point.

"Wouldn't it be nice if it were that easy?"

"I have nothing to offer you. You're a psychologist, damn it, you should have seen that."

"You have everything to offer, but I should have seen that you wouldn't offer it," she corrected him. "It's a funny thing about love, though, it just happens, and analyzing the whys and wherefores doesn't seem to help."

"I should never have touched you."

"No," she agreed, "you shouldn't have. But you did, and I fell in love with you." She met his gaze directly. "It wasn't such a bad thing, Sam. Love is worth giving, even if it's not returned."

"I'm sorry."

"Don't be sorry. I'm a big girl." She pushed her chair back from the table and gave him a smile that didn't even tremble. "I love you, Sam, but I love myself, too. I'm not going to punish myself for what happened, and I'm not going to beg you to change your mind. I'm going to walk out of here and get on with life. And the next time I fall in love, I'm going to be more careful."

She stood, hesitant for a moment, then stepped to his side and bent to kiss his cheek. She wasn't sure whose benefit the gesture was for. She only knew she wasn't going to end this with anger, even if it would be easier for them both. "Good luck on the Omega Oil case. Call me when it's over and let me know how it turned out." She straightened and walked away, without looking back.

Sam watched Antoinette stop at the bar to pay their bill. She had been in control of the whole scene, right from the beginning. He'd been through scenes with other women, wheedling, tearful scenes that had left him stone cold and glad to escape. This time he felt empty.

He had avoided Antoinette because he hadn't wanted to face the end of their relationship. Now he had to face it. She was gone. His life could return to normal. His energies could go back into the job that needed them.

A brunette with a pouty expression was watching him from the bar. Antoinette was no longer in sight, and the brunette made it clear that she would welcome his company. She was attractive in an overblown, soap-opera-vixen way, and Sam knew he could have her in his bed before the night was over. He stood and walked out the door without a backward glance. He had been ruined by the combination of class and compassion that was Antoinette Deveraux. He knew it would be a long, long time before he looked at another woman.

Chapter 13

Sam looked up from the patch of water hyacinth where his fishing line was tangled, in time to see the familiar form of his uncle's pirogue move soundlessly through the water. Nonc Claude rarely visited him at his cabin, judging accurately that, if Sam was there, he needed his privacy. Now Sam watched his uncle pole through the water and step onto the barge deck.

"I hope you're here to tell me the case I've been working on is solved and the chief called Didi's house to let me know I can take an extended vacation." Sam's line came unsnagged with one vicious tug, and he reeled it in, setting the rod beside him.

"*Mais non.* I jus' heared you was here, Sam-son. Came to find out if it was the truth."

"I'm here." Sam felt ashamed that he hadn't even left his uncle a note when he'd gotten his canoe. That had been two days before. He had paddled straight to his cabin, and he hadn't been anywhere else since.

"Been a while since we seen you here."

It had been exactly a month. One hellish, miserable month. "I've been working around the clock on the Omega

Oil case," Sam apologized. "This is the first weekend I've had off. I probably won't have another one for a month."

"Don' have to say sorry to me, Sam-son. Didya think I was askin' why?"

"No, I didn't." Sam faced his uncle and tried to smile. "You never pry."

"Not even when you was sixteen and mad as a mosquito who can't find nuthin' good to eat."

Sam hadn't thought about being sixteen for a long time. "I was mad all the time that first year," he recalled. "Mad because you made me get up every morning and paddle miles down the bayou to the school bus, and because I had to come back to Bayou Midnight every afternoon."

"Mad 'cause I made you fish, mad 'cause you never caught nuthin'."

"I learned, though. In school and out."

"Nobody could tell you nuthin', but I was stronger'n you. Only way to git you to do anythin'."

"I'd be in jail somewhere now if you hadn't taken over," Sam said. "Instead, I put people in jail. When I can find them," he added, thinking about the Omega Oil case.

"Mebbe sometimes you look in the wrong places."

"Maybe I do."

"Gotta look for answers where you don' think they gonna be."

"Do you know something I don't?" Sam searched his uncle's face, but Claude's expression was as carefully neutral as Sam kept his own.

"Nuthin' I can put a finger on. Talk. That's all."

"Talk about what?"

"Omega Oil."

"I know there's no love lost for the company here."

"I was a boy, swampers made the laws here. Some things, they change. Some things don'."

"We worked on that angle," Sam said finally. "We had reason to suspect a man from down here somewhere was involved, at least on some level, but nothing turned up. The sheriff tried to help."

"Sheriff." Claude spat in the water at their feet. "Don' know nuthin' 'bout what's here. Come in on the weekends, does a little fishin', throws a few nets. That's all."

"Have Martin or Leonce talked to you about any of this?"

"Martin, he don' talk 'bout nuthin'. Leonce, he don' talk 'bout nuthin' serious. *Mais non,* this, it's only a say-so. Stuff I heared 'cause I keep my ears open and my mouth shut."

And having said the last, Claude turned back to his pirogue.

"Nonc Claude. I'll throw what you said into the gumbo pot."

"You do that, Sam-son." Claude hesitated and then faced his nephew. "Where's 'Toinette? I could git to like that one. Might not have Cajun blood, but she's good enough to be Cajun."

"She won't be back."

"Life without a woman, nuthin' harder."

The sentiment seemed strange coming from Claude, the perennial widower. "You made it all these years," Sam reminded him.

"You never saw your Tante Louise. Looked a little like 'Toinette. I still hear her voice in my dreams. She be waitin' for me when I die."

Sam was moved by the longing in his uncle's voice. In all the years they had been close, his uncle had never mentioned his aunt. Now Sam understood why. "I always thought you didn't remarry because you didn't want a woman messing up your life."

"I'm still married. Always was, always will be."

Sam watched Claude's descent into the pirogue. The long boat disappeared into the trees as silently as it had come.

Sam felt strangely restless. For two days he had felt perfectly content to sit and brood. He'd brought a case of beer and a cooler of junk food with him, and he'd consumed more of both than he should have. He had lain on the mattress where he and Antoinette had made love and listened to the sounds of the swamp. He'd heard them—as if through her ears but with none of her enthusiasm. Her presence was tangible everywhere.

He was right to have ended their relationship. One weekend together and he could think of little else. A month had passed since that weekend, and two weeks had passed since he'd last seen her. It had taken a week to put his guilt in perspective, another to convince himself that she would adjust. How many weeks was it going to take before she wasn't the first thing he thought of in the morning and the last thing he thought of at night?

There was no point in continuing this self-imposed exile. Being here made matters worse, not better. Sam stood and headed inside the cabin to get the few things he would take back to the city with him. He had come here to force himself to forget Antoinette Deveraux. The trip was an unqualified failure, just as working night and day at his job had been. Time and only time would take care of his problem. Now he just had to find a way to make it pass more quickly.

Antoinette blew a smoke ring over her head and watched it float toward the light fixture in the ceiling. She was getting good at smoke rings again, almost as good as she'd been before she quit smoking. And she didn't cough anymore when she inhaled deeply. She was firmly back on the path of self-destruction.

The return to cigarettes was only temporary, or at least that's what she told herself every time she lit one now. Physiologically, a month or two more of smoking couldn't make much difference in her health. And right now it was making all the difference in her mental health. She was sleeping, eating, concentrating—all the things that a normal person does. Without the cigarettes she wasn't sure she could have managed to do any of them.

Smoking was one little setback, but that was all. When Sam was out of her mind for good, she'd quit again. Rosy could make another strudel, and life could get back to normal.

Antoinette put her head in her hands at the sound of a knock on her office door. She may have started smoking again, but no one in the office knew it yet. That was about to change. "Come in."

Rosy took one look at the smoke-filled room, marched to the window and threw it open to let in fresh air. For once, however, she had no comment to make. "I'm going. There was a phone call for you while you were in session. It was long-distance, and I didn't want you to miss it." She handed Antoinette the pink message slip and stood by her desk as she read it. Antoinette was surprised to find that it was from Didi. "She says she's been trying to reach you at home, but she couldn't get you," Rosy said helpfully.

Antoinette heard the curiosity in her secretary's voice. "I haven't been home a lot. My friends have never seen so much of me."

"Better than working too hard." The self-control that had allowed Rosy to avoid commenting on the obvious ended. "Better than smoking."

"I know."

"Why don't you come home with me for dinner, dahlin'? I'll fry some soft shell crabs. You can eat them on French bread if you want," she added generously.

"I'm okay." Antoinette flashed Rosy a smile to convince her. "I really am. Lonely sometimes, and sad a lot, but I'm okay. And I'm not the only woman in the world who's had an unhappy love affair."

"If that weasel ever sets foot in this office, I'll . . ."

"He won't."

Rosy nodded, fists still clenched. "Good thing."

"Thanks for the message and the invitation. If I don't go home tonight, though, my dog will think I'm a stranger and gobble me up next time I walk through the door."

"Have a good weekend, dahlin'."

"I'm going to, I promise."

Antoinette denied herself another cigarette before she dialed Didi's number. The call was a link to Sam, and as such, she wanted to get it over with quickly.

The phone rang ten times before Didi answered. Antoinette pictured the pretty blonde outside hanging the laun-

dry or scrubbing the porch with whirlwind energy. She
might even have been fishing for dinner.

"Didi, it's Antoinette. It's nice to hear your voice."

"'Toinette. I been callin' for days. Glad I got smart and
called you there."

Antoinette sat back in her chair and listened to Didi
chatter at full speed. In a minute she had been caught up on
all the bayou news. "Sounds like you've been busy," Antoinette said at the first break. "Leonce is on the rig this
week?"

"*Mais* yeah. That one, he couldn't wait to go. Workin' an
extra shift just 'cause he loves it so—" she paused, and her
voice softened "—and 'cause the money will buy things for
the baby."

"Baby?" Antoinette smiled. "You're going to have a
baby?"

"About time. We been tryin' for years. I think it's Omega's fault we don't have one yet. Leonce's never home at the
right time."

Antoinette decided that was the most unique gripe she'd
ever heard against Omega Oil. "Sounds like that changed
somewhere along the line."

"Must have," Didi agreed. "Anyhow, I don't know how
to ask you this, so I'm just gonna ask. I wanna talk to you.
And I can't do it over a phone. I hate phones. Never got no
news I liked over the phone. Never said anything I wanted
to say, neither. Could you come here, 'Toinette? I know it's
a long way to drive...."

"Didi, did you know that Sam and I aren't seeing each
other anymore?"

There was a short silence. "Yeah, *chere*. I guessed."

"I don't know if I should come under the circumstances."

"Sam, he won't be here. He was here last weekend."

Antoinette thought of all the reasons she shouldn't make
the trip. The time involved, the hassles, the reminders of
Sam. And then she thought of the young woman who obviously needed to talk to her. Being needed by somebody

connected to Sam suddenly seemed a very precious thing. "When did you want me to come?"

"Tomorrow? I'll make a bed for you here."

"May I bring my dog?"

"*Mais* yeah. Lemme give you directions."

Antoinette hung up a few minutes later, wondering what had possessed her to agree to such a long trip. The answer was perfectly obvious, however. She still wanted to be close to Sam. She was willing to inflict pain on herself just to be with someone who would talk about him. It didn't seem a very healthy thing to do, but falling in love with him hadn't been healthy, either. She would survive this, just as she'd survived that. And maybe it would be easier to put him out of her mind after she'd been back to Bayou Midnight. It would be one more way of saying goodbye.

"Paging Dr. Martane."

Joshua Martane ran his hands through his hair and said words that neither a minister nor a psychologist normally indulge in. He was both a minister and a psychologist, but he was a man first. The man was bone-deep weary and finally finished with a shift that had stretched three hours beyond the norm. At home waiting for him was the wife he adored and the daughter who already knew how to get around her father's stern philosophy of child rearing. He wanted to go home before Bridget went to bed and in time to take Maggie *to* bed. He ignored his page, striding toward the City Hospital parking garage.

"Dr. Martane. Didn't you hear your page?"

"I heard it." Joshua spun around to face the physician who had called his name. "I was ignoring it."

The man's lopsided smile was understanding, but he sobered quickly. "You'll want to know about this one. A friend of yours was brought into ER a little while ago. I just finished stitching him up. He's going to be fine, but I thought you might want to go talk to him. He's upset, I think, though he hasn't said much."

"Who is it?"

"Sergeant Sam Long. He asked if you were still here."

Joshua had never known Sam to ask for anything. He was down the hall and through the doors of the emergency room before the doctor could finish his report.

Sam was sitting on a gurney in one of the little emergency cubicles, his shirt off and his shoulder bandaged. His expression was unfathomable, but his face was a ghostly white.

"What happened to you?"

"I almost got to meet Tante Louise."

"What?"

"And the Grim Reaper."

Joshua whistled softly. "That close? What in the hell were you doing?"

"Daydreaming."

Joshua had a feeling that it was going to be a long story. He looked around for a chair, turned it backward and pulled it close to the gurney. "Why don't you start from the beginning."

"Got all night?"

"As long as it takes."

"I turned my back on a suspect today." Sam's voice was filled with self-condemnation. "I turned my back like a rookie recruit issuing a parking ticket. I almost got my partner killed."

"And here I thought you were beyond mistakes."

Sam grimaced at the gentle sarcasm. "You don't make mistakes in my line of work, Josh. You make a mistake and you don't have to worry about regretting it."

"You survived."

"Because I have a partner who was a little faster than our suspect and a lot better shot."

"He killed him?"

"No, in fact, the guy's up in surgery now. He should make it, although it wouldn't be any loss to the world if he didn't. He's a real lowlife. Name a crime, any crime, and this guy's been involved."

"Well, he's off the streets now."

"Off the streets and on the critical list. It'll be days before we can interrogate him."

Joshua suspected that Sam regretted that as much as his own wound. "At least he'll be here waiting for you."

Sam thought about Omega Oil. They'd been close to a break. He'd felt it in his bones. The guy they'd gone to talk to had been tried and set free on two different counts of arson in the past three years. He was a known if unproven arsonist, and he was living in New Orleans—had been, it turned out, for months. Furthermore, he'd been seen hanging around the Omega Oil building several nights before the fire. Things were adding up nicely. Adding up nicely until Sam had turned his back on the guy because he'd suddenly thought of Antoinette and how much he'd like to be able to tell her what they'd found.

Joshua watched Sam's face contort in disgust. "How important was talking to him immediately?"

"We think he was our link to a big case that involves one of the oil companies. We can't wait for answers. If this guy's guilty, somebody hired him. We have to find out who."

"It isn't going to do you any good to rake yourself over the coals for one error. So you're not perfect, and because you're not, this case is going to take longer to solve. You're still alive and so is your suspect. Things will work out."

Sam snorted. He could forgive himself for almost anything. He was not the type to worry unduly about past actions. Worry took energy, and energy was better used for his job. This time, however, his job was affected, and in Sam's mind that was the bottom line. "People may die because I was daydreaming. Do you have any idea what that does to me?"

"Suppose you tell me what you were daydreaming about."

Joshua was a hard man to fool. Sam imagined that on some level that was exactly why he'd chosen him to talk to. "You're a winning combination, Josh," he said, trying to smile. "A little bit the minister demanding a confession, a little bit the psychologist probing beneath the surface."

"Let's see if it works tonight."

"I was daydreaming about a woman. Antoinette, if you want the whole truth and nothing but."

"She's a woman worth daydreaming about." Joshua watched his friend brood over his own admission. For the first time in his life, Joshua was absolutely certain that Sam was going to be all right. The man was going to live a long, happy life, teased out of his compulsive devotion to duty by a woman any man would be lucky to have.

"We're not seeing each other anymore."

"Oh?"

"To think someone pays you a fortune to give one-syllable answers," Sam said with disgust heavy in his voice.

"Well, I'll do better, then. I'll tell you that it couldn't have happened to a more deserving guy. I'd about given up hope that you'd get off that pedestal you built for yourself."

"What in the hell does that mean?"

"It means that if Sam Long the perfect policeman no longer exists and Sam Long the human being has taken his place, I'll bring out the champagne."

Sam knew only too well what Joshua meant, even if he didn't agree with his friend's assessment. "My job is my life. I make no apologies for that."

"No apologies are needed, and no explanations. I've known you longer than anyone else. We've both struggled most of our lives to be free of our backgrounds. I went into the ministry and psychology to understand myself better. You went on the force to put as much distance as possible between you and the life you almost fell into. I know about the work you've done trying to rehabilitate juveniles in trouble. I know how you've worked night and day to clean up this city."

Sam's eyes were narrow slits. "Are you saying that my life's been a pathetic attempt at gratitude? That everything I've done has just been some sort of compulsion?"

"I'm saying that you can let up now. You've paid your dues, Sam. You can live like everyone else. You can have it all and still be a good guy. You can have Antoinette if you want her. When you're done with work every day, you can go home to her and forget about everything else until the next morning. The side benefit to all that pleasure is that you'll be a better cop, too." Joshua combed weary fingers through his hair. The day had been much too long.

"Maggie must be wondering where you are."

Joshua knew that Sam wanted no more insights thrown at him. He stood. "Let's get you checked out of here. Is somebody from the station here with you?"

"I sent them back to file a report."

"I'll drive you home." Joshua waited for Sam to refuse, to insist that he was perfectly capable of getting home by himself.

Instead, Sam stood, holding on to the gurney until he was sure he was steady. "All right."

"Antoinette's a beautiful woman," Joshua said as they walked to the nurse's desk. "She needs you almost as much as you need her. She hasn't had much loyalty or devotion in her life. You could give her both."

"She's through with me."

"Maybe."

"She'd be a fool to give me another chance."

Joshua didn't ask for details. "Maggie gave me more chances than I deserved."

"Maggie's damned special."

"So's Antoinette."

"I know."

Joshua knew better than to push. He'd already given Sam more to think about than Sam wanted. On the way home he told stories of Bridget's latest antics, coaxing a halfhearted smile from the proud godfather before he dropped Sam off at his house. Joshua remembered what it was like to be caught squarely between the brain and the heart. Silently he wished his friend well.

Inside his apartment Sam threw a week's collection of newspapers off the sofa and stretched out, too tired to go through the motions of getting ready for bed. His shoulder throbbed, his head throbbed, his entire being throbbed. He let himself imagine what it would have been like to come home to Antoinette tonight, instead of to an empty, unattractive apartment.

He could no longer deny the obvious. If he'd been coming home to her tonight, none of this would ever have happened. His mind would have been on his work. He wouldn't have been daydreaming about the impossible pleasure of sharing his triumphs with her. He'd thought that, without Antoinette in his life, he could get back down to business. He'd believed that all it would take to recapture his single-mindedness was to tell her goodbye. Had he always deluded himself that way?

He turned a little to ease the ache in his shoulder. He had been born to become a cop. There was nothing about his job—except, perhaps, the endless paperwork—that he didn't find fascinating. He was energized by the contact with people of all kinds; he was constantly challenged by the demands of solving cases. There were days when nothing happened, but those days were always a prelude to excitement. His job had been enough for him. Enough until now.

His needs had changed. Maybe Joshua was right and he'd spent these years paying fate back for giving him another chance. If so, it hadn't been a bad way to spend this part of his life. He'd been happy, and if he'd been lonely, he'd been too busy to notice. But he was not the person he had once been. Evidently he was a man first, not a cop. And that man inside the cop's uniform needed a life away from the police station. He needed Antoinette.

He needed her. Just the thought of needing someone repulsed him. He had never needed anyone. No one. No one.

No one except his uncle. No one except Martin and Leonce and, later, Didi. No one except Joshua and Skeeter. No one except Maggie and Bridget. No one except little Laurie Fischer, who, for a brief time, had taken the place of the child he should have had himself.

God, he'd been filled with needs. And he'd never even seen it. He'd thought he was the man of iron, the cynical cop who watched but never joined in. He was just a man.

Just a man. The words didn't come with the wrench in his gut that he'd have expected. He tried them out loud. "Just a man." Funny thing, they didn't sound so bad after all.

He'd always been just a man. On some level he must have known it all along.

He wondered if the blood he'd lost was doing funny things to his head. His eyes were blurred, as if by tears. He hadn't cried since he was a child. He hadn't expected to cry again, ever. He fell asleep wondering if he would feel better in the morning.

He wasn't sure he wanted to.

Chapter 14

The route to Bayou Midnight seemed to have been stretched by the hands of some unseen giant. Antoinette was sure that the trip was exactly twice as long as she remembered it. But then, the first time she had traveled these miles, she had been sitting next to Sam. Now she and Tootsie were alone in the car, and the trip was interminable. She tried to take her mind off the differences in this trip and the last by enjoying the picturesque scenes she was passing. Today, however, the swamps looked fetid and decidedly evil, the marshes were stultifying, endless sweeps of grass and water. Even the occasional fisherman was a testimony to foolish optimism.

She passed cane-processing and chemical plants and cursed man's nonchalance about destroying the environment; she passed the place where she and Sam had twice eaten breakfast and remembered only that the coffee had been too strong. She smoked all her cigarettes and stopped to buy a carton before she turned onto the clamshell bayou road. Didi's directions were excellent, but as the road twisted along the water, finally becoming the dirt track that led to Claude's and then to Didi's, she wondered what would happen if she made a mistake and took a wrong turn. Today nothing seemed welcoming. She tried to imagine what it would be like to be lost in the middle of this desolate, snake-infested countryside.

With gratitude she realized she was not to find out. Claude's cabin was around the next bend. She continued following the track, making a sharp left about five hundred yards past Claude's, and soon Didi's house appeared in the distance. In a minute Antoinette was knocking at the back door. At the first joyous sniff of bayou air, Tootsie had taken off for Claude's.

"'Toinette." Didi gave Antoinette a spontaneous hug and guided her inside the house. "I got no right to make you come all this ways. But I got to talk to somebody."

"I guess I needed to come, too," Antoinette reassured her. "I think the trip down here helped clear the romantic cobwebs out of my brain."

"Just tell me one thing. Was it you or Sam-son that said 'no more, thank you'?" Didi motioned to the sofa, and Antoinette sat down. Didi disappeared only to return in a minute with two big glasses of iced tea.

"Sam." Antoinette took the glass and enjoyed a long drink before she continued. "He doesn't want a woman in his life. He doesn't want anybody in his life."

"That one, he don't know what he wants."

"I'm afraid he does. It's not me."

"Did you want Sam-son?"

"Yes."

"Did you want marriage?"

Antoinette had asked herself the same question for the past month. Had Sam sensed some pressure from her that she wasn't even aware of? "Didi," she answered finally, "I really don't know. I was glad to be with him, but I had a lot of doubts that Sam would let our relationship grow. I wasn't thinking marriage because it seemed so impossible. Someday, though, I'd like to marry somebody with all of Sam's good qualities."

Didi waved aside her words. "You want Sam-son. Stubborn and blind as he is. He's like *le poisson arme,* the garfish. He don't seem like much of a catch, hardly worth the time, but he's a prize fish, that one. No one better out there than Sam-son.''

Antoinette chuckled at Didi's simile. "Well, let's just say that after he got off the hook the last time, I decided to give up fishing altogether.''

"Sam-son, he was here. Didn't say nuthin' to nobody. Didn't come to supper, didn't show his face.''

"I'm sure he was tired. He's been working night and day on the Omega Oil case.''

"Not tired. Sad. Mad at himself, and he should be, him.'' Didi called Sam a few lyrical names and shook her head. "But why talk about Sam-son? Let's talk about 'Toinette.''

Antoinette couldn't think of anything she'd rather not do at the moment. "No, let's talk about Didi. Tell me about the baby.''

Didi was glad to oblige. She told Antoinette everything about what was obviously the most thrilling event that had ever happened to her.

"So the baby's due at Christmas.''

"Leonce, he says it's gonna be a girl, but I tell him it's his son, through and through.''

"Son?''

"*Mais* yeah. That's what I been askin' for.''

Antoinette suspected that Didi had been practicing some of her father's gris-gris. "You won't be disappointed if you're wrong, will you?''

"Oh, I'm not wrong,'' Didi said with a giggle. "And I want a girl next. I get sick of all these men.''

"How is everybody else?''

Didi sobered instantly. "That's why I called. 'Toinette, somethin' bad, it's goin' on here. Claude won't listen. He says I'm like Mamselle Damsel Fly who's so busy watchin' out for the gator she forgets about the bullfrog.''

"In other words, you should mind your own business?''

"Claude says if I keep talkin' 'bout problems Martin has, Leonce is going git very mad at me.'' Didi pouted a little, obviously perturbed that her beloved husband might not like her interference in his brother's life.

"What does Leonce say when you talk to him?"

"Nuthin'. He just looks at me like I stabbed him with a nife. He don't believe nuthin' could be wrong with Mar-n. Martin, he could set fire to the house, and Leonce would ast a pig in the ashes, then thank Martin for dinner."

Antoinette found the idea of that kind of loyalty touch-g. She also saw the problems. "What did you think I could o, Didi?"

"I gotta know if this problem with Martin, if it's just in y head. If you think there's a problem, too, then I'm onna go back home and talk to my mama and papa and git em to talk to Claude."

"You haven't told them anything about this yet?"

Didi shook her head. "I don't want it talked about till I now somethin' is wrong. The bayou world, it's a small orld. Word gits out that Martin's head's not screwed on ght, people, they'll look at all of us funny. Don't wanna ke no chances."

Antoinette could understand exactly what Didi was say-g. She imagined that Martin's problems would cause a lot f gossip, but she also imagined that there might be more olerance for him here than in a city where he would be a tranger to those around him. "If I think Martin might have ome serious problems, what are you going to suggest?"

"Martin, he's a veteran. We can git him help at the VA ospital. They could treat him, he could come home at ight. He'd really go crazy if they tried to put him some-here else than the swamps."

Antoinette nodded. Didi was not trying to get rid of a roublesome family member. Her concern was obviously enuine. "Okay, suppose you tell me what kind of things ou've noticed."

Half an hour later it was clear to Antoinette that Martin as increasingly troubled. According to Didi, the behavior hat Antoinette had noticed and worried about during her ast visit had escalated. His self-control was slipping. He was xploding with rage over little things, and he was acting out is rage by disappearing for days without a word to his amily concerning his whereabouts. He rarely spoke to Didi,

but she had heard bits and pieces of conversations wit
Leonce that worried her. Omega Oil's closing of the mars
where he had always trapped was a prime topic of thei
conversations.

Didi was not trying to change a man who was differen
from her own particular preference. She accepted and sup
ported her brother-in-law's reclusiveness and his devotio
to nature. What worried her now was his mood swings, th
silences that went on for days and then the explosions o
temper. She was concerned about Martin for his own sake
but she was also concerned about the effect his behavior wa
having on Leonce.

"Leonce, he don't talk to me no more," Didi said sadly
"I say somethin' about Martin, he leaves the room. Used t
be when he weren't on the rig, he'd go off in the mornin'
and then come back for dinner with a mess of fish or crabs
Now he don't come home till dark. Half the time he go
nuthin' to show for goin'. He's doin' it to git away from
me."

"Does Martin have any friends who've talked to yo
about his behavior?"

"Leonce has friends, men he works on the rig with
Leonce goes off with them two, three times a week to drink
and play Bourré. Martin? Well, everybody likes Martin
nuthin' about him not to like. But nobody's close to Mar
tin, so nobody but a few people he's lost his temper with'v
noticed anythin'."

"Do you suppose I could see him while I'm here?" An
toinette asked.

"I was hopin' you'd wanna. I told Claude and Martin yo
was comin' and that we'd make dinner for them tonight
'Course, I don't know if Martin, he'll be there. S'posed t
be, but then, who knows?"

"Let's wait and see. After I've seen him myself, I can giv
you better advice."

Didi volunteered to take Antoinette to visit a small com
munity about five miles away by boat. The two wome
packed a light lunch and traveled to the little town, whic
officially consisted of a general store and bait shop,

school-bus shelter and a tiny church that seated no more than twenty. Swampers and fishermen sat on the banks of the bayou behind the general store, swapping yarns. Antoinette decided that the scene resembled something from a Cajun edition of *The Saturday Evening Post*.

Down the road and through a thicket of palmetto and scrub oak was the cottage of a friend of Didi's. The three women sat on the front porch talking and enjoying the warm spring air. Didi's friend, Mathilde, was a native of the bayou country who had gone away, gotten several degrees and returned to her roots. A free-lance writer, she now lived in the old family home, a genuine Acadian cottage constructed of split cypress and bousillage, a mixture of mud and Spanish moss used to fill in cracks and protect the wood. Mathilde had more education than her friend and more experience in the rest of the world, but she was very much like Didi in her enthusiasm and her openness. Antoinette enjoyed the afternoon thoroughly.

By four-thirty Didi and Antoinette were on their way back to Didi's to begin dinner preparations. Sam's name came up again while they chopped onions for crawfish bisque.

"Did Claude think it was strange having me come to visit here without Sam?" Antoinette asked, giving the cutting board a resounding whap with her knife.

"No. Claude said, 'That Sam-son, he's too stupid to see *une bonne femme* when she stands in front of him. Me, I marry her in a second if she look at me like she look at Sam-son.'"

Antoinette smiled. She hadn't expected Sam's uncle to be an ally. "Well, I'm glad you invited me down for the weekend, though I'm sorry you're worried about Martin."

"I wanted you to be my sister-in-law."

Antoinette ignored the fact that Leonce and Sam weren't really brothers. There was something about coming down to the bayous, something about being here with Didi doing traditional women's work and feasting on gossip as they would feast on crawfish bisque and catfish later that night, that made Antoinette realize just how much she had wanted the same thing. She hadn't admitted it to herself before this moment, but she realized with a sudden surge of vulnerability that she had probably wanted to marry Sam almost from the beginning.

No wonder he'd run. He had sensed her desire for permanency even before she had. It had scared him to death.

"The board, it's not s'posed to go in the bisque."

Antoinette looked down at the onions, which were now nothing more than juice. Didi was right; there were splinters mixed in. "I'm sorry," she apologized.

"I didn't mean to make you angry."

"You didn't. I made myself angry."

"Sam-son, he's gonna realize what he's missin'."

"The day M'sieu Gator, he learns to fly," Antoinette answered sadly.

The ache in Sam's shoulder was worse the next morning, but surprisingly the rest of him felt better than it had in a month. His dreams had been of Antoinette. They had been hopeful, joyous dreams of a reunion. He realized just how impossible those dreams were, but he had awakened knowing that he had to try to make them come true.

Antoinette would be crazy to give him another chance. Sam knew just how badly he had treated her. His only hope was to throw himself on her mercy and woo her with the single-mindedness he'd always reserved for his job. The phone rang while he was making his plans, and for one heart-stopping moment he believed it might be her.

It was Joshua. "How are you doing this morning?"

"I'm fine," Sam assured his friend. "Better than you know."

"Oh?"

Sam allowed himself a smile at Joshua's obvious curiosity. "I've got nothing to report, but maybe I will later on."

"You're not going to work, are you?"

"They won't let me near the station today. I've been ordered to take the weekend off."

"Make sure you rest. I've had to hog-tie Maggie to keep her from coming over to fluff your pillows and make you chicken soup."

Sam hesitated, then decided to go ahead and share his plans with Joshua. "Tell her if everything goes the way I want, Antoinette will do it for me."

Joshua whistled softly, and Sam could almost see his smile over the phone. "I'll be sure to tell her."

Sam hung up, looked at the phone for a full minute and picked it up again. He'd learned the folly of hesitation early in his police career. He dialed Antoinette's number without looking it up. It, like everything else about her, was burned permanently into his brain.

His heart gave an uncharacteristic thump when he heard the click of a receiver. But the voice that answered wasn't Antoinette's, or rather it was Antoinette's, but a recorded version that was as unlike the real thing as a plastic rose. He was so disappointed that he had to redial the number again just to listen to the message.

She was out at the moment, but he was to leave his name and number at the sound of the tone.

He hung up, leaving nothing except a loud click.

It was early in the morning, not even ten. Where was she? He wanted her. He was in no mood to wait.

One shower and meager breakfast later he tried again. This time he pantomimed along with the message. At the end he gave in, leaving his name and phone number in a voice that sounded strangely like a plea. Lunchtime came and went. He spent the afternoon cleaning the apartment and shopping for something he could cook for dinner, just in case she agreed to see him.

Dinnertime came and went, and the message was just the same each time he called. For entertainment he watched ridiculously stylish television cops play at catching bad guys who were fashion-conscious, too. He wondered if most of the viewing audience really believed that police work paid that well or was that simple.

After the late-night news he tried her again. He wondered if she'd found someone new, someone who could give her everything she needed. It was his last thought before he fell asleep.

* * *

Claude was the first to arrive for dinner. He wiped his feet carefully before coming inside, as if he was somehow intimidated by Didi's housekeeping. Seated on the sofa with a beer in his hand, however, he was just Nonc Claude, bayou patriarch.

Martin came in just as they were about to give up and sit down to dinner without him. His face was a road map of scowls. He mumbled a good-evening to everyone, but it was the last word of English that he spoke during the meal, even though Claude reminded him that Antoinette didn't understand Cajun French.

Antoinette evaluated Martin discreetly as she ate the mouth-watering meal. There had definitely been a change, although it was subtle enough to make her wonder how serious it was. Martin was the picture of an angry man, a man with an ax to grind, but not necessarily a man who was mentally ill. There were many ways of determining just how disturbed he was, but none of them were things she could do while sitting at the dinner table. Her inability to speak his language was also a definite problem. Without being able to understand the meaning and nuances of the few sentences he uttered, it was impossible to analyze more than the tone of his voice. She wondered if that had occurred to him.

He left immediately after dinner, followed closely by his father. Didi was quiet as they cleaned up, obviously waiting for Antoinette to give her opinion when she was ready. Antoinette went over everything in her head, but there was little she could add to what she'd already told Didi.

"Didi," she said finally, "I just don't know what to tell you. I never make a diagnosis unless I'm really sure I'm right. I don't know what's going on with Martin. He's obviously angry, but you didn't need me to tell you that." She leaned on a counter, trying to put her feelings into words. "I don't think you have to worry about Martin hurting himself. His anger is turned out, not in."

"The day he dumped crawfish on Mr. Simoneaux's feets, I got worried about him hurtin' someone else."

Antoinette nodded. It was a legitimate worry, and it had occurred to Antoinette. "That's possible, I guess, though from what you've said, Martin has so little contact with people he doesn't have much chance to use his anger."

"You don't think he's crazy?"

"Crazy can mean a lot of things. If Martin doesn't resolve what's bothering him, it might make him mentally ill. How close he is to that point now, I can't say. You're going to have to use your own judgment about telling your parents. I wish I could be more help, but I can't be, not without doing a thorough psychological evaluation. Making guesses wouldn't help any of you."

Didi was philosophical, although it was obvious that she would have preferred a definitive answer. "*Mais non*, making guesses isn't good." She scrubbed the counter until it was clean enough to do surgery on, finally beginning a new topic. "Claude, he likes you."

Antoinette wasn't sure how the two thoughts connected, but she made a noncommittal sound of agreement.

"He'd listen to you," Didi continued.

Now Antoinette understood. Her first inclination was to refuse to become involved. Her second was that perhaps it wasn't such a bad idea after all. Of course, she wouldn't approach Claude as a psychologist who was there to tell him that his son was mentally ill, only as a concerned friend who was worried about Martin's behavior. As careful as she had been not to unfairly alarm Didi, she was concerned about Martin. Something was wrong here. She could feel it, and she had great respect for her own intuition. She hated to leave Bayou Midnight without making an attempt to help.

There was one other thing to consider. If she spoke to Claude, that fact might get back to Sam, and Sam would be angry that she'd interfered. But Sam's anger couldn't be much worse than his indifference. In the long run she had to do what felt right. Talking to Claude about her concerns felt right. She would be the soul of tact, stopping immediately if she sensed any resistance. She was experienced enough not to worsen the situation.

"All right," she agreed, "I'll talk to Claude. But I'll only tell him what I've told you. I'm not going to tell him what he should do."

Didi's smile was so filled with gratitude that Antoinette was sure she had made the right decision. Until now Didi had carried this burden alone. It was a big burden, even for someone so strong and self-assured.

"Martin, he gits up and goes out before the birds sing. Claude, he gits up later. Tomorrow bein' Sunday, he'll be home in the mornin' till nine."

"Then I'll go over about eight-thirty and try to catch him. I'll head home from there."

"I gotta go to early Mass. I promised the Virgin I'd git up and go to early Mass every Sunday if she'd send me a son."

Antoinette gave her a spontaneous hug. Didi was one of a kind and very special. "I'll be gone when you get back. I've had a lovely day. Thanks for inviting me."

"Me, I'm the one to say thank you. I just want my family smilin' again. You gonna help it happen."

"I hope so, Didi."

Didi was gone when Antoinette woke up the next morning. She had been lulled to sleep by the chirping of crickets and the croaking of frogs, sleeping better than she had in the past month. After she dressed, she sat on the front porch smoking the first cigarette of the day and watching the glossy surface of the water, still and calm and infinitely mysterious.

Didi had left homemade cinnamon rolls and fresh coffee in the kitchen. Antoinette resumed her place on the porch and watched a pileated woodpecker scrounge for his breakfast in a dead tree at the water's edge as she ate her own.

It was a little past eight when she loaded her overnight case into the car and headed toward Claude's cabin. She wasn't looking forward to confronting him, but she still believed it was the best thing to do. She had dreamed all night of Martin. Foggy dream fragments where Martin was always just out of reach. The truth about Martin was just out of reach, too. There was something wrong, but it, like the dream, was just out of her grasp.

The time was right to tell Claude about her concerns. They would talk, and then she would drive back to New Orleans. She would not come again. Now when she remembered Bayou Midnight, her memories would be diluted with memories of this weekend here without Sam. Eventually that would help her put things in perspective. But coming back once was all the coming back she needed. More would only bring up thoughts of Sam, thoughts that were better buried. If Didi needed to talk to her again, and Antoinette doubted that she would, it would have to be in New Orleans.

At Claude's cabin Antoinette parked her car and got out, expecting Tootsie to greet her. But there was no sign of the big sheepdog or her canine friend, Claude's hound. There weren't any signs of Claude or Martin, either. Antoinette knocked on the back door of the house, waited a minute and knocked again. It was apparent that no one was inside.

She walked around the side of the house, calling for Tootsie as she went, but the only signs of life anywhere in the vicinity were the occasional songs of birds and the leaping mullet in the bayou.

The one place left to try was the boathouse. Sam had told her that his uncle built pirogues the time-honored Cajun way when he could get a cypress log large enough to hollow out. Since such logs were few and far between and skilled artisans were a thing of the past, Claude's pirogues brought top dollar. Antoinette hoped she would find Sam's uncle out in the boathouse working on one. It would be an ideal place to talk, casual enough not to put pressure on Claude.

Antoinette hesitated at the boathouse door. She was surprised to find a heavy padlock, unsnapped but still unwelcoming, hanging from a shiny metal clasp. She supposed that the bayou wasn't immune to crime, but it still surprised her to find such evidence of distrust from Claude LeBeaud.

Knocking once, then twice, she pushed open the door. No one was inside, but there were signs that someone had been recently. There was a pirogue in progress that looked as if it had recently been shoved to the side, judging from the redistribution of sawdust. Boot tracks led to the other side of the roomy building, and tools, sawhorses and rubbish had been moved to make a clear trail. Another padlock gleamed silver-bright from a closet on the opposite wall. It was the final thing Antoinette needed to set her curiosity into full gear.

What did Claude or perhaps Martin feel he had to keep under double lock and key? She had no business wondering, but the part of her that had become a psychologist to solve puzzles wanted to know. Were there valuable furs from their seasons of trapping in the closet? Were there traps, equipment, outboard motors that might be prime targets for bayou theft? Or was there something more insidious?

She walked across the room, aware that she was snooping but unwilling to stop. She felt compelled to find the answer, and she wasn't sure why. Somewhere in the back of her brain suspicions were beginning to form. Closer to the closet door she could see that this lock, too, was not shut. It was a warning that someone would be back shortly, but the warning went unheeded as she removed the lock and opened the closet door.

The sight of wooden crates of explosives stacked as neatly as canned goods in a grocery store made her shut her eyes in horror. There were times when the final piece of the puzzle dropped into place and the solution was much worse than not knowing had been. She was only surprised that she hadn't seen this particular solution to several puzzles long before this.

Martin, with his hatred of Omega Oil and the personality profile of a loner, was the Omega Oil arsonist. Martin, with his training in Vietnam and his experience as a hunter, had moved in and out of the Omega installations with skill and cunning, destroying that which he felt was destroying him. He had never murdered purposely—he had even saved Laurie Fischer's life—but he was nevertheless guilty of killing a man. And judging from the size of this cache of dynamite, he was on his way to killing others. Everything fit neatly. Her dreams of the night before came sharply into focus. She only wondered why she hadn't been suspicious before.

Sam had to be told. Antoinette couldn't believe that he hadn't seen the truth, that none of them had seen the truth. Sam, protective and loyal to those he loved, however, would never consider his cousin a suspect. Just as he couldn't see that Martin's anger was eating away at his sanity, he couldn't see that his cousin was capable of taking revenge on the company that, in Martin's opinion, was destroying a way of life.

Sam would have to believe it now. The evidence was frighteningly clear. Martin fit her profile. He had the motive. He had the skill. And here, stacked neatly in front of her, he had the weapon.

Her heart rate accelerated, and her hands began to shake. She had to get to a telephone and call Sam before something else happened. She couldn't wait until she returned to New Orleans. Sam had to be told right away. The closest phone was Didi's. She would call Sam from there, and then she would leave. There was nothing she could do anymore. Sam would have to take care of this situation by himself, and she was sure he would rather take care of it without her.

She was also aware that she was in danger. If Martin was still nearby, he would know that she'd been inside the boathouse. With danger quickening her thoughts, she remembered that both locks had been unsnapped. No one had been expected, but she imagined that, if Martin had planned to be away for long, he would have locked them tight. He could return momentarily, and at this point there was no telling what he would do if he found her there. Didi had been right all along. Martin was much, much sicker than any of them had seen.

A tiny noise behind her increased her heart rate until it was pounding like the hooves of a runaway horse. It had been nothing more than the faintest whisper of sound, but every one of her faculties, magnified by a huge surge of adrenaline, was working overtime. Under normal circumstances she wouldn't have even heard it. Now she knew for certain that she was no longer alone.

She turned, an act that took more courage than anything she had ever done in her life. In the darkness of the boathouse, she thought her eyes were playing tricks on her for a moment. The man standing in the doorway was shorter than Martin and heavier. Then relief flooded through her, making her knees turn to Jell-O.

"My God," she said, her eyelids dropping shut and her hand coming to her chest to cover her heart. "Leonce. You have no idea how happy I am to see you."

Chapter 15

"What are you doin' here, 'Toinette?" Leonce's face was stern, and Antoinette knew he didn't appreciate what surely looked like snooping, what surely *was* snooping.

"I came to find your father. I wanted to talk to him about Martin." She felt such a wave of remorse at having to be the one to tell Leonce about his brother that she stopped for a moment, trying to find the words. "Martin's in serious trouble, Leonce," she said finally. She stepped aside and gestured behind her to the closet filled with dynamite. "Martin's the Omega Oil arsonist." She watched Leonce's face, but not a flicker of expression showed on it.

"You shouldn't be here. No one told you to come and start messin' around in our lives."

She was surprised by his reaction, but the surprise was slowly turning into something else. She would have expected Leonce to be upset at what she'd found; she would never have expected this cold anger directed at her. "Leonce, I came at Didi's invitation."

At the mention of his wife's name, Leonce shook his head, his face still carefully expressionless. "You shoulda minded your business, 'Toinette. You shoulda."

"I know you're upset. I don't blame you. But we can't change the truth. Martin's in deep trouble, and you have to help me stop him before the trouble gets so bad he'll never be able to get out of it." For one moment Antoinette watched Leonce wrestle with her statement. Then his face changed back into a mask.

"I can't help you."

She couldn't believe that Leonce's loyalty to his brother was making him so blind. What was it about this family that they couldn't see the truth when it was neatly stacked in wooden crates in front of them? "What are you going to do, then?" she asked in frustration. "Throw me in the bayou so I can't tell anyone, either? Think, Leonce. Martin could get himself killed. He could end up in jail for the rest of his life. We've got to stop him."

"Leonce?"

Antoinette watched a shadow deepen behind Leonce. She had jumped at the sound of another voice. Now she stared at the man standing behind him. He was tall and freckled, with a brown crew cut and eyes as cold as a bayou winter.

"Who the hell is that?"

"She's a friend of my cousin Sam's. The policeman," Leonce added for emphasis, never taking his eyes from Antoinette's face. "She knows."

"Damn it to hell, this was supposed to be a safe place! You said nobody ever came out here except your father and brother."

"I know what I said."

Antoinette felt her body flood with fear again. "Leonce?"

"Shut up," the man with the crew cut snapped at her.

"What's going on?" A third man came up behind the other two and stared over their shoulders, his eyes narrowing behind wire-rimmed spectacles. "Damn, a woman."

"It's been bad enough wondering if your father or brother were going to catch on and open this closet last night after we put the dynamite in," the man with the crew cut said, "but now we're stuck with this. You know she's going to have to go," he said matter-of-factly.

Antoinette knew he wasn't talking about a pleasant walk back to her car and a leisurely trip home. He was talking about murder. She refused to let them see how the words affected her. "So it was you and not Martin," she said calmly to Leonce. "That thought never entered my mind."

"Shut up!" the man with the crew cut snarled again.

"But it will enter Sam's mind when I don't show up in New Orleans this afternoon," she went on, praying that Leonce didn't know that she and Sam were no longer seeing each other. "He'll come looking for me, and he'll be suspicious if I've just disappeared off the face of the earth."

Leonce had never resembled his brother more. His expression was a scowl, his eyes haunted. "Sam would come," he agreed. "If he knew you was here, he'd come."

"We're having dinner together tonight," she lied.

"We'll have to arrange an accident, then," the man with the spectacles concluded.

"No." Leonce was adamant. "No killin'. We agreed."

"Everything's changed." The man with the crew cut pushed past Leonce and stood, hands on hips, observing Antoinette. "Too bad, too."

Antoinette wasn't sure how it happened, but a split second later Leonce was in front of the other men again and the situation seemed to be firmly in his control. "No killin'. Anyone lays a hand on 'Toinette, they gonna have to kill me first. And killin' me might not be a good idea because it would lead right back to you two."

"What do you plan to do with her, then?"

Leonce appeared to be wondering the same thing. Finally the man with the crew cut spoke again. "There's a place in the water right off the bayou road that's real deep. Lew, you can drive her car to the edge and push it in so it looks like she left here."

"With her in it?" Lew, the man with the spectacles, asked.

Leonce answered. "I tol' you. Nobody gits killed. We'll take 'Toinette with us, leave her on one of those cheniers down in the marshes on the back way to the rig. Somebody'll find her next day or so."

Lew and the man with the crew cut looked at each other and nodded. Antoinette could see what was going through their heads. The spot they'd choose would be hopelessly remote. They fully expected her to die there. Or perhaps they would come back for her. Without Leonce.

"Leonce," she pleaded, "just give yourself up before you get into so much trouble you'll never be able to get out of it."

"I'm in that kinda trouble now," he said sorrowfully. "This is the last thing we're gonna do. After this we're gonna git out of this place forever."

"What about Didi? What about your baby?"

"Better off without me."

"No, Leonce, you're wrong. You can still get out of this. Sam will help. I know you, you didn't start any of those fires yourself. You can turn state's evidence. You're the one who saved the little girl's life, aren't you? That'll sway any jury."

"She's not dumb, is she?" the man with the crew cut said admiringly. "But, honey, you're wrong about one thing. There ain't no way that Leonce here won't take his share of the rap if we're caught. That's the way the system works, and your friend here knows it."

"He's wrong!" Antoinette's eyes begged Leonce to believe her. "Don't get in any deeper."

"We're due to leave in twenty minutes," Lew told Leonce. "If we're going to get rid of her car, I'd better do it right now."

Leonce pulled a bandanna out of his jeans pocket and walked toward Antoinette. "You shoulda stayed out of this, 'Toinette," he said sorrowfully. "Omega's a bad company. They worked us till we dropped, left a crew of men to die in that hurricane, shut down the marsh and now they're shuttin' down the rigs because oil prices went down. Didi don't know it, but I haven't worked for weeks. Lew and Jerry haven't worked for months."

"That's no reason to kill people." She tried to reason with him.

"No one was supposed to git killed. Lew and Jerry, they wanted to teach 'em a lesson." He was one step away. "No one was even supposed to git hurt.'' His arms circled Antoinette in an embrace that was sadly affectionate. Then he lifted the bandanna to her mouth. *"Sa me fait de la pain. C'est ein affaire a pus finir."*

Antoinette still wasn't home. Sam banged down the telephone receiver, missing the cradle entirely. It was Sunday morning. Apparently she had gone somewhere for the weekend. Where? Why? Alone?

He realized he was being irrational. Antoinette had every right to spend her weekends away from the city. He had no rights over her. He had very carefully, very methodically, made that clear from the beginning of their relationship. He had wanted nothing from her. That's exactly what he had now. And nothing was a terrible thing to have.

He'd spent a restless night rehearsing what he'd say to her when she answered the phone this morning. The words, with no one to hear them, stuck in his throat as if they were objects waiting to be expelled. He went into the bathroom to shower and shave, and the man staring back at him from the fogged-up mirror was someone he didn't know. The man was vulnerable, emotional, eaten up with regrets. It was going to take some time to get used to him, but Sam figured he had the rest of his life.

He was selecting clothes to wear when he realized that he didn't have to continue suffering. Finding out where Antoinette was wouldn't be hard. He was, after all, a policeman with a policeman's skills. He had a mind that filed everything away in case he needed it. He remembered the name of Antoinette's secretary. He could call her, tell her it was police business and find out what she knew.

A listing for R. Madison on Banks Street, right off Carrollton, looked promising. When a woman answered, he recognized the voice instantly. Succinctly he explained that he needed to get in touch with Antoinette right away. Did Rosy know where to reach her?

Rosy was less than accommodating. Sam listened to a long lecture about what a good woman Dr. D was and about how badly she'd been treated. He had the grace to wince when Rosy told him that Antoinette had started smoking again and that he was the cause.

"I don't care what kind of business you think you have with her," Rosy said finally, "I'm not telling you where she is!"

Sam was sitting by now. "Not even if I tell you I want to propose to her?"

Rosy didn't miss a beat. "She called me yesterday morning to tell me she was going to visit some woman down in the bayous. And it sure took you long enough to make up your mind, dahlin'."

Sam hung up, happy that Antoinette was not with a new man somewhere, and confused about why she'd be with Didi. It was Didi's phone number Rosy had given him; he'd recognized it immediately. He tried the number, not even sure what he would say to Antoinette when she was so far away, but he was anxious to make contact. There was no answer, and he decided to try again in a half hour.

He had just finished dressing when the doorbell rang. He knew it wouldn't be Antoinette, but he couldn't keep himself from hoping. Skeeter stood at the door instead, and Sam motioned him inside.

"I have to look twice these days to believe it's you," Sam told his friend. "You're actually respectable."

Skeeter was dressed in a conservative suit. Only his tie, a tidy repeated print of Mickey and Minnie Mouse holding hands, said anything about the real Skeeter. "I am respectable," he said with a grin. "So respectable that I've been asked to do a one-man show at the Harrigan Art Gallery. I've just been negotiating the details over breakfast at Brennans."

Sam whistled softly. Skeeter had come a long way in the past years. Of the three boyhood friends, it had taken longer for Skeeter to find himself than it had for either Sam or Joshua. Skeeter had been the least lucky. No one had reached out a hand to pull him out of the mire of his background. Prison and his own indomitable spirit had made the change in Skeeter. And it seemed that now he had taken one more step. "So you're finally going to get serious about your talent?"

Skeeter shrugged, and his grin turned sheepish. "I've been discovered. One of the portraits I did for a customer on Jackson Square was sold to a gallery owner in New York. Looks like I'm going to be in demand."

"Congratulations."

Skeeter flopped down on Sam's sofa. "I hear you were wounded Friday."

"News travels fast." Sam sat across from him and waited for Skeeter to get to the point. The two were firm friends, but neither of them had much time for social calls. When Skeeter visited, there was always a reason.

"Are you all right?"

Sam nodded.

"While you were getting shot, I was getting information."

This wasn't the first time that Sam had been grateful for Skeeter's talent for sleuthing. Skeeter wasn't personally involved in the New Orleans underworld, but he always seemed to be places where he heard things that even Sam's best informants didn't hear. He drew portraits at a bar on Bourbon Street in the evenings; he lived in a neighborhood that was not the best; in pursuit of subjects to sketch, he haunted areas of town where even the bravest cops didn't want to go. He was just available. And his availability often paid off. "What kind of information?" Sam asked him.

"I sat in a bar across the river last night and drank with a Cajun fellow who's up here looking for work."

"And?"

"This guy says that everybody where he comes from thinks the Omega Oil sabotage originates from down there."

"That's nothing more than a rumor."

"Try this, then. The guy's from the area around Bayou Midnight." Skeeter had been down to Sam's cabin enough times to know exactly what the information would mean to his friend. His expression was sympathetic.

"I don't believe it."

Skeeter shrugged. "Do you have any better leads?"

"The guy who shot me is a professional arsonist. He was seen in the vicinity of the Omega Oil building several nights before the fire." Sam was thinking out loud. He didn't want to believe that anyone he knew—and he knew everyone up and down Bayou Midnight—could have been involved in the campaign of arson against Omega.

"You haven't seen the paper this morning, have you?"

Sam looked up and saw compassion in Skeeter's eyes. "No."

"The guy who shot you confessed to killing somebody up in Shreveport the night of the Omega fire. He couldn't have been two places at once. He's a lowlife, but not the right lowlife. You're back to square one, pal."

Sam hadn't even called the station to find out what was happening. He'd been so preoccupied with Antoinette. And no one had called him because they knew he was recovering. He slammed his fist into his open hand. "Damn!"

"I'll leave you to ponder the eccentricities of your job. Take care of yourself." Skeeter stood and waved Sam back to the sofa when he started to stand. At the door he turned as if he'd thought better about leaving without saying one more thing. "Loyalty's a fine thing, Sam, but I think this guy at the bar last night knew something. Don't let your personal blinders keep you from checking out what's going on down south. Even the safest haven has its share of problems."

Sam sat with his head in his hands long after Skeeter had gone and wondered how many other times in his life he'd let his loyalties and his prejudices determine his actions. The Omega Oil case had been full of twists and turns and an overwhelming amount of evidence that had led him in circles. But all along he had ignored some of the most important evidence he had. Laurie had repeated a phrase spoken in Cajun French by the suspected arsonist, but he had let other clues lead him in a different direction. His uncle had warned him that something was going on in the basin, but he had only paid the most minimal attention to Claude's words. Now the warning was being repeated, and he had tried, once again, to discount it.

What other warnings had he discounted?

The answer was so shocking that he winced in pain. *Martin*. Antoinette and Didi had both tried to tell him that something serious was bothering his cousin. But Martin was his beloved friend and teacher; Martin had been on a pedestal since Sam was sixteen years old. He had refused to see the truth of anyone's observations about him, just as he had refused to give Laurie's phrases or Claude's words the attention they deserved.

Martin, who spoke Cajun French better than he spoke English, Martin with his hatred of Omega and his training in Vietnam. Martin who fit the description in Antoinette's profile exactly.

Sam had ignored it all because he didn't want to believe that anything bad could touch the people and the place that he loved best in the world.

Had he always had this blind spot? He'd believed that good was good and bad was bad. It made his job easier to do. Antoinette had tried to tell him differently.

Antoinette...

Antoinette was down at Bayou Midnight right now, visiting Didi. Sam felt a jolt of fear. The woman he loved was in the place he loved, and yet nothing was as it had always seemed. The facts were muddled now with emotions; he was no longer sure of his own name. He was only sure of one thing: he had to get to Antoinette, and he had to get there fast. And once he was there and sure she was safe, he had to investigate what Skeeter had said and interrogate Martin.

He stopped only long enough to call Didi's number once more. When there was still no answer, he grabbed his keys and rushed out the door.

Antoinette lay under a heavy tarpaulin on the bottom of a wooden skiff and tried to untie the ropes binding her hands. It was a useless attempt, but she couldn't keep herself from trying. The tarp smelled of fish, and it was constructed of stiff black canvas that absorbed the day's bright sunshine. It was difficult to breathe the fetid, smothering air that filtered through the canvas, and there were moments when she wondered if she would die before they reached the chenier, where death would come slower but even more inevitably.

They had been traveling for a long time before she felt the weight of the tarp being lifted off her. Leonce's bandanna made it difficult to gulp the air she needed, but she was able to breathe more efficiently. Slowly she felt better. The tarp was replaced, then lifted off several more times before she felt the boat slow. She had lost all concept of time. It might have been days or only an hour since the men had tied her and dragged her into the skiff. The tarp was removed once more, and rough hands pulled her to a sitting position. Leonce bent over from his seat in the skiff to untie her feet.

It took precious moments for her eyes to focus. They weren't in the marshes. The area was a desolate swamp, rank and evil looking with dry land almost nonexistent. "This place usually got more land this time of year," Leonce was saying to Lew. The other man, Jerry, was nowhere to be seen. She imagined he was in another boat, loaded with dynamite, on his way down to the Gulf.

"It'll have to do. We don't have time to look for something else."

Leonce hesitated, his gaze flicking quickly over Antoinette's face before he looked back at Lew. "All right."

She implored them both with her eyes and made sounds deep in her throat, but they ignored her. Lew maneuvered the skiff as close to one tiny little rise of land as he could, and Leonce stepped out, sinking almost to his waist in sucking black mud. He stepped up on a cypress knee, pulling the skiff closer until he could reach Antoinette. With one strong jerk she was beside him on the knee, then she was shoved to the dubious support of spongy ground.

Leonce helped her rise to her feet, then touched her cheek, wiping away one errant tear. "I'm sorry, 'Toinette," he said loud enough for Lew to hear. "I'll be back," he promised under his breath as he turned and stepped back down in the mud to climb into the boat.

She stood on shaking legs on the narrow bank and watched the skiff pull away. Her hands fumbled frantically with the rope that tied them. Her bonds seemed looser, and she remembered Leonce had pulled her up by the rope after he'd shoved her off the cypress knee to the ground. She wondered if he'd purposely loosened it. The skiff was far in the distance when she finally managed to slip the rope off her hands. In a second her mouth was free, and she stood, gratefully gulping the heavy, foul-smelling air as the boat finally disappeared from sight.

Leonce had said he'd be back. Had he meant it? Lew wouldn't be back, nor would Jerry. They had chosen a spot so remote, so isolated, that if someone stumbled on her in the next week, it would be miraculous. They had talked about leaving her on one of the cheniers down toward the marshes. She knew enough about the terrain to realize how much more preferable that would have been. The cheniers were high ridges of dirt deposited by the Mississippi on its way to the Gulf. Once established they often grew wind-twisted oak trees to further hold down the soil and keep it from eroding. At her most optimistic she had pictured herself waiting under the shade of one of those trees for a fisherman or a trapper to rescue her.

At her most pessimistic she had expected Lew or even Leonce to kill her. Instead, she was somewhere in between life and death, in the middle of a horrible, pestilent backhole cypress swamp that no one would ever choose to come into. If Leonce didn't return for her, it would be the last place she would ever see.

The ground she stood upon was no more than twelve feet in diameter. There were cypress trees all around her, most of them out of reach unless she waded through the mud. None of them was large enough to climb. Trees that size had been logged for their rot-resistant lumber, and even in this hellhole there were skeleton trunks testifying that the loggers had been there sometime this century.

She suspected that until today the loggers had been the last people in this swamp. Leonce had pretended to know this place, but she wondered if even he had really ever been there before. If people had been few and far between, however, the swamp was still teeming with life. The birds she had found so beautiful around Sam's cabin were there. As she turned to examine the tiny island, she watched a gray water snake slither off into the muck that had been behind her. She stifled a cry, forcing herself to breathe deeply. There were dozens of varieties of snakes that lived in the basin. Only a small percentage of them were poisonous. If she allowed herself to panic each time she saw one, she would die of the fright.

She tried not to think about the snakes. There would be alligators here, too, and insects that most people didn't even know existed. She swatted at a deerfly that persistently buzzed around her head and tried not to think about dusk and the onslaught of mosquitoes that would come. Sam had told her once that mosquitoes were usually worse at dusk, fading away as day passed resolutely into night. If she was lucky, there would only be an hour or two of mosquito torture. And, of course, by dark she would be surrounded by this hostile environment without light to see what was around her. Mosquitoes would be the least of her problems.

She started to cry then. There was no way of controlling the helpless, strangling fear that rolled over her in waves. She gave in to it, sinking to her knees and covering her face with her hands. As she sobbed, she began to pray.

Sam slammed on the brakes of his Toyota, narrowly missing the big sheepdog who stood in the middle of the dirt road leading to Didi's house. Sam had driven the familiar roads to Bayou Midnight examining every car coming from the opposite direction in fear that he would miss Antoinette. Now Tootsie's presence assured him that she was still there.

He rolled down his window and shouted a few succinct words. The dog barked sharply several times as if offended by Sam's rough treatment before she moved to the side of the road to lie with her head on her paws and stare down into the bayou. Sam drove on, parking behind Didi's house. He sat at the steering wheel for a moment, trying to figure out what was going on. Antoinette's car wasn't here, nor had it been parked at Claude's house. Didi's car was gone, too, indicating that they weren't together. Perhaps he had missed Antoinette after all, and yet Tootsie was still here. He couldn't imagine Antoinette leaving Bayou Midnight without her dog.

There was no explanation inside the house, either. He found a brief note of thanks from Antoinette to Didi, with a promise to call later that day to tell Didi about her talk with Claude. He puzzled over the cryptic message, feeling more and more uneasy. Something was wrong, but nothing fit well enough to form an answer.

When no other information turned up, he took a short-cut back to his uncle's house. Berry brambles tore at his pant legs, but he paid no attention. In the woods beside his uncle's house, he stood gazing toward the water. Nonc Claude's skiff was gone, and one of the two pirogues that usually sat on the dock was gone, too. He walked down to the water, looking for something out of the ordinary, but everything was in place. He was just about to try the house when he noticed that the door to the boathouse was locked tight.

The lock was new and shiny, an intrusion in a world where everyone trusted everyone else and things were always as they seemed. When had Nonc Claude taken to locking the boathouse? Or had locking it been Martin's idea?

Locking an isolated boathouse was the kind of peculiar behavior that was to be expected from his cousin now. It could be an example of Martin's paranoia, an attempt to lock out a world that was increasingly infringing on his way of life.

Or it could be something worse.

The sixth sense that had failed Sam so often in his search for the Omega Oil saboteurs was working overtime. If he was wrong, he would kiss the ground at his cousin's feet in apology. If he was right and Martin was in trouble, was, in fact, making trouble, he didn't know what he'd do.

At the door of the boathouse, he pulled out the one piece of equipment that identified him as a cop better than any other and shot off the lock. Inside, his worst fears were confirmed. There had been a scuffle here. The signs were unmistakable. He scanned the room as he approached the closet door and prepared to shoot off that lock, too. But there was no need. The lock was not snapped shut. He lifted it and opened the door. The closet appeared to be empty. It was only just before he turned away, when his eyes had finally adjusted to the dim light, that he saw one single dynamite cap tucked into a crack in the corner.

"So now you know."

Sam wasn't surprised to hear Martin's voice. He had, after all, been the one to teach Sam to move with the silence of the hunted. Sam turned slowly and faced his cousin, gun still in hand. "What is it I know, Martin?"

Martin narrowed his eyes. "You, you're the big cop, Samson. The truth, it's all around you, heh? You should smell it like the coon smells the new young in an egret's nest."

"What I smell is the stench of evil." Sam threw his gun on the floor between them. He began to stalk his cousin, his hands tightly knotted into fists. "Where's Antoinette?"

Martin watched his cousin advance. His eyes were sorrow filled. "Me, I taught you better, Sam-son. Can't you see what's happened?"

"I can see you're not the man I thought you were." Sam's tone was deadly. In that moment he knew his control was almost gone. "What have you done with her? Where's Antoinette?"

"With Leonce."

Sam advanced another step. "Don't make it worse by lying, Martin. Leonce is on his rig. Where is she?"

"Do you think you can beat me, Sam-son? Will it bring back your woman?" Martin threw up his hands in a Gallic gesture as old as civilization itself. "Listen to the truth, *l'imbecile.* 'Toinette's with Leonce. I got here too late to stop them. Me, I deserve a beatin' for lettin' this happen!"

Sam stopped a foot from Martin. "You have thirty seconds to tell me what you're babbling about."

"Leonce, he knows about those fires. He didn't set them, but he knew who did, and he wouldn't go to the police."

Sam sucked in a breath. He knew that, no matter what Martin had become, he would not protect himself by incriminating his brother. "Go on."

"I been tryin' to watch out for him. It's been makin' me crazy knowin' the trouble he's in. He don't know I know what he's done, but I do. He changed, got eaten up inside, and no one saw it but me. So I followed him and put the story together from little pieces of talk."

"What did you find out?"

"Two men he works with, friends, were settin' the fires. Leonce found out and tried to stop them. He didn't wanna turn them in. He found out they was gonna blow up the Omega Oil buildin' in New Orleans, and he followed them there, but he was too late. He went into the building, even saved a little girl's life, but she saw his face. Then he knew he was in it, too."

"Why didn't you come to me?"

"You, you're a cop," Martin said simply. "I had to try and protect my brother. Even from you, Sam-son. Even from you."

Sam knew enough about family loyalty to understand what Martin had done. His shoulder throbbed, and he felt unutterably weary. The rage he'd felt was turning into fear. Where was Antoinette? "You made a bad decision."

"Worse than you know. I thought it was all over. Then las' night I came in here late. Leonce, he's been keepin' that closet locked. Said he wanted to keep his traps there under lock and key. Didn't make no sense, he's got his own house, but Papa agreed. Las' night I saw the lock was new. I picked it and found a closet full of dynamite. Leonce, he's been staying down on Bayou Sorrel, so I went there at dawn to talk to him. But he was gone. By the time I got back here, the dynamite, it was gone, too."

"How much dynamite was there?"

"Enough to blow up an oil rig. Leonce's rig, it's empty now, no one on it but a few watchmen. But if it goes, Omega'll go, too. Poof, no more cheatin' oil company."

Sam could feel his whole body sag. "What makes you think Antoinette is with Leonce?"

Martin's expression was compassionate. He reached across the space between them and rested his hand on his cousin's shoulder. "Pray to *le Bon Dieu* that she is," he said softly. "'Cause if she's not, she's in her car. And her car is at the bottom of Bayou Midnight."

Chapter 16

The parish sheriff stood at the bayou's edge, staring down into the water that had been named only too well. It was as black and as mysterious as midnight. He shook his head slowly. "There's nothing we can do until the scuba team gets here and goes in to investigate. Only a damned fool would have gone into that water without the right equipment, son."

Sam stood beside him on the bank, clenching and unclenching his fists. His clothes still dripped from his own pathetic attempt to find what lay under the murky surface covered with a torn patch of water hyacinth. He had never felt so helpless. Now, as he watched, two deputies knelt on the ground behind him, measuring tire tracks and jotting down notes. "She could be down there," Sam said, shoving his fists into his pockets.

"If she is," the sheriff answered kindly, "getting her out fast ain't gonna help."

Sam was holding himself in rigid control, but he knew if he could see his own face, it would have the look of a man who has just seen the worst life has to offer. He wished he could break down and release the lump in his throat that threatened to choke him. It would be better than this terrible restraint.

The sheriff was still speaking. "Why don't you go back to the house, son. We'll come up and tell you as soon as we know something."

Sam gestured in the general direction of the Gulf. "If I can't be out there looking for her, I want to be here."

"There wasn't anything you could do about looking for anybody. Those men had hours on you. And the coastal police are waiting for them at the rig."

Sam knew the sheriff was right. He had fought for the right to be in on the chase, but in the end Martin's and the sheriff's common sense had won out. It was more important for Sam to stay close to Bayou Midnight in case Antoinette was found in her car or somewhere in the vicinity. One other thing had influenced his decision. When he had called the coastal police to report what he'd learned from Martin, he had found they already knew about the planned explosion on the oil rig. Leonce—finally choosing law over loyalty—had managed to alert them. There was no way that the men could escape. Leonce had helped save the rig from destruction. Sam could only hope that he had saved Antoinette from the same.

"It'll be her car down there, but 'Toinette won't be in it." Martin came around the corner and stood on the bayou bank, next to the spot where Tootsie lay peering down into the water as if she expected her mistress to rise from its depths. Martin spit in the water for emphasis.

"Someone drove it off the road . . . or worse," Sam said, hating the opaque, tannic-stained water, hating the bayou that had once given him a new life.

"I think the car was pushed in." One of the deputies stood, gesturing at indentations in the dirt between the parallel tracks. "These look like boot heels. Someone puts it in neutral, then they give it a big shove or two. Over it goes."

"I'm afraid you're right," the sheriff said, not even turning to examine the marks. Sam knew the sheriff had seen them immediately. He had, too. The sheriff didn't even flinch at the deputy's words. "Get some pictures. It's gonna rain."

The sky had darkened prematurely, not with twilight, which was still a good two hours away, but with the portent of a ferocious bayou storm. No one had to say out loud just how much more difficult it would be to get any leads if the storm hit. All of them knew. And if the scuba team didn't get there fast, they'd have to wait until morning to find out the truth about the car.

"She's not in that water," Martin reaffirmed. "Leonce, he wouldn't let her die."

"Hope you're right, son," the sheriff said, scratching his belly. "Your brother's in enough trouble as it is."

"Martin! Sam!" Didi's voice drifted toward them at the same moment the staticky squawking of the sheriff's radio cleared and a message for him to call in came over the airwaves.

Sam turned to watch Didi running toward them, waving her arms to catch their attention. She had arrived home from church right behind the sheriff's car. Sam hoped he would never have to be the one to break this kind of news to a loved one again. She had cried and refused to believe it at first, but in the end she had accepted Sam's words with courage and faith in Leonce. She would not believe that her beloved husband had done more than show ill-advised loyalty, and she could not believe that he would have let anything happen to Antoinette. Sam hoped to God she was right.

Now Didi stopped in front of Sam, gulping for air and talking twice as fast as usual. "The police called. Leonce and the others, they're in custody."

Sam couldn't even feel relief that his cousin was all right. He couldn't feel anything except the lump in his throat. He pushed past it to ask the question he was afraid to have answered. "Did they know anything about Antoinette?"

"I got to talk to Leonce." Didi's words were delivered so quickly it took a moment for them to sink in. "'Toinette's all right. She was in the boathouse when they went to load the dynamite. The others, they wanted to kill her, but

Leonce made them bring her with them. They dropped her off in the old egret rookery, the one where you used to go to look for plumes. He said he wanted her hid good in case the others, they got away and decided to go back and look for her. It was the only place he knew where they'd never find the way back. Leonce said you better git her fast. She was scared to death. He's on his way there with the police, but he says you can reach her faster.''

It was a funny thing. When feeling returned, it returned in one electric rush. Sam felt as if his body was buzzing with sensation. For a moment he couldn't move.

Martin had no such problem. He was already sprinting down the road toward his house. "Lemme git my airboat," he shouted over his shoulder.

The sheriff pushed his considerable bulk out of the front seat of his car and stood, peering over the roof. "They've got the men in custody. The gal you're looking for is..." He blinked. Both men were gone. "Think they'll need us to help look?" he asked the deputies. "We could go get a boat."

"We can try, but I think they're halfway there already," one of the deputies answered. "From the look on that city cop's face, he'd swim to that rookery and back if he thought it would do any good. She'll be home before nightfall."

Antoinette watched the storm roll in. She had cried all her tears, prayed all her prayers. Now she just waited. After a brief bout of hysteria, she had forced herself to be calm. Seeing the outlines of a monstrous alligator in the water ten feet away hadn't helped, but she had diligently recited the facts she knew to be true. The alligator would sense her presence and stay away. There were few actual cases of alligators attacking humans; they preferred smaller animals. The alligator was more afraid of her than she was of it. She could only hope that the last fact was the only one that was a joke.

Even knowing all that, she watched the alligator with the intensity of a woman whose life depended on it. Gradually he moved farther and farther away, nothing more than two eyes and a long ripple of water that indicated the length of his tail. When he was gone, she scanned the island again. She had managed to break off a branch from the closest small cypress, and although it would be no good at all against an alligator, it might help protect her from snakes.

The storm was a different matter. She had no shelter, but getting wet would be the least of her worries. She'd lived in Louisiana all her life, and she knew how quickly water levels could rise and land could flood. Her tiny island was already losing ground with the inevitable ebb and flow of the bayou water. It would submerge in a bad storm. Then she would be left with no alternative except clinging to the trunks of one of the cypress trees.

The mosquitoes had gotten worse as the storm darkened the sky. So far she'd killed a dozen that had tried to feast on her body, but she knew that soon they would be unbearable and defending herself would only be an exercise in futility.

When jagged streaks of lightning split the dark clouds above her, she listened to the fierce cries of the birds nesting nearby. She had never seen so many egrets. This was obviously the place they came each year to nest because it was so isolated they had no fear of human intrusion.

Sam had shown her the channel that led to an egret rookery the day they had gone crawfishing. She wondered if this was the same one. Leonce would have known about it, too. Perhaps it was the same one, but what did it matter? Sam was in New Orleans doing the job he loved, Leonce was blowing up an oil rig out in the Gulf somewhere and she was standing on an island surrounded by the densest swamp she'd ever seen with a storm about ready to break.

The first drops of rain were almost a relief. She tipped her head back and opened her mouth. She was thirsty and hungry, although neither had seemed important considering everything else. As the rain increased its tempo, she swallowed again and again. The rain cooled the heat of her skin and took the sting out of her mosquito bites. But as it began to pelt her harder and harder, she knew the relief it offered was only a prelude to the misery it would bring.

The lightning and thunder seemed to move directly overhead, and the noise was deafening. The sky was so black now and the rain so dense that she couldn't see anything farther than six feet away. Even if people were searching for her, they would never find her in this storm. The tiny hope she'd had that Leonce would really come back for her was washed away. He wouldn't be back, and she would die of exposure. She wondered just how long it would take.

"Antoinette!"

For a moment she was sure she'd imagined the shout. It had been sandwiched between two claps of thunder, and in comparison it had sounded like a whisper. Earlier she had screamed for help so loud and so long that she'd gotten hoarse. Now she summoned up the volume she had left and shouted, "Here!"

The thunder drowned out her attempt. Lightning split the air so close that it seemed to dance along the top of a nearby tree. In the burst of light she saw a boat in the distance, one like Martin sometimes used. An airboat, Sam had called it.

"Here!" she shouted again. "I'm here."

The boat was going in the wrong direction. When the lightning flashed again, the boat was gone.

Someone knew she was there. Someone had come to rescue her. Or perhaps someone had come to kill her. She clapped her hands over her mouth and rocked back and forth with a new surge of terror.

Whoever had come for her had disappeared back into the swamp. Shouting might bring them back, but she might be making a terrible mistake if she allowed them to locate her.

"Antoinette!"

She heard the voice again from the same direction. Faced with the worst decision of her life, she could only stare through the rain at the spot where the boat had been.

It was gone as surely as if it had never been there. She couldn't stand on the island knowing that her one possible chance for survival had just passed away. And yet she was helpless. She could not shout; she could not swim to the spot where the boat had been. Without knowing who was on the boat, she could simply wait. She stared at the spot, willing the rain to part so that she could see if the boat was to be her salvation or her doom. The lightning flashed, the thunder roared and she could feel the cold swirl of water around her ankles.

"Antoinette!"

This time the voice was behind her. She turned, disoriented, and stared into the darkness. She watched a boat pull up, and through the heavy sheets of rain she saw a man leap into the water, his arms spread wide. She was against his chest, shivering and crying, before she could let herself believe it was really Sam.

On the trip out of the rookery, huddling under a tarp was a luxury. Sam held her tight, and the rain beat down over them as Martin, oblivious to the elements, steered the boat back toward Bayou Midnight. Antoinette was so spent that she couldn't find words to ask how she'd been found or how Sam had come to be involved. She just accepted the reality of his presence and the fact that her life had been spared. She tried once to tell him that Leonce and friends were headed somewhere to blow up an oil rig, but he stopped her with his lips against hers in a gentle kiss. "Don't worry about anything," he had said. "It's all been taken care of."

She was surprised when the boat came to a stop. Sam and Martin held the tarp over her and encouraged her to step onto a platform. It took her a few moments to realize that she was on the deck outside Sam's cabin. The storm was ending, and once inside, she turned for a quick glance out the window. The black clouds of the storm were giving way to a more natural twilight. Soon it would be night. She tried not to think about what would have happened if no one had found her.

"I'll take it from here," Sam told Martin, his arm still around Antoinette for support. "Can you bring me the skiff tomorrow morning?"

Martin clapped his cousin on the back and disappeared back outside into the rain, which now resembled nothing more than a heavy mist. Sam guided Antoinette toward a chair. He left, but he was back in a moment with a heavy towel and a large T-shirt. He knelt beside her, drying her face and hair, whispering soothing words.

She was too exhausted to respond. She sat in the chair, eyes shut and let him continue. She felt his fingers at the throat of her shirt, and then she felt each button give way. The shirt was parted, and she leaned forward a little at his coaxing as he slipped it off, along with her bra. The towel was rough as he smoothed it along her shoulders and breasts. It was replaced by the soft knit of the T-shirt. She felt Sam unsnap her shorts, and she got up so that he could remove them. She slipped her panties off herself, smoothing down the T-shirt as she did. As tired as she was, she wasn't oblivious to the intimacy of this. Sam dried her legs, and then he picked her up as if she were Bridget Martane or Laurie Fischer and carried her out to the porch to his bed.

The last thing Antoinette remembered was the feel of something warm covering her. She drifted into a deep sleep immediately.

It was much later when she awoke. She'd been dreaming that an alligator wanted to share her island. She was fighting him with her pathetic little stick, and he was croaking, opening his mouth to show rows of huge yellow teeth. She sat up, her hands covering her face, and for a moment she couldn't remember where she was or why.

Strong arms pulled her back down, and she was cradled against the long length of Sam's body. "Bad dreams?" he asked softly, his warm breath caressing her ear.

"Am I really here?"

"You really are."

"I thought I was going to die."

His arms tightened around her. "I thought you were dead," he admitted. "I stood on the bank of Bayou Midnight and looked at the place where your car went over the side, and I thought you were in it."

"I almost was. Leonce wouldn't let them kill me. But then, he was the one—" the words caught in her throat and she had to force them out "—he was the one who took me to that horrible place."

"He was afraid that if he left you somewhere the others could find easily, they might return for you. Leonce had already alerted the police about what the men had planned before they even stumbled on you. I imagine he hoped the police would be waiting at the rig, but he didn't know for sure. He was trying to protect you."

"I didn't feel protected." She shuddered.

"I know, love." He stroked her hair. "You're safe now." His hand drifted down to her back, and he began to caress it in a motion that wasn't quite comforting.

"Why did you bring me here?"

His hand stopped, then slipped to the side of her breast, slowly smoothing a fluid line along her torso, down to the narrow indentation of her waist, along the graceful swell of her hip. "Because I wanted to be alone with you."

And tomorrow he'd go on his way, she thought. Sam was grateful she was all right. The fear he'd felt was making him overreact in his relief. She knew him well enough to know that tomorrow he would be silent and withdrawn. Her car was gone and he would drive her back to New Orleans, but once there they would say another goodbye. The pattern was too clear for her to ever be fooled again. "Please don't do that." She rolled over so that she was facing away from him.

He turned, too, pulling her body to fit into the curves of his own. His hand began to stroke her breast. "Let me love you. I know you're here in my arms, but I just can't quite believe it yet."

She needed to believe it, too, but she tried to struggle free. "Please, Sam."

"When I thought you were dead, I wanted to die, too."

She had thought of him constantly on the island. She had remembered the way his hands felt stroking her body, remembered the way his lips felt on hers. She had thought of him because, with him, she was completely alive. Facing death, that memory had been crystal clear.

"I kept thinking of this," she whispered. "Lying here in this bed with your arms around me. I kept remembering." Her voice caught in a sob.

"Don't cry. Let me love the tears away."

She stopped struggling. Making love to Sam wasn't a question of right or wrong. It was a question of being willing to face the truth: when morning came, they would once again go their separate ways. But, oh, she needed this right now. She needed to melt into him and feel his strength. She needed to feel the heat flooding her body and the miracle of merging with the man she loved. It wouldn't be wrong, only dangerous. And after this day the danger seemed a small consideration.

"Antoinette, I—"

"No!" She turned to face him again. "Don't say anything. I don't want you to say anything. Just love me. And don't be gentle."

He pushed her to her back, covering her face with kisses. His mouth traced a path to her ear, lingering there as his hands pulled up the T-shirt and found the silken skin of her breasts. There was nothing gentle about his caresses, but he took painstaking care to arouse her. She would know she was alive when he was finished, and she would be his in a way no one had ever been. That thought alone was enough to inflame him until he was so ready to sink into her that his control was stretched to the limit.

Sam had always been a thoughtful lover, but tonight Antoinette felt as if he were inside her head, reading her thoughts and acting on her desires. She had never felt this sense of oneness with him. He knew what she needed and gave it to her with nothing held back. His hands touched her in ways she hadn't experienced before, and she felt herself moving closer and closer to an explosion of fulfillment. His mouth tormented her breasts and traveled down her stomach to rest at the juncture of her thighs. He lingered there only long enough to bring her one step closer before he lifted her hips in his hands and fit himself slowly inside her.

She groaned when they were one. She knew, finally, that she was really there, that everything that was happening was real. She felt his life pulsating in the deepest part of her, and she knew that, whatever tomorrow brought, this was where she needed to be tonight.

She stroked his chest, then felt the firm, muscle-padded skin of his back, the cool, smooth skin of his buttocks. She let her hands drift to his neck and shoulders. Her hands encountered gauze and the unmistakable feel of adhesive tape.

Suddenly she was afraid. "Sam? Were you hurt looking for me?"

"No, I was hurt looking for me." He kissed her, cutting off more questions. He leaned on his elbows, cradling her face in his hands. He wanted this moment to go on forever. She was his now. It was indisputable. But after they made love, after he explained his new insights to her, would she still be?

He began to move, slowly but with strength. They fit together as if constructed for that purpose alone. He could feel her warmth mold to him. Each time he moved away, he could feel the loss. She was part of him in a way that was so elemental, he understood that, even if she left him, she would only be taking him with her.

Antoinette shuddered with the force of each thrust. She never wanted this to end. She held back, trying not to spur him to finish quickly. She gloried in each movement, in every touch of his skin, in every twist of his body. She was floating, but not away from him—no, never away from him again. She was his. He was making her his. And if that was only true for tonight, it was more than she had ever expected to have again. Much, much more.

Finally there was no control. Perhaps in heaven pleasure was limitless, but on earth it was destined to end before it could begin once more. Wrapped together, they found their release, holding on as if in the finding they might lose something even more precious.

Antoinette didn't want to talk. She wanted to lie there in Sam's arms and pretend that what she'd felt as he made love to her was more than just a reflection of her own needs. She lay very still, willing herself to fall asleep. Sam was stroking her hair, and she tried to relax and give in to the weariness of body and soul. But she could not.

Sam knew she was still awake. He could feel a slight tension in the body that had been so totally relaxed. He had hoped they could both get some sleep before they tackled the problems between them, but he knew now that wasn't going to happen.

"Are you hungry?" he asked, still stroking her hair.

She hadn't thought about it—there had been too many other needs to have met. But she was hungry. She realized she was starving, and she didn't want to talk until she'd had something to eat. "Yes."

"I have some canned vegetable soup that'll probably taste like gourmet fare about now." He kissed her forehead and slid to the side of the bed. Standing, he took dry jeans from a peg on the wall and slipped them on. The soup was already heating when he heard her behind him.

She was still wearing the T-shirt and nothing else. He realized he'd never gotten around to taking it off her, and he admired the way the well-washed knit clung to the curves of her body. He almost liked it better than the very feminine gown she'd worn the last time they were there. In the gentle glow of his kerosene lantern, she was the most compelling vision he'd ever seen. He knew, without a doubt, that for the next fifty years he would think exactly the same thing each time they were alone like this.

"How did you know where to find me?" Antoinette sat at the small cable-spool table and watched Sam at the stove. The light from the kerosene lantern illuminated his hair with burnished highlights and set off the tanned fitness of his body. Only the white patch of gauze spoiled the perfect image.

"Leonce told the police. They called Didi, knowing that Martin and I could get there before they could."

"What were you doing down here?"

"Looking for you."

Antoinette couldn't comprehend his words. Why had he come to Bayou Midnight to find her? How had he even known she was there? His answer gave her hope, but she'd learned the hard way just how foolish hope could be where her relationship with Sam was concerned.

"What's going to happen to Leonce?" she asked to cover up her feelings.

"I don't know."

"He didn't set any of the fires, Sam. He knew what was going on, but it was Leonce who saved Laurie's life. He went to New Orleans to stop his friends, but it was too late. Then, when he rescued Laurie and she saw his face, he realized he was involved, too.''

"He was a fool not to come to me.'' Sam banged his spoon on the pot of soup. "I could have prevented all this from happening.''

Antoinette imagined she knew what Sam was feeling. As deeply as he loved his family, he felt guilty for what had happened. She tried to reassure him. "Leonce saved my life as well as Laurie's. I think all along he acted in ways he thought were the most moral. He hated what Omega was doing to Martin and to his friends, and he carried his loyalty too far, but he didn't commit any crime himself except withholding evidence.''

"If that's all true, and I suspect it is, he'll probably get off. Especially since he turned himself and the others in.''

"I'm glad. For Didi's sake, and for your family's.''

"Didi'll stand by him, no matter what. We all will.'' Sam poured the soup into a bowl and brought it to the table. He sat down across from her and propped his chin on his hands to watch her eat. "Do you remember the night we had dinner and I told you that anyone who commits a crime doesn't deserve a second chance?''

"I remember you saying that good is good and bad is bad and that motives mean nothing.''

"I was wrong.'' Sam hesitated. "And it's not the only thing I've been wrong about.''

Antoinette concentrated on the soup, savoring the flavor as if it were homemade. She wanted to ask him what else he'd been wrong about, but she wasn't sure she'd like his answer. Instead, she finished her soup. Without a word Sam refilled her bowl, and she finished the second bowl in silence.

"Do you want anything else?''

A cigarette, but she didn't ask, knowing it was useless. Besides, she didn't want Sam to know she'd begun smoking again. It was almost like proclaiming how much stress she'd been under since he'd said goodbye.

"I'm fine." She pushed her chair away from the table and stood, unsure what was expected of her now. Her eyes fell on Sam's bandaged shoulder, and she used it as an excuse to begin a different conversation. She had a feeling it was going to be a long night, and she wasn't ready to go back to bed with him. They had just made love, and yet she wanted to be in his arms again. Her pride wouldn't let her admit that to him. "You never did tell me how you hurt your shoulder."

"I got shot."

She sat abruptly, her knees caving in. She hadn't felt this faint on the island. "Sam!" she wailed.

"Does that mean you care?" he asked, the corners of his mouth lifting in something that resembled pleased relief.

She couldn't believe he was smiling. What was there to smile about? She ignored his question. "Who shot you?"

"Nobody you know." He couldn't seem to stop smiling at her. She had been so upset at the thought of his being in danger. Even though he'd just made love to her, he hadn't been sure she still loved him. Now he knew she did. He suspected his silly smile was permanent. He didn't care. "It was your fault, you know."

"No!"

He stood, coming to her side to kneel and take her into his arms. "I was thinking about you, and I let my guard slip. I've been thinking about you day and night since the last time I saw you. I've been a basket case. If you don't take me back, I'll have to quit the force. I'm no good to anyone anymore, Antoinette. Love me, marry me, so I can get on with my life."

At first she wasn't sure she'd heard him right. She'd been expecting anything except this. Sam was asking her to marry him so that the thought of her would stop interfering with the job he loved! She gave him a hard shove and stood. "As proposals go, that's one of the crassest I've ever heard!" Antoinette was pleased that her surge of anger had strengthened her knees. She marched out to the back porch and stared out the windows, her arms folded in front of her.

Sam followed, clasping his arms around her waist. He refused to let her pull away. "Now what do you expect from a man who never intended to ask anyone to marry him?" he asked, his voice a silken caress against her ear. "If I'd had any warning you were going to be here, I'd have practiced. But I called you all day yesterday and last night, and I couldn't get you. I had all kinds of things to say, wonderful, romantic things, but they just slipped away when I ended up having to rescue you tonight."

Antoinette took a deep breath to steady her voice. "Sam, you're wallowing in guilt. I absolve you. None of what happened is your fault. I chose to come back here to see Didi, and I chose to meddle about Martin and to snoop around the boathouse this morning. It's my own fault I got into trouble, and I do not hold you responsible."

"I'm glad."

"I know you were worried about me, but that's relief you're feeling. Not love."

His arms tightened, and he pulled her hard against his chest. "Once we're married," he said evenly, "you will stop analyzing me. I'm going to write it into our wedding vows. Yours are going to say, 'I, Antoinette Deveraux, promise to love, honor and cherish thee, and also to stop telling thee what thee is feeling. Forever and ever.'"

This was a man she didn't know. He seemed almost giddy. "Sam . . ."

"And I'll answer like this, 'I, Sam Long, promise to love, honor and cherish thee, and also to never, never doubt the absolute specialness of what I feel for thee and how much I need thee in my life. Forever and ever.'"

"Sam, I wouldn't put it past you to leave me at the altar!" She waited for him to release her, but instead he began to nibble on her earlobe. "Did you hear me, Sam? You're going to change your mind again. I feel like a Ping-Pong ball! First you want me, then you don't want me. You want me, you don't want me! Stop that!"

"No." He turned her slowly to face him, his lips tracing a leisurely path along her jaw as he did so. "I admit I've been occasionally indecisive—"

"Occasionally!"

"And that I haven't shown the sense of a damsel fly." Sam's gaze locked with hers. He could see that her eyes were suspiciously watery. He saw his advantage and pressed it. "It took getting shot to make me realize what a fool I was. But once convinced, I'm unshakable."

Antoinette trailed her fingers up his chest, touching the gauze. "I can't stand the thought of you being hurt."

He knew he'd won. "I love you. I have all along, but I've never loved anyone this way before. Please understand, it just had to sink in. Forgive me. Love me forever. Is that asking too much?"

Her hands crept up to his neck and into his hair. "You called me yesterday?"

"All day."

"What were you going to say?"

"Just exactly what I just said. Probably with a little more finesse."

"How do I know you called? This could just be remorse."

He smiled, cupping her face in his hands. " 'Hello,' " he said, imitating the pitch of her voice, " 'this is Antoinette Deveraux. I'm sorry I can't come to the phone now, but if you'll leave your name and number at the sound of the tone, I'll return your call as soon as I'm able. Thank you.' " He stopped, kissing her nose. "Right after you say your name," he finished, "Tootsie starts to bark. She barks three times, then stops."

"You did call."

He kissed her forehead. "Did you really start smoking again because we weren't seeing each other?"

She sighed. "And you called Rosy, too."

"If you marry me, I'll keep you too busy to think about cigarettes."

She shook her head, but her fingers tunneled deeper into his hair. "I'm in no shape to make a decision like that."

"You're right. What could I be thinking about?" His eyes held hers as his hands skimmed the soft fabric of her T-shirt.

At the hem he slipped his fingers under it and began to inch it along her hips.

"What are you doing?"

"Helping you get in shape to make your decision."

"That's unfair." She rested her hands on his arms, but she applied no pressure.

"Absolutely unfair. Do you want me to stop?"

Antoinette examined the direct warmth of his gaze, his pleased smile. Most of all she examined the utterly relaxed lines of his face. Sam Long was a man totally at peace for the first time since she'd known him. In that moment she believed, finally, that he was never going to change his mind again.

And just in case she was wrong, she was going to marry him quickly before he wavered.

"When M'sieu Gator, he learns to fly," she said, lifting her hands over her head in invitation, "that's when I'll want you to stop loving me."

"Not even then," he promised as the T-shirt fell to their feet. "Not even then."

*　*　*　*　*